RENEGADE

RENEGADE

NANCY ALLEN

GRAND
CENTRAL
PUBLISHING

New York Boston

Cover design by Jerry Todd
Cover image of woman (center) by Miguel Sobreira/Arcangel; other images by Getty Images
Cover copyright © 2022 by Hachette Book Group, Inc.

Grand Central Publishing
Hachette Book Group
1290 Avenue of the Americas, New York, NY 10104
grandcentralpublishing.com
twitter.com/grandcentralpub

First edition: March 2022

Grand Central Publishing is a division of Hachette Book Group, Inc. The Grand Central Publishing name and logo is a trademark of Hachette Book Group, Inc.

The publisher is not responsible for websites (or their content) that are not owned by the publisher.

The Hachette Speakers Bureau provides a wide range of authors for speaking events. To find out more, go to www.hachettespeakersbureau.com or call (866) 376-6591.

Library of Congress Cataloging-in-Publication Data

Names: Allen, Nancy (Lawyer) author.
Title: Renegade / Nancy Allen.
Description: First edition. | New York : Grand Central Publishing, 2022. | Series: Anonymous justice ; 1
Identifiers: LCCN 2021041416 | ISBN 9781538719176 (trade paperback) | ISBN 9781538719183 (ebook)
Subjects: LCGFT: Thrillers (Fiction)
Classification: LCC PS3601.L4333 R46 2022 | DDC 813/.6—dc23
LC record available at https://lccn.loc.gov/2021041416

ISBNs: 9781538719176 (trade paperback), 9781538719183 (ebook)

Printed in the United States of America

LSC-C

Printing 1, 2022

To Ben and Martha

CHAPTER 1

THE HANGING OVERHEAD lights cast a greenish tint on the face of the jury foreperson as she passed the verdict form to the bailiff. As I stared at her, I wondered: Was the color green a good sign? Or a bad one?

I was hungry for an omen, some visible indication regarding the outcome of the trial. I wanted the woman to look at me. My eyes bored into her profile as I leaned in, the palms of my hands flat on the wooden surface of the counsel table. With all my might, I sent her an unspoken message: *Look over here. At me. Do it.*

The foreman didn't glance my way. But I saw her briefly cut her eyes at the defense table before turning her attention to Judge Callahan.

I exhaled, my shoulders sagging as I released the breath I'd been holding. Because that was a bad sign. Bad for me as the prosecutor, anyway.

Judge Callahan reached out his black-shrouded arm. When the bailiff handed the verdict to him, the judge pushed his eyeglasses up over the prominent bump on the bridge of his nose and peered through them to read. I'd often wondered how he got the big bump on his nose. It looked like something or someone had broken it for him in the past. With every prejudiced ruling he'd made during the trial this past week, I'd fantasized about breaking his nose again. It would be simple, just a sharp blow with my left fist. I imagined seeing blood spurt from his nostrils every time he ruled against me.

He turned his gaze to the jury box. Giving them a small smile, just a twist of his lips, he asked, "Ladies and gentlemen of the jury, is this your verdict?"

Several of them nodded. One juror, a young woman I'd pinned my hopes on, wore a defeated look as the foreman said, "It is, your honor."

The judge shook the sheet of paper, and it crackled into his microphone. He read, "We, the jury, find the defendant, Maxwell Alfred James, not guilty."

The two defense lawyers flanking the defendant broke into jubilant grins. One of them slapped Max James on the back, snickering like a teenage boy. The sound of his laughter had an ugly ring.

When the judge dismissed the jury, the young woman I'd been counting on shot me an apologetic glance. I wanted to shout, *Why didn't you hold out, for God's sake?*

Because the verdict of the jury had to be unanimous to convict or acquit. Even one juror who refused to buckle would have meant a hung jury. If she'd hung them up, we would get a new trial—and I'd get another shot.

And I wanted another shot at Max James. I despised that

man. As long as he walked free, he was a threat to the women of New York City.

Once the jury departed, I saw James break away from his exultant legal counsel and beat a path straight to the bench. The sight of the defendant reaching out for a handshake from the judge almost made me lose my shit.

Someone tapped me on the shoulder. I swiveled and came face-to-face with Anna Sung, the victim in the felony assault case. She'd been present in court for the verdict.

At the sight of her tearstained face, my stomach twisted. I said, "Anna, I'm so sorry."

"Why did he win, Kate?" she asked me. She hung her head. "The jury didn't believe me."

I took her hand and squeezed it. "Anna, you were an excellent witness. And you were strong during cross-examination…they never made you back down. But with a jury trial, there are no guarantees. Sometimes the jury doesn't make the right decision."

"They think I am a liar."

Though Anna spoke with an accent, her English was excellent for a woman who'd been born and raised in China. I wasn't lying when I told her she'd done well on the stand. And the medical evidence of her injuries was compelling—injuries she'd received from the brutal beating inflicted by Max James.

But James had the best defense team money could buy, and they were cronies of Judge Callahan. I had passion on my side—had that in spades. But they outgunned me. At twenty-eight, I was still a neophyte in the DA's office. And the defense lawyers knew every dirty trick in the playbook.

Max James's girlfriend sidled over. She had been eavesdropping on us. At trial, the girlfriend had provided an alibi for James. As she drew near, I gave her the evil eye. She stared back with a sneer on her face. I broke eye contact first. A woman who would willingly perjure herself to defend a scumbag like Max James probably deserved my pity.

In an undertone, I told Anna I'd call her in the morning. She nodded and left the courtroom, shooting a fearful glance at Max James as she departed.

As I packed my laptop into my briefcase, shoving my file folders in beside it with angry thrusts, Judge Callahan called to me from the bench.

"Ms. Stone, don't forget to pick up your exhibits."

I walked over and snatched up a packet of X-rays and photos from the table beside the court reporter. Max James was still snuggled up to the bench with his buddy the judge. I was determined not to look his way, but when I heard James laugh, my eyes flew up to his face.

He was grinning—actually smirking at me. My heart began to pound, and I felt the blood rush up my neck. A common criminal, a serial assaulter of women, had the gall to laugh in my face because he had beat the justice system once again.

Judge Callahan knew Max James's reputation as well as I did. I glared at the judge with a silent challenge. He swiveled in his high chair and turned his back on me.

Returning to the counsel table, I swallowed the angry accusations I longed to toss at the judge. In a lot of ways, the miscarriage of justice was his fault. How many times had I jumped out of my chair during the trial to make valid objections to the smarmy tactics of the defense? Too many to count. I got a workout just flying out of and back into that chair. And Callahan had overruled me, time after time. Then he let the defense counsel shut me down without cause. I didn't get a fair shot.

I'm a great believer in the US Constitution but sometimes I wish they'd omitted the language about double jeopardy in the Fifth Amendment. Because I deserved a second chance when it came to Max James.

In addition to the X-rays, a couple of color photographs taken at the hospital spilled out when I tossed the packet onto the counsel table. Angry tears burned my eyes as I looked at Anna Sung's bruised face, broken nose, black eye, and swollen mouth. My left hand squeezed into a fist. With an effort, I relaxed my fingers and used them to massage the web of skin between my right thumb and forefinger. *Chill*, I thought.

I picked the photos up with a careful hand and slipped them into my briefcase. Prolonged examination of her injuries was bad for my mental health. But even though I locked the pictures into my bag, I couldn't unsee them. The images were burned into my head.

As I left the courtroom, carrying my briefcase along with my personal failure, I just wished I could have the opportunity to strike the same blows into Max James's smirking face that he'd enjoyed inflicting on Anna Sung. I thought of how cleansing it would feel, how supremely satisfying.

CHAPTER 2

IT WASN'T 5:00 P.M. yet, but I was done—done for the day and ready to down a drink. I rode the elevator to the lobby, planning to dash from the courthouse. But when I stepped out, I was confronted by the sight of Max James. Again. Laughing with his attorneys while his girlfriend tagged along behind him.

I briefly considered returning to the DA's office but I knew that my coworkers would ask about the outcome of the trial, and I was in no mood to enlighten them.

And my boss, the district attorney, would be certain to rub my nose in the not guilty verdict. Frank Rubenstein, the DA, had discouraged me from pursuing the felony charge, had warned against presenting it to a jury. He said the case boiled down to a swearing match between an immigrant and a Wall Street businessman, and the reasonable doubt standard would work in the defendant's favor. As it turned out, he was right. But I wasn't ready to hear him say "I told you so."

So I dawdled in the lobby. I walked slowly along the marble wall. I stopped to check the time in the hanging clock: 4:34 p.m. I watched the second hand tick down and up again.

When I finally figured the coast was clear, I left the lobby and emerged outside. But James was *still* there, continuing his victory lap on the sidewalk.

The sensible choice would have been to avoid him, head to the subway and go home. But I wanted to cross the intersection and walk over to Walker Street; there's a bar there that I like. And Max James was in my direct path. I almost changed direction and walked the opposite way. Unfortunately, the pit bull in me wouldn't permit it. "Fuck that," I muttered as I barreled down the sidewalk and swept past James and his entourage.

I kept my chin up, didn't look their way. But I heard the heavy footfalls as he broke away from his lawyers and came after me.

"Look who's running out. Hey! Kate Stone!"

Increasing my stride, I walked faster. So did he.

"Got your tail between your legs, Stone? Looks like it to me. What else have you got between your legs?"

At that point, he was directly beside me, keeping pace. As he shouted in my ear, I felt the spit spray from his mouth and land on my face. I wanted to wipe it off my cheek, but I wouldn't give him the satisfaction.

He said, "I saw you giving me the eye in court. Why won't you look at me now? You afraid of me?"

That stopped me in my tracks. I spun and looked back at the courthouse steps, where his lawyers stood watching us.

I called out to them, "You need to control your client."

One of the defense attorneys shrugged. The older one shook his head and looked away.

But I had lit a fire under James's girlfriend. She trotted toward us on stiletto heels. When I tried to move on down the sidewalk, Max blocked me. It must have looked incongruous to the casual observer, this street brawl ignited by a man whose haircut cost more than my monthly rent. He stood so close I could smell his breath. In a tight voice, I said, "Back off, Mr. James. I have nothing to say to you."

His eyes bulged with an artificial look of disbelief. "I can't believe that. You've got nothing?"

His girlfriend slid to his side. Wrapping her fingers around his forearm, she tried to intervene. James snatched his arm away. She took a step back, watching him with apprehension in her eyes. James worked for a glossy asset management firm; I wondered whether his fellow traders on Wall Street had seen this side of his character. Maybe they didn't care.

He said, "Oh, so now you've got nothing to say. You've been slandering me all week."

People were staring. Even in New York, this was a note-worthy spat outside the Criminal Courthouse, and I wanted nothing to do with it. I pushed past him and strode to the street corner but the light was red. I'm a New Yorker, more than willing to jaywalk. But the rush hour traffic was thick.

His voice was directly behind me. "I'd like to see a ball gag in your mouth. That's what it would take to shut you up."

The ball-gag remark almost did it. I tensed, clenching both fists. But I held off, thinking, *They're only words*. He can't hurt me with words. Sticks and stones and all that bullshit.

That's when I felt it. Two fingers in my back, shoving me. Shoving so hard I almost stumbled forward into traffic.

Then he did it again. Harder.

"Hey! I'm talking to you!"

My vision tunneled, graying out on the edges of my sight. I spun around. Without thinking it through, I acted on pure instinct. I landed a nasty uppercut to his chin. Seeing the surprise explode in his eyes, right as the blow was struck, was delicious.

James went down hard. I saw the back of his head bounce off the concrete when he landed on the pavement. Time had slowed for me. It felt like I waited a long stretch for him to react. But once he did, I was ready.

He sat up. Growling, he rose from the sidewalk with his fists clenched. I broadened my stance, prepared to fight. Looking forward to it, in fact.

But his lawyers were on the run and quickly separated us. The girlfriend gave me a kick in the leg before it was over. I didn't even feel it. Our brief altercation evolved into a shouting match; James and I exchanged insults as his lawyers pulled him toward the far end of the block. Like a soprano in an Italian opera, the girlfriend shrieked curses at me.

When I pulled myself together enough to look around, I saw that a circle of onlookers had their cell phones out, undoubtedly recording every second of the confrontation. Some of the amateur reporters looked disgusted, a couple appeared amused. One young man with tousled blue hair lifted a fist in a salute.

"You rock," he said.

I laughed a little at that. As the light changed, I limped

into the crowd crossing the street. My laughter quickly faded as my leg started to throb; the girlfriend had kicked me harder than I realized.

I should have seen it coming. I am, after all, an avid student of martial arts. And kickboxing. And my dad taught me how to defend myself with my fists when I was in grade school. Dad spent thirty years as a cop in the NYPD, and he had been determined to ensure I could handle myself when the situation called for it. Before his untimely death, he took a lot of pride in my prowess. And living in the city, it's a valuable skill to possess. My expertise is common knowledge around the criminal courthouse.

Maybe Max James's lawyers should have mentioned that to him.

I never made it to Walker Street. Instead, I ran for the subway, where I took the train uptown. When I arrived in my own neighborhood, I went straight to my regular watering hole and ordered gin. Followed by more gin.

CHAPTER 3

I HONESTLY MEANT to be on time for work the day after the James verdict. Before I'd collapsed onto my Murphy bed the night before, I set the alarm on my phone. Rookie mistake: I passed out before I had the chance to plug the phone into the charger.

So I was hustling down Centre Street at a trot, the courthouse looming before me like a granite prison. Storm clouds gathered overhead, promising a heavy April rainfall. If I wanted an omen, the threatening sky could be read as a bad one. But the sight disappeared as I trudged up to the DA's entrance on Hogan Place and made my way through security. In my windowless office, I wouldn't see the angry sky again until five o'clock.

When I dropped my briefcase on the floor next to the battered desk of the office I shared with Bill Parker, he looked at me with suspicious eyes.

"Morning. You look like shit," he said.

I didn't reply. Sitting in my sprung office chair, I buried

my head in my arms on the desktop. I was thinking about a short nap.

"Kate?" he said.

Quiet, I thought.

"Kate. He's looking for you."

"Oh God," I moaned into the vinyl desk pad. Lifting my head, I contorted my face. "Not today."

Bill spoke in a hushed voice. "He stuck his head in here twenty minutes ago. He said he already texted you, but you didn't answer. I tried to call, give you a heads-up. It went straight to voice mail."

I didn't have to ask who was looking for me. I knew. Francis, aka Frank Rubenstein, or "Ruby" to his friends.

We weren't friends.

When I swiveled the chair to face Bill, he was picking at his cuticles—one of his nervous habits. "You need to go up there. If he has to come down here again, it'll just make things worse," he said.

I nodded. Digging in my bag, I found a compact and checked my face. The reflection wasn't encouraging. Blood-shot eyes stared back at me. And my hair, scraped back into an elastic band, looked like a mug shot coiffure, but there was no time to remedy it. I pulled a box of breath mints out of my top drawer. Popped two.

When I approached Frank's office, I shot what I hoped was a winning smile at his administrative assistant. She responded with a knowing look.

"Go on in, Kate. He's been waiting for you."

I walked in. He looked up from his computer monitors.

"There you are."

"Good morning, Frank." I waited to be invited to sit. Like I said, we weren't close.

He waved at the chair adjacent to his massive desk. I slid into it. A hank of hair had escaped from the elastic band and fell over my right eye. I tucked it behind an ear.

"I know why I'm here," I said.

His brow lifted. "You do?"

He leaned back in his chair and set his feet on top of the desk. He wore a slim black suit, and his brown calfskin oxfords were so shiny, they looked like they'd just come out of a pristine shoebox. The sight of his footwear made me want to tuck my own worn shoes under the chair.

Instead, I stretched my legs out and crossed my ankles, so Frank could get a good look at them. He knew my pay scale.

"I know you heard about the not guilty verdict in the Max James case. And you're probably recalling that you told me it was unwinnable. Because she worked in a massage parlor."

He was just sitting there. As he regarded me through hooded eyes, he twirled a pen between his fingers.

I forged ahead. "The judge was prejudiced against the prosecution. Totally unfair. I don't mean to cast blame, but we should consider disqualifying him from future cases involving violence against women. I wanted to clue you in about that."

He set the pen down and brought his feet back down to the floor. "I didn't call you in here to talk about the verdict. Not precisely."

That took me aback. I blinked, rubbed one of my bloodshot eyes and blinked again, waiting for him to continue. When he didn't, I spoke up.

"So why am I here?"

Rubenstein's face lit up, like I was a dull student who had finally asked the right question. He picked up a remote from his desk and said, "I have something to show you."

He pointed the remote at a giant TV screen hanging on the far wall of his office. I shifted in my chair and watched, apprehensive.

The sound on the video was garbled; too many people on the sidewalk, too many conversations. But the image was clear. The video recorded my altercation with Max James outside the courthouse. Whoever held this particular iPhone came in close, just in time to see me throw the punch. The videographer followed James down to the ground, where the back of his head smacked on the pavement. Then the video returned to me, my clenched fists at the ready, and zoomed in on my face. The angle was not kind.

Rubenstein lifted the remote and hit pause. My face was frozen in a snarl on the screen, enlarged to a frightening degree.

He dropped the remote onto the desk. "So," he said.

When he didn't say anything else, I tried to go for a laugh. I said, "Honestly? I'm relieved. I thought for a minute you were going to play a sex tape. Of me," I hastened to add.

It fell flat. He pointed at the screen. "What's your reaction to that?"

I looked at it. It wasn't pretty. But I'm stubborn. Got that from both sides of the family tree.

"That's my resting bitch face," I said. And laughed.

Frank wasn't laughing. "Do you know who has seen this?"

Actually, I didn't. There was a television in the bar where I had drowned my sorrows the night before, and I had been aware of the local news droning in the background. The scuffle apparently hadn't been significant enough to catch their attention.

Rubenstein said, "That footage has made its way to every law firm and judge in New York City. Hell, the paralegals and interns are watching it by now." His voice had a note of malice when he added, "I'll bet even your mom has seen it."

My left hand rubbed the web of skin between my thumb and forefinger in response to the suggestion. The revelation that the video was circulating in legal circles horrified me, and not because I worried about New York legal interns. *Not my mother, please God, not that.*

"How do you think this makes me look?" he said quietly, angrily.

At that, I held my tongue. Because the tension in the room had grown palpable. Even the weather reflected it. Raindrops pelted the windows of Frank's corner office. I heard the crack of thunder. A bad sign, my superstitious mind warned me.

"You understand that with the video evidence, Max James could press charges against you for assault."

That suggestion sent my blood pressure soaring. I could feel my pulse beating in my ears. "Is that a joke? You're kidding, right? Because Max James provoked me. *Threatened* me."

Rubenstein raised a hand. I fell silent. "I've talked to his lawyers. They're not bringing the police into the matter."

I settled back into my chair with an eye roll.

"But this video is troubling. I can't ignore it. And it's part of a larger pattern. Do I need to remind you? There was that time you threw the stapler at Bob."

It was true; I had. But I apologized later.

"And you were almost held in contempt in Judge Callahan's court last year, after he ignored your recommendation on sentencing. And I almost forgot—remember when you knocked the coffee out of the defense attorney's hand during a pretrial conference?"

"The guy was an asshole."

Frank fixed me with a somber look. "Kate, you need to seek assistance for anger management."

"What?"

"Anger management. There are a number of professionals and organizations in the city that provide counseling. You will sign up for one. And attend."

The suggestion was laughable. And it made me angry. I rubbed the skin by my thumb again, harder.

"I don't think so."

Rubenstein remained calm. "You will."

"I don't have the time. And I don't need any help."

He pulled his chair up to the desk and fixed me with a sad look. "That's exactly what people who need help the most always say."

My mind was racing. I already had a full schedule. As an assistant district attorney, I regularly prepped for jury trials. Trial preparation was a grueling process; the term "overtime" didn't begin to describe it. In addition, I tried to devote one or two nights a week to kickboxing.

And then there was my extracurricular bar time. It was high on my priority list, too.

"What if I refuse?"

His smile was rueful. "If you refuse, you'll have to find another job."

When I started to sputter an indignant reply, he cut me off. "Kate, I'm trying to help you. And I won't accept any resistance to the proposition. It's nonnegotiable."

I sagged back into the chair. He had me.

"Where do I sign up?"

CHAPTER 4

THE SUPPORT GROUP met in a building on Forty-Fourth Street, on the western outskirts of the theater district. I walked into the building promptly at 7:30 p.m., nobly ignoring the bars that beckoned me along the way.

Once inside, I followed the signs directing me to the meeting room. The building design was early flophouse, but that didn't bother me. I'd chosen this particular anger management support group based on its affordability factor. Frank had provided me a list of highly recommended therapists in Manhattan, but when I checked them out, I didn't like their price tags. The city's benefits covered a finite number of therapy sessions, and Frank's counseling form had a lot of signature lines for me to fill.

And Frank made it clear he wasn't backing down on the decree. He'd called me just after I arrived at work that morning, demanding to know which therapist I'd chosen from the list. He got snippy when I explained I'd found a more economical choice from my own research, even though I assured him that the therapist on Forty-Fourth and Ninth was legit.

Entering the meeting room, I spotted the group leader instantly, a slight man with a Sigmund Freud beard. But it wasn't the beard that gave him away. It was his voice. A middle-aged woman asked a question, and he answered in a voice so soothing it sounded like he was reading a bedtime story.

I walked up. "Mr. Schmidt?"

He looked at me through round, horn-rimmed glasses. "Call me Duncan."

"Hi, Duncan. I'm Kate." I thrust a folded sheet of paper at him. "I need your signature on this form. Actually, I don't need it. My boss does."

Duncan gave me a cryptic smile. "Let's take care of that after the session. Sound good?"

I didn't want to hang around after the session and wait for him to sign the verification sheet, but I was trying to avoid getting off on the wrong foot. So I took my seat in one of the folding chairs set in a loose circle on the dirty tile floor.

Next to me sat a guy in his thirties wearing a messy man bun. His hair looked as bad as mine had the day before. He nodded at me.

"I'm Flynn."

"Hi, Flynn," I said.

"What are you here for?" he asked.

He pulled his chair closer to mine, making it screech on the floor. I already regretted my seating choice. He needed a shower.

"My boss sent me," I said.

He nodded thoughtfully, as if I'd said something profound.

The others—ten or eleven people—were drifting into the chairs. The majority were men, with a couple of angry women in the mix.

Duncan, the group leader, was the last to join the circle. "Good evening," he said. The group echoed the greeting. I kept my mouth shut. *I'm just gonna observe and learn the ropes*, I thought.

"Did we bring our journals?" he said.

Some of the men were holding small spiral notebooks. The women reached into their handbags. Flynn pulled a crumpled sheet of paper from the front pocket of his pants.

"Don't you have your journal?" Flynn said in a whisper, his brow furrowed.

"No…?" I whispered back.

Duncan must have seen the interaction. He said, "We have a new member tonight. Would you like to introduce yourself?"

A dozen pairs of eyes zeroed in on me. Like a jury, but even less chummy. Then again, I've won over some pretty hostile juries in my time. I flashed a toothy, fake smile.

"Hi, nice to be here. I'm Kate."

"Hi, Kate," was the patchy response.

A woman in a pilled, gray sweater turned to Duncan with a worried face. She was twice my age and looked like someone's grandmother. I was curious to learn who grandma had punched out. "But she doesn't have a journal," the older woman said.

"It's fine, Mona." To me, Duncan said, "We meet on a revolving schedule, you can join at any time. I like clients to keep a journal. You'll need to pick up a notebook or notepad this week."

"Got it," I said.

"Who would like to share something they recorded in their journal this week?" Duncan asked in his honeyed voice.

Mona flipped pages in her notepad. "My goal for the week was counting to ten. When my husband said something that made me angry, I counted to ten before I reacted."

She turned to Duncan, hungry for his reaction.

"And how did that work out?" he said.

"Good. It was good. I did it six times this week." She checked her notebook. "And we didn't have any fights. I never got physical."

The people in the circle snapped their fingers. After a moment, I snapped too.

Flynn was next in line. He smoothed the crumpled sheet of paper on his thigh.

"My goal for this week is 'Don't take the bait.' Because I lost my last job when I broke my boss's jaw. I told you about it, that I landed in court for assault. But the dude was always baiting me."

I listened with growing interest. I was warming up to Flynn. Who wouldn't like to break their boss's jaw?

"And I've got the new job at the deli, and I want to keep it. But people really get under your skin. This guy working the line with me is always fucking with me. 'Faster,' he says, like I'm his bitch."

I nodded. So did a couple of others in the circle. But not Duncan.

"And the customers can piss you off. A guy comes in, he wants breakfast, and we've already got the lunch stuff put out, and he freaks the fuck out. But I said to myself, 'Don't take the bait.'"

He put the sheet of paper back in his pocket. The circle snapped again.

Duncan focused on me through the round lenses of his glasses. "Kate, is there anything that you'd like to share?"

"Well, it's my first time here. I don't think I've formed a precise goal yet."

The faces around the circle were stony. I'd given the wrong answer. Hastily, I tried to correct my mistake. I wanted Duncan's signature on that form.

"But I'm hearing great stuff here tonight, advice I can use. Flynn's thing about not taking the bait—I should adopt that one. One of my problems is that I let people make me mad, then I get physical when I'm baited. And what Mona said—I should try counting to ten. Sounds good to me."

I fell silent. Duncan blinked.

"Would you like to share with the group the particular event that led you to join us?"

Uncomfortable, I shifted in the metal chair. It squeaked.

"Okay, I guess. I'm a lawyer. I work in the DA's office here in New York. After a jury trial this week, I had an argument with an individual outside the courthouse. A heated argument. And anger management therapy seemed like a good idea."

The faces in the circle exhibited skepticism. They knew I was holding out. I had failed the show-and-tell portion of the meeting.

"Oh, hell—the case is a matter of public record. I guess I don't need to be so mysterious."

I wanted to unload, but it seemed prudent to give James a pseudonym. Again, I wriggled in the chair, trying for a more comfortable position, but without success.

"There's this guy. Let's say his name is…Jones. He's a Wall Street trader—big time, big money. A guy who can afford to buy whatever he wants, including female company, if that's his thing."

Only one person in the circle nodded: a young woman who had a full sleeve tattoo down her right arm. I made eye contact with her.

"So, Jones was in a massage parlor on the Upper West Side. He wanted a happy ending but the woman, Anna, wouldn't do it. She's not a prostitute, she's a licensed masseuse. When she refused, he beat the shit out of her. Even after he knocked her out, he kept on hitting her."

In my head, I saw the photographs of her injuries. My breath was coming faster.

"It wasn't a great case because the other employees at the massage parlor refused to testify. They said they didn't see anything, hear anything. Which is total bullshit."

During my pretrial preparation, I took the information from the police report and hunted down the women individually. I haunted the massage parlor where they worked. I went to their homes. They were too frightened to cooperate. They were unwilling to take on a powerful man with unlimited financial resources. They knew what Max James was capable of doing.

"But I talked the assault victim into testifying, because it was so important to proceed with the case. Do you know how many times the police have been called on Jones for assault? Do you have *any* idea?"

There was silence in the room.

"He has a rap sheet as long as my arm! Domestic violence,

assault, aggravated assault. All arrests, no convictions. Because the women he beats up are too scared to go to court."

Flynn scooted his chair away from me at that point, but I wasn't paying attention.

"The jury cut him loose—I still can't fucking believe it. He could've killed that woman. I'm sick of it, seriously. Sick of law enforcement and the courts turning a blind eye when powerful men abuse women. It makes me crazy. That's why I work so hard at my job. The pay is shit…people think lawyers make good money, but assistant DAs live on a shoestring. But it's an important job. Only the DA's office can make those abusive fuckers pay."

My face was hot. Was I loud? Some of the people looked kind of scared. But one guy was listening intently.

"When he was acquitted, I tried to stay out of his way. But he confronted me. And that's the truth. *He* confronted *me*. He pushed me. Like that."

I held out two stiffened fingers to illustrate. As I did, I relived the moment, felt the jolt in my back from James's shove.

"I didn't think, I just acted. I swung at him, knocked him down. It felt great. God! I wish I could do it again. That *fucker*."

I stopped, breathless. No one spoke for a moment. Duncan coughed into his fist.

My heart was pounding so hard, I barely heard Duncan say, "Who else would like to share?"

I sat in the chair as the voice next to me droned. Perched on the metal seat, I fretted silently over the impact of my monologue. I needed that verification form signed.

Sometimes a person can say too much.

24

CHAPTER 5

WHEN THE MEETING finally ended, Mona dashed to Duncan's side. I sat in the metal chair with my verification form and waited, the heel of my foot tapping on the floor in a nervous dance. When two other group members lined up behind Mona, that did it. I decided I would intercept him on his way out.

As I hit the door, I wadded the form into a ball and shoved it inside my bag. Once outside the building, I saw a glorious vision: a stout man wearing a lemon-yellow polo shirt. He was lighting up a cigarette.

Approaching the man with a smile, I bummed one. He was happy to oblige. Based on his bright yellow shirt and accent, I guessed that he probably hailed from the Midwest. He politely asked whether I wanted a light. I did.

Keeping a respectful distance from the door, I inhaled the brown weed with gratitude. Because I'm an infrequent smoker, the tobacco had an immediate kick. By the third hit, I leaned against the stone exterior of the building, relishing the nicotine's calming effect on my brain. It struck me that the tourist's cigarette had done more to manage my anger than the ninety-minute session in the support group. No wonder my dad used to like his Marlboros.

A tall, lanky guy strolled up to me.

"You're going to be late to the smoking cessation support group."

I checked out his expression, trying to see whether he was messing with me. Because the building I had just fled offered a plethora of meetings for alcohol and drug abuse, eating disorders, hoarding, smoking. And, of course, anger management.

But he had a nice voice, with a teasing lilt to it. A hint of a Latino accent. I ashed my cigarette onto the sidewalk.

"I thought I'd skip that one. Hoarders Anonymous looks more interesting."

"Really?"

"Absolutely. Entire reality shows have been dedicated to hoarders. Smokers get no positive publicity these days. It won't even give me a shot at Dr. Phil."

He was staring at the half-smoked cigarette I held. I misread his interest.

"Sorry I can't offer you one. I bummed this off some guy."

He laughed. "Smoking isn't my personal weakness. I'm a doctor. The medical profession is united in one proposition: smoking is hazardous to your health."

I deliberately took another drag and blew the smoke out in a thin plume before I replied. Out of courtesy, I aimed it away from his face.

"How about mental health?" I asked.

He shrugged. "There may be a professional split of opinion on that. I'm Steven, by the way. I was in the anger management meeting."

I nodded. I recognized him. "I'm Kate."

"Kate, the angry DA."

I barked a laugh. Dropping the cigarette butt on the pavement, I crushed it with the tip of my shoe. "That's me, for sure. Kate Stone, the angry DA."

He stuck out his hand. "Steven Salinas, the angry MD."

He leaned his shoulder against the stone wall and spoke in a low voice. "I found the story you told in the meeting really interesting."

At that, I tensed up. Where was he going with that remark? Clearly, my angry tirade hadn't been a hit with the circle of men and women who were working out their inappropriate impulses. I looked away from Steven, casting my eyes around in search of another friendly smoker.

My body language shouldn't have encouraged him to move closer to me. But he bent his head close to my ear.

"Your story was compelling."

I pulled my bag onto my shoulder, giving him notice that I was about to move on, even though I was still waiting for Duncan. But as I stepped away from the wall, wearing a see-you-later expression, he said something that made me pause.

"I don't think you have an anger problem. I think the problem is our society's acceptance of violence against women."

My surprise must have registered on my face because he smiled. "Let's talk. Do you want to get a coffee?"

"No," I said in a decided voice.

He looked wounded by my quick response. I decided to

backtrack; he was pretty attractive, and I liked his stance on domestic violence. And Duncan was nowhere to be seen. "I'm not up for coffee. But I'll drink a beer with you. It's better for my health than coffee."

We started walking up Ninth Avenue, where plenty of venues provided hot and cold beverages. The traffic was thick at that hour. Steven had to raise his voice to be heard over taxis honking their horns.

"I think it's your anger that fuels your work as an assistant DA. The rage you feel gets funneled into the cases you handle, the arguments you make to the jury. It's part of why you're good at what you do."

His comments were a balm to my injured spirit; nothing sets a lawyer's confidence back like a disappointing jury verdict. Still, it was hard to accept such extravagant praise from a stranger.

"How do you know I'm good at what I do? I could be a piece of shit in the courtroom, do an uninspired job, for all you know."

He said, "I can tell by the way you command attention, the way you conduct yourself. Like when you told your story to the group tonight."

My face must have conveyed skepticism. He gave me the side-eye, grinning. "Okay, I confess. I googled you during the meeting. Found the verdict in the Max James trial."

That gave me a lift. I thought that the only person who's ever googled me was me. A neon light winked at us, and my new buddy steered me to the entrance of the bar. As he held the door, I spoke over my shoulder to him. "Google probably didn't tell you, but there's a reasonable explanation for my tendency to be contrary. My dad was a cop. And my mom is a big defense attorney in Jersey. So it's possible that conflict is an inherited trait in my family tree."

We bellied up to the bar. I ordered a Stella. Steven actually requested a cup of coffee, to my undisguised amazement. When the bartender delivered his coffee, Steven wrapped his fingers around the mug as if he needed to warm his hands.

He looked at me with genuine interest. "One thing I don't understand—how did you punch out an asshole like that James guy? I looked him up. He's a big dude."

I swigged the Stella from the bottle, ignoring the frosted glass next to it on the bar.

"I neglected to mention one detail in the meeting."

"Oh yeah?"

"I have some hobbies." I took another sip, just to prolong the suspense.

"Hobbies other than smoking cigarettes and drinking beer? Because I already know about those."

"Ouch." I took a big gulp from the bottle and stared him in the eyes. "Hobbies in addition to my vices, thank you very much," I said with a smile after swallowing.

"Okay. I'm officially intrigued." He pushed the coffee mug away to demonstrate that I had his complete attention. "Tell me about these hobbies of yours."

"Kickboxing. And karate."

His eyes widened. Which was the reaction I was aiming for.

"That's fascinating. But it strikes me as overkill. Kickboxing *and* karate?"

"I've been training in karate for years. My dad got me started when I was in middle school. The kickboxing has been a more recent pursuit. I took it up after my dad passed away. It was a tough time." Focusing on the beer bottle, I scraped the label with my fingernail, unwilling to confide the extent of my trauma to a stranger. Though three years had passed, I couldn't block that image from flashing in my brain, the picture of my father's body twisted on the sidewalk outside his walk-up apartment on the West Side. The *New York Post* published the picture the morning after he died.

My stomach knotted up. I kept talking, hoping my discomfort wasn't too obvious. "It gave me another outlet to work through some frustrations. The anger, too. I can work out a lot of hostilities with kickboxing."

I drained the bottle and signaled the bartender for another. "Steven, I don't mean to question the effectiveness of your little club with Duncan, but you might want to try kickboxing. It sparks a lot of endorphins."

"I bet it does."

"And the anger management meeting tonight? It sparked zero endorphins. Zero."

The bartender set a cold bottle down in front of me. Casting a quizzical glance at the pristine glass beside my empty beer bottle, he said, "You want a fresh glass?"

"God, no." I swigged, to give him the nonverbal cue that I didn't need a glass at all.

The beer eased my stomach.

Steven sipped his coffee. He made a face. "That…is not a good cup of coffee."

I shrugged. "You shouldn't have caffeine at night. It's not good for you."

He dragged his barstool a few inches closer to mine.

"I know what you mean about the support group tonight. It wasn't particularly inspiring."

I lifted my bottle in a toast. "Here's to that."

"I think you'd benefit from another meeting."

I let out a sound that resembled a hoot. Apparently, Steven hadn't been listening to me.

"I'm not sure I can sit through another meeting with Duncan."

"I didn't mean that group. There's another one, at a different location. I promise that you'll find it more meaningful."

I wasn't even tempted. Not in the least.

"I don't think support groups are my thing," I said.

"This one's different. You'll connect with us."

"No, thanks."

His voice was earnest when he said, "I guarantee it."

Steven had moved so close to me that his face was inches from mine. I leaned back; he was invading my space.

"I don't think you can guarantee that kind of thing. We don't even know each other."

To my relief, he straightened up on his stool, putting some distance between us. But his next words were unsettling.

"I know you better than you think."

It was time to go. I was getting a little creeped out. Groping in my bag for my wallet, I felt a crumpled wad of paper: the form that Frank Rubenstein had given me. The one I neglected to have the group leader sign before I bolted from the meeting.

After a moment of hesitation, I said, "Okay. Tell me the time and place for the other support group. I may drop by sometime."

He made an apologetic grimace. "It doesn't really work like that. You can't just drop in. It's a single invitation kind of thing."

"Huh?"

"If you miss it, you won't be invited again."

He wasn't making any sense. I was no expert on support groups but to my best knowledge, they had an open-door policy. Duncan had *just* stressed that new members could join at any time.

"What is this? Some kind of exclusive club? Do I need to know a secret password to get in the door?"

Apparently, he had no comeback to my jab because he didn't respond. Silently, he watched my face, as if waiting for something.

Pulling out my debit card, I lifted a hand to signal the bartender, but he was already standing in front of us. The bartender's proximity was also unnerving. It felt like the guy had been watching our exchange. I wanted to leave, to escape the funk of the bizarre night.

But Rubenstein's form still required a signature. And I wanted to keep my job. *Needed* to keep it.

Without feigning enthusiasm, I said, "Okay. Very mysterious. Tell me where."

He gave me an address and time. Whispered it in my ear, for God's sake, like it had to be supersecret. Feeling his breath in my ear sent a shiver through me. My shoulders twitched.

"So I'll see you there?" he asked.

"Cross my heart."

I paid my tab and got the hell out of there before he could talk me into anything else.

CHAPTER 6

AT LUNCHTIME, MY coworker Bill Parker and I stood in line at a food truck near the Criminal Courts building. While we waited, Bill appeared to study the brightly colored pictures that decorated the side of the truck, depicting various menu items.

"What looks good to you, Kate? I'm trying to decide."

I gave Bill an eye roll. He always ordered the same thing: the lamb gyro with red onion. By the end of our lunch hour, white tzatziki sauce would speckle his shirtfront.

When Bill's turn in line came up, he said, "I guess I'll have the lamb gyro with red onion and a Diet Coke."

I hid my smile.

After Bill paid, I also hesitated for a second before I ordered. The smell of chicken and spice inside the truck made my mouth water. I was hungry for chicken curry and could almost taste it.

"Hot dog deal," I said.

The proprietor looked unimpressed. "Two hot dogs with free soda for three ninety-nine. What kind of soda?"

"Diet Coke." I handed him a wrinkled five-dollar bill and watched as he counted out my change. "I need mustard. Four packets."

When we sat on a bench in Thomas Paine Park, Bill clucked with sympathy as I struggled to open the mustard packets. "If it's hot dog day, you're low on cash."

"I'm always low on cash." It didn't bother me to admit my financial strain to Bill. He was almost as poor as I was. "And I actually like hot dogs. They're an excellent source of protein."

We ate in silence for a while. Bill took a swig of Diet Coke and cleared his throat. He asked: "Did Rubenstein give you a hard time? About your jury trial?" Hastily, he added, "We don't have to talk about it if you'd rather not."

I had not been disposed to discuss it inside the DA's office, but I decided to make an exception for Bill. "Yeah, he gave me some shit. Not so much about the verdict. He was pretty unhappy about what happened after."

Solemn, Bill nodded to show he understood. He had seen the video, I was sure of that. It seemed like everyone in the city had watched it. Bill looked down at his gyro and took a big bite. While he chewed, we both stared ahead at the Supreme Court building.

Bill nudged me. "That's where Barzini was assassinated. In *The Godfather*."

If so, I'd never heard it. "Nah, I don't think so."

"I'm sure of it."

I didn't argue; maybe he was right. Bill was a huge cinema fan.

Deliberately casual, he asked: "So what did Rubenstein say?"

Sparks of resentment flashed through my chest. I had been very closemouthed about the meeting with Frank. I hadn't told anyone about his ultimatum. Having therapy imposed as a job requirement was embarrassing. But Bill was my best friend in the office. I decided to come clean.

"Frank thinks I have an anger problem."

I waited for Bill to profess disbelief, to voice a denial of the charge, but he made no response. When I turned to measure his reaction, his eyes slid to the left.

"Shit," I whispered. "You agree with him."

"Kate, I'm on your side. You know that."

"You think I'm unbalanced. That I can't control my rage."

His voice had a defensive ring. "I didn't say that. Don't put words in my mouth."

As if I had spoiled his appetite, he tossed the messy sandwich onto the paper bag crumpled next to him on the bench.

We sat in uncomfortable silence. I refused to speak, because I wanted him to take it back, to tell me that Frank was wrong.

Bill sighed. "Maybe what you need is a change."

That suggestion rattled me further. "What's that supposed to mean?"

"I mean, a change within the office. Working violent crime really takes a toll, and we have a daily diet of it. Doesn't it get you down? It makes me crazy sometimes. Some nights, I wake up and my heart is beating so hard I think I'm having a heart attack."

I listened, dumbfounded. Bill had never confessed his frailty before. We had worked together for almost three years.

"You know what I wish? That we could get into the

white-collar crime division. I have a friend who's working over there, and he makes it sound great." His voice held a wishful note.

I snorted. Bill's face darkened. He grasped my wrist and squeezed it.

"I'm serious. The pay is better, you know that. And they get a lot more respect from Frank. It would also pave the way to more job opportunities for us when we're ready to move on."

Resolutely, I shook my head. I had no desire to spend my days combing through financial statements, hunting for numerical irregularities. The very idea sent a shiver of distaste down my back.

I said, "So you think that it would be a more valuable way to use your time and energy as a district attorney. Trying to build cases against poor people who sneak money away from the rich people."

"That's not what it's about."

With a scoff, I said, "That's exactly what they do. Every time the DA files an embezzlement charge, that's what it is about. Some underpaid clerk funnels the rich man's money into her account. Frank Rubenstein's white-collar henchmen come after her so they can put her head on a spike. And she will serve as an example to others, a harsh reminder. No, thank you."

"That isn't all they do. Sometimes they go after the Bernie Madoffs."

"Bullshit." Our debate had grown heated. I could feel blood pounding in my ears. "My dad used to warn me, that rich and powerful people want to manipulate law enforcement to serve their personal needs. Dad never let them make a puppet of him. And neither will I."

"Your mom doesn't share the opinion, I guess."

I refused to respond to the jibe. I knew what he hinted at. In her defense practice, my mother was more than happy to come to the rescue of anyone willing to pay her hefty fee. She'd secured an acquittal in a high-profile white-collar case prosecuted by our office in the past year. I'd been forced to listen to her crow about it last November over Thanksgiving dinner.

When the silence stretched out, Bill broke it, saying, "I respect your loyalty to your dad. In your position, it's got to be hard. It put you in a tough spot when Frank lost the manslaughter case three years ago because your father couldn't testify."

My stomach twisted. I was afraid the hot dogs would come up.

Bill paused to pick up the remains of his sandwich. When he took a bite, the white sauce rolled off the pita bread and onto his shirt. I handed him a napkin.

While he blotted at the mess on his blue shirt, he said, "But damn, Kate, that stuff about the white-collar division being a puppet for rich people? That's nuts. I never knew you were a conspiracy theorist. That whole man-behind-the-curtain thing. Didn't know you bought into that."

There it was again: the cinema reference. At least I caught it this time. When we were kids, my mother watched *The Wizard of Oz* with us repeatedly. She claimed to be a Judy Garland fan. I privately suspected she was rooting for Margaret Hamilton.

I managed to keep the hot dogs down. As my stomach relaxed, I took a cautious swig of warm Diet Coke.

While I nursed the soda, Bill made his case one last time. "You ought to think it over, Kate. If we both got transferred to white collar, we would still get to work together. That's a big plus for me. And I could sleep at night without panic attacks." He paused, wadding the sticky napkin inside the foil wrap.

After a moment of hesitation, he continued, his voice sincere: "And you wouldn't be so inclined to lose your temper. Knocking a guy out after an acquittal is pretty extreme, Kate."

"I didn't knock him out."

That denial was truthful. To be accurate, I knocked him down. But not out. Max James did not lose consciousness.

"Just promise me you'll think about it. Sometimes you get too personally involved with your cases, like getting obsessed with Max James. It could genuinely be better for your health."

"My health is fine." When Bill didn't look convinced, I said it again, louder. "I am absolutely fine."

I jumped up, ready to put an end to the conversation. When I tossed my trash into a nearby can, I saw that I had a bright yellow stain down the front of my shirt: mustard.

Unaccountably, I began to tear up, thinking: *It's impossible to get mustard out. I ruined it.*

Bill stood at my side, looking into my face with concern. "Kate? Are you okay?"

"Fine. I told you, I'm fine."

He tossed his wrapper and we turned to walk back to the office. Halfway there, he said, "Want to get a beer after work?

My treat. It would be nice to have a chance to talk, away from the courthouse. I always feel like someone's listening in in the DA's office."

I would have liked to. Bill could almost always make me feel better. But I had a conflict.

I had to attend another anger management meeting. The second one this week.

Maybe I wasn't just fine after all.

CHAPTER 7

THAT NIGHT, I stood under a streetlight, studying the map on my screen. The address Steven had given me was in the East Village—not my neighborhood, but I knew the place was nearby. So I strolled the sidewalk, keeping my eyes peeled for a public building, like a YMCA.

When I reached the corner, I paused, uncertain. I'd arrived at the location; my phone said so. But it wasn't a community center. It was a church built of ancient red brick. A shuttered church that looked unoccupied. No illumination lit the outdoor sign which identified the house of worship as "Our Lady of the Forgotten."

Maybe Steven was messing with me.

Still, I walked up the crumbling stone steps and reached for the handle of the door, just in case. To my surprise, it opened.

Once inside, I stepped into a foyer marked "Narthex." The vestibule was dimly lit by a single pillar candle encased in glass. I let the door close behind me. Its rusty hinges creaked out a greeting.

Through the narthex, I could see more candles lighting the front of the nave. The flickering light illuminated a number of people sitting at the front of the church, near the altar. I caught snatches of conversation, but they spoke too softly for me to hear what they were saying.

The gothic setting put me on edge, but I'd already come this far. As I walked down the aisle that divided the wooden pews, I called to them, to make sure I wasn't crashing a cult meeting.

"Am I in the right place? Is this the support group?"

Heads turned toward me, but in the near darkness, I couldn't see whether Steven was among them. I took a backward step, prepared to make a quick exit.

A woman's voice said, "Are you Kate?"

"Yeah," I answered. I was only partially reassured. The backdrop was creepy as hell. "Steven told me there was an anger management group here tonight, so I came to check it out."

I thought I heard someone laugh, which seemed like an inappropriate response. But another voice in the darkness invited me to join them, so I made my way to the cluster of people gathered down in the front.

Some of the men and women sat in the pews; others were scattered across the carpeted steps leading up to the chancel. Two altar candles and a collection of votives were the only source of light. I took a seat in an open spot on the pew and took a look around. When no one spoke, I plunged right in.

"I'm Kate, and I have anger issues."

A scant few responded. "Hi, Kate."

After an uncomfortable pause, the woman sitting to my right said: "I'm Diane, and I'm a sex addict."

I jumped to my feet. "Oh…well, there's been a miscommunication then, I guess. I'm looking for the anger management group. Am I in the wrong place?"

When no one volunteered information, I asked, "Is Steven here? Because he told me the anger support group was at this address."

A big guy who looked like a bodybuilder leaned against the lectern. I could just make out a US Marine Corps "Semper Fi" tattoo on the dark skin of his shoulder. "We're a special group. We represent a variety of self-help programs. I'm Rod. PTSD."

"Hi, Rod." Drawing a deep breath, I said, "Where's Steven?"

"He'll be here," the sex addict said. I'd already forgotten her name. "Let's do the intros," she said.

A paunchy middle-aged man seated beside her said, "I'm Larry, and I'm an alcoholic."

"Hi, Larry." The group chorus was stronger that time.

A guy across the aisle from me who barely looked old enough to shave spoke next. He wore high top dreads. "I'm Devon, and I'm a gaming addict."

A young woman with a mane of blond hair sat on the top step to the chancel, close to the candles flickering on the altar. "I'm Millie. Anxiety."

She made the announcement with mournful resignation, but I was confused by it.

"Isn't anxiety a psychological condition?"

"I'm *addicted* to anxiety." Her voice rang in the vaulted space.

I nodded; who was I to question someone else's quirk? The man seated beside Millie put a supportive arm around her. Even in the uncertain light, his clothing appeared to be spattered with paint.

"I'm Edgar. Anger."

"Excellent. Hi, Edgar." I was so relieved to find a fellow member suffering from the anger issue that I stepped up to offer a fist bump. He responded, but with a lack of enthusiasm. As I sat back down, I wondered how quickly I could take my leave.

Behind me, a gray-haired woman stretched out along the pew. "I'm Whitney, and I'm a gambler." She rolled onto her side, cushioning her head with her arm.

"Hi, Whitney. Can I ask a question?"

She looked at me with suspicion, but said, "Sure."

"Why don't we turn the overhead lights on? So I can see who I'm talking to."

"This is a deserted building. The utilities have been shut off." Whitney closed her eyes, as if she might doze.

I was trying to get my head around their choice of an abandoned church as a meeting place when Steven's voice called out behind us.

"Sorry I'm late."

He strode down the aisle, joining the cluster of people on the carpeted steps. When I caught his eye, he broke into a smile. "Kate! So glad you made it. Have you met everybody?"

"I think so." It was possible that others might be lurking in dark corners, but I'd picked up on the group dynamic.

I sighed, then spoke false words of gratitude. "Steven, I really appreciate you including me here tonight, but I don't think this group is what my boss had in mind. So I'm going to head out."

I draped the strap of my purse across my chest, more than

ready to depart. Steven held his hand out in a restraining gesture.

"At least give us the opportunity to explain, Kate."

"Explain what?" I'd developed a bad case of restlessness. My knee began to jiggle.

"Everyone in this room shares an important quality," he said. His voice was solemn.

I smiled to show I understood. "Right. We're all addicts, or have a behavioral problem."

When I stood up, the woman reclining on the pew behind me spoke out in a commanding tone. "Steven hasn't finished talking. Sit down and hear what he has to say."

I sat, despite my desire to leave—and despite my general disregard for following orders. It felt like I was stuck in a bad dream, in which my legs wouldn't propel me away from danger. To fortify myself, I massaged the spot between my thumb and finger.

Steven said, "The real bond among us is that every person in this group has been wronged by the justice system."

His statement took me by surprise. My knee stopped jiggling. "Really."

"Yeah, really. Our court system is flawed. Law enforcement is riddled with corruption. And every one of us here has been injured by it."

The individuals in the room nodded and murmured in assent.

"Kate, you know what I'm talking about. Your experience this week, with the not guilty verdict. It's a miscarriage of justice."

They were all looking at me. The candlelight shadowed

their faces, but I could feel the intensity of the stares. When the gambling addict leaned over the back of my pew to eyeball me, I shuddered.

A defensive impulse kicked in. "The law is my professional calling. Sure, the scales of justice are imperfect. Sometimes it doesn't work, and the guy walks, or the wrong person pays. But it's the only system we've got, the only way to right the wrongs in our society."

Silence fell in the sanctuary except for a rustling noise. I began to worry about pestilence. If rats were roaming the corners, I resolved to take off like a shot.

The big guy, Rod, took a seat by the blond anxiety girl. To her, he muttered, "Law enforcement in this country damn near killed me. And it totally failed you." She snuggled up to him, resting her head on his shoulder.

The guy with paint-covered clothes—the one who shared my anger problem—spoke up next.

"You say the system is the only way. But it's not."

"What do you mean?" I was curious, in spite of myself.

Steven left the steps and stood in front of me. "We believe we can make things right. But we do it outside of the law. We work as a team, all of us in this group. We choose one case a month, and do everything in our power to create a just result. And we succeed because the people in this room have some exceptional talents."

He reached out to take my hand in his. "This month, we've chosen your case."

I shook my head because I didn't understand. "My case?"

"Max James. We've chosen to serve real justice to Max James, if you're willing to join us."

I jerked my hand from Steven's hold and grabbed my purse. "No. Thanks. But no."

I stood, pushing past Steven, who looked at me with disappointment.

"You sure?"

"Absolutely." I made my way through the people and hurried down the aisle.

The muscle-bound guy said, "Who's going to stop this James guy if we don't do it? He's not going to change."

I turned around to answer. "You're right. He'll do it again. And when he does, I'll get him. But I'll do it within the system. Because I still believe in it."

The blond girl lifted her head from Edgar's shoulder. When she spoke, her voice echoed through the sanctuary. "If you believe that, you're nuts."

I laughed. "I'm pretty sure you're nuts. All of you."

I walked out of the church, letting the door shut behind me with a rusty creak. Safely back on the street, I squared my shoulders and left the wannabe Batmen and -women behind. As I walked away, literally shaking my head in disgust, I thought I must be losing my mind. Why did I stay for their freak show in the first place?

CHAPTER 8

BY THE TIME the car service dropped me off in front of my mother's house in New Jersey the following Thursday, I was nursing a bad case of resentment.

She'd sent a series of texts to me over the past week, demanding my presence at her dinner table. I'd tried to dodge her, but she was relentless. It wasn't difficult to divine the reason for the invitation; I knew she must have seen the video of my altercation with Max and wanted to use it to extract a pound of my flesh.

I pressed the intercom next to the front door of her McMansion. After a protracted wait, my brother's voice crackled through the speaker.

"We're in the kitchen." The door buzzed, unlocking as it did so.

I opened the door and dropped my bag on an elaborate carved bench in the entryway. With a sigh of resignation, I made my way through the formal dining room and into the kitchen. My brother sat at a barstool, hunched over the large island in the center of the room; my mother was nowhere in sight. "Kate's here, Mom," he called.

"Hi, Leo," I said and took the barstool next to him. Resting my elbows on the granite island, I spoke in a hushed voice. "How is she?"

His eyes darted to the doorway. Lowering his voice, he said, "She's in a total mood. Be careful, that's my advice."

The warning put me on edge; even though I'd been out from under my mother's thumb for years, she retained a certain power to intimidate me.

The clacking sound of her heels on the tile provided fair warning of her approach. She trotted into the kitchen, saying, "There you are. We've been waiting."

I heard the defensive note in my voice when I spoke. "It's not exactly easy to get here from Manhattan. I have to take the subway, catch a train, and get a car service."

"It would be easier if you didn't insist on living on that filthy island," she said. She lifted a stack of foam boxes from Whole Foods delivery bags and set them on the counter. Giving me the side-eye, she added, "Get your elbows off the table."

My arms jerked away from the surface as the bubble of resentment in my chest expanded. "Mom. It's a countertop. A kitchen counter."

She acted like she hadn't heard me. Pulling plates and flatware from the dishwasher, she ordered my brother to set the table in the breakfast room. As he walked out of earshot, she sidled up to me.

"I saw it, you know."

A stubborn streak took possession of me. "What's that?"

"The video."

I gave her a poker face. "What video?"

She reached out and pinched the fleshy part of my upper arm. I let out an involuntary cry.

Rubbing the sore spot, I said, "I hate it when you do that. It hurts."

"Don't mess with me. I saw the video of your humiliating street fight with Max James."

My eyes stung as I inspected the red mark on my arm. She knew how to make me feel ten years old again. "The video made it look worse than it was. Really, it wasn't a major thing."

"Really?" She looked over at my brother, who hesitated in the doorway. "Put the food out. No grains near my plate." To me, she said, "Keto. It's amazing. You should try it."

I resisted the urge to roll my eyes, thinking that if my mother would ingest some carbohydrates, her brain might produce serotonin, and we'd all be happier.

"Is that why we're not drinking? Because you're doing keto?" I gave the full wine rack a look of longing.

My mother ignored the hint, leading the way into the breakfast room. "I think we can enjoy a family dinner without medicating ourselves with alcohol." She stopped short, staring at the table. "Where are the napkins?"

My brother rushed to correct his misstep as Mom took her place at the head of the table. She spooned a small piece of salmon onto her plate before passing the box to me.

As Leo hustled back, extending a napkin to Mom, she said, "This is why you can't seem to pass the bar exam, Leo. You're never quite prepared."

His fair skin flushed as he slid into his seat. Heedless of

his discomfort, she continued the harangue. "Maybe if you spent less time on your skateboard and more time studying the bar materials I purchased for you, you'd see a different result."

Leo's face was scarlet. His test anxiety was a long-standing issue, and I felt a rush of sympathy for him. "Have you ever asked him whether he wants to practice law, Mom? Seems like you handpicked the career for both of us."

"I like being a paralegal for her firm," he said quickly, handing me a napkin as he sat.

Mom focused on me, ignoring Leo's defense. I watched as she tried to raise her brow but the fillers she used in her face interfered with the expression.

She said, "You should thank me. With the right direction, the practice of law can be a lucrative profession." Then she jabbed her fork into the fish, adding, "Though when I picked up the tab for your education, I certainly never envisioned you throwing it away on prosecution. Law enforcement is bloodsucking—a ruthless task, and it changes people. Look where it got your father."

The arrow struck home. I looked down at my plate, working hard to keep from crying. Even after three years, the wound felt fresh.

To spite her, I wrinkled my nose and said, "Does this fish smell a little off to you?"

She chewed deliberately and swallowed. "Delicious."

Leo took a wolfish bite from his plate, nodding his head and making appreciative noises.

We sat in silence as they ate and I toyed with the food on my dish. When I reached for the loaf of bread at the far end of the table, my mom spoke, her voice deliberately casual. "Are you ready to come to work for me yet?"

I ripped a chunk of bread from the heel with my teeth, grinning as I chewed. Bad table manners grated on my mother; she glanced away.

At length, I responded, "What in God's name gave you that idea?"

"Oh, I don't know. The fight outside the criminal courts building, the black eye you received on social media." She picked up her knife with a manicured hand. "Kate, you are an effective trial lawyer, but the prosecution role is making you a little unhinged."

I was about to launch an outraged denial when a thought tickled my brain. Hadn't my boss said essentially the same thing? And my friend Bill?

My mother continued. "Your brother and I discussed it. Didn't we, Leo?"

His face flushed again, and he avoided my eye as his head bobbed in agreement.

"I'll pay you whatever you say is fair. It's time, don't you think?"

The fork fell from my hand with a clatter. "How many times do I have to tell you? I'm not working for you." When her eyes narrowed with displeasure, it still had the power to make me backpedal. "I don't think it would be healthy for our relationship, Mom."

"It would be healthy for your legal career. Your reputation and standing in the legal community."

Pushing the chair back abruptly, I stood. "I'm gonna leave now."

"But you haven't eaten your dinner."

"I'll eat at my apartment. I've got some food in the fridge."

It was a bold-faced lie. I had a twelve-pack of beer in there, resting beside some expired condiments.

She followed me to the entryway. "I hoped you'd stay longer. We need to talk."

"Gotta head out. It takes forever for me to get home, Mom. As I've explained."

Her tone was tart. "Maybe if you didn't live in Harlem, you wouldn't have these transportation challenges."

I sighed. It was an old argument. "I live in Morningside Heights."

"It's practically Harlem. And it's not safe there. Not for you."

"Jesus Christ," I muttered. I hit the car service app on my phone. When I saw that my ride was ten minutes away, I wanted to howl. Ten minutes would feel like a lifetime.

"You don't have to live in squalor. I've offered to put money in your account on a monthly basis. You only have to accept my generosity. And be appreciative."

Briefly I envisioned the food truck outside the courts building. With Mom's help, I could order everything on the menu, chicken curry and falafel sandwiches every day. My rent would always be paid right on time. But I pushed temptation aside. "No thanks. That's your money, not mine."

My brother lurked in the hallway. I waved at him. "Take care, Leo. Good to see you."

Heading out of the house, I stood in the driveway, checking my ride's progress on the phone. It still predicted a ten-minute wait.

"Kate."

I looked over my shoulder at my mother, silhouetted in the doorway. Though her face was hidden, I could imagine the set of her jaw.

"What?" I said, expecting her to repeat the same demands, bribes. Denunciations.

So when she took her parting shot, it surprised me. "Punishing me won't bring your father back."

She pulled the door shut and left me in the dark.

CHAPTER 9

BY THE TIME I made it back onto my own turf, my evening was shot. And I still hadn't eaten. There's a little Italian place in my neighborhood; it has a friendly bar, where one of the bartenders slips me free drinks. When a person lives in Manhattan on a government employee salary, every little bit helps.

I sat at the bar and ordered bruschetta while the bartender made a stout gin and tonic for me. "Thanks, Nick," I said, taking a long pull on the straw. My eyes watered after I swallowed; it was well gin, not call liquor. But beggars can't be choosers.

He leaned on the bar, giving me a longing eye. "Where have you been all week, Kate? I missed you."

"I was here this week. Where were you?" I had to pick up my tab on that occasion, and it was substantial. That was the night I'd drowned my sorrows following the Max James verdict.

"I must have been off. We need to coordinate our schedules better."

"Absolutely. Agreed." The gin had started to work its magic; the tension in my shoulders began to ease.

He dropped his voice to a low whisper. "Maybe we should meet up outside of here. Go to some clubs."

Nick had made the suggestion before, but I hadn't taken him up on it. Keeping things friendly between us required an artful maneuver; I wanted to keep the liquor flowing without having to dodge a sexual overture. I flashed him a smile, withholding anything that could be interpreted as flirtatious.

"Nick, I don't want to join your harem. It would take a toll on our friendship."

He backed off, to my relief. Seriously, Nick wasn't my type. He was a little too pretty and clean-cut for my taste.

My appetizer appeared, and Nick moved down the bar to serve another customer. As I devoured the food, I focused my attention on the television set poised behind the bar. The local news was on; I was curious to see whether any catastrophes had transpired in the city while I was traveling to and from New Jersey.

When a new mug shot of Max James appeared on the small screen, I almost spilled my cocktail. "Nick," I said, "turn up the volume."

By the time I could hear the reporter's voice, she was wrapping up the story. But from the visuals on the screen, it appeared that James had committed another assault. The coverage made reference to his recent acquittal, flashing stock footage of the Criminal Courts building. The reporter's voice was icy as she related the outcome of my unsuccessful felony prosecution. The implication was clear: If James had been convicted of that offense, it could have prevented his latest attack.

They moved on to another story: Subway commuters had been infected with bedbugs. "The suspected source of transmission was a fellow passenger," the anchor said. Usually, a subway horror story would snag my attention, but on that occasion, I tuned it out.

I pulled out my phone and texted Bill.

Max James in custody. wtf

Swigging the drink, I waited impatiently for his reply. As the minutes ticked by, I caught Nick's eye and pointed at my empty glass. *Refill required.*

When Bill responded, the message was unsatisfactory.

??? Don't know what you're talking about

"Shit," I whispered. After a moment's hesitation, I sent a text to Frank. Surely the DA would know what was up. Whether he would deign to enlighten me was less certain. I wasn't in my boss's information network.

Chugging the fresh drink Nick provided, I shoved the half-eaten plate of bruschetta out of my space. My knee jiggled under the bar as I waited for Frank to respond. Despite the gin, I was growing edgy. As my anxiety increased, I tried rubbing the skin between my thumb and forefinger, but it didn't provide any soothing effect.

While I waited, I googled the TV station, to see whether I could access the newscast on their website. When I found it, I hit the video, maxing the volume on my phone, and ignoring the frowns of the people seated beside me at the bar. The video showed the story in its entirety, including the identity of the victim. When it flashed across the screen, I literally yelped with surprise. The name wasn't familiar to me, but her face most certainly was: it was Max James's girlfriend, the woman who'd provided his alibi at trial. I still had a bruise on my shin from the kick she'd delivered to my leg when we were outside the courthouse. According to the reporter, she was hospitalized; she'd been beaten to a pulp.

My heart pumping, I tried calling Frank, but he didn't pick up. "You asshole," I whispered. He was intentionally ignoring me. But he underestimated me if he thought he could keep me away from the case. I had a vested interest in the crime, a right to know about it. I dialed Frank again; this time, I left a message: "Just saw the news about Max James. Waiting for your call."

The minutes ticked by but he didn't call back. I cursed Frank in language so awful that Nick shot me an alarmed glance.

I would sure as hell chase Frank down at the courthouse the next day. He'd have to bring me up to date on the deets. But twelve hours seemed like an interminable time to wait. I sucked on the ice in my glass as I tried to think of something I could do. I was itching to take action. Waiting around wasn't my style; I wanted to do something proactive. And then I had a thought.

I pulled up Steven Salinas's contact info. With my thumbs, I composed a hasty text: a brief yet compelling description of the newest turn of events in the Max James case. Then I asked him to meet me at the bar, to discuss what we could do about Max with the assistance of Steven's group.

I almost sent it. Almost hit the button on the screen before I thought better of it. Instead, I deleted it, and signaled Nick for another drink.

CHAPTER 10

ON THE SUBWAY the next morning, I grasped the metal pole for balance, shoving my free hand into the pocket of my trench coat. A wadded sheet of paper scratched my skin. I pulled it out, planning to toss it.

The sight of the paper made me groan. It was the form for my anger management sessions. The form that didn't bear a single signature.

I had attended not only one but two of the damned meetings, yet I had failed to get anyone to sign on the line. Frank would be sure to nag me about it. He was a stickler for minutiae and loved to obsess over unimportant details. On the other hand, I've always prided myself on being a "big picture" person. Our basic contrasts in vision were probably part of the reason that he and I didn't see eye to eye.

And I planned to encounter Frank that very morning. I intended to hunt him down as soon as I arrived at the office. He'd never returned my texts or calls about Max James.

The train stopped, and a woman vacated her seat. I nabbed

it. It would have been polite to wait and see whether an elderly person was boarding, but I make it a point to avoid checking people out on the subway. Generally, it's best not to look too closely.

Smoothing the sheet of paper over my knee to get the wrinkles out, I tried to remember the name of the therapist who'd overseen the first meeting I'd attended. Was it Duncan? Was that his first or last name? It struck me that it didn't really matter whether I correctly recalled the name, since I was planning to forge the signature anyway.

With a pen poised over my knee, I was about to scribble the sham verification when a distraction stopped me. As the doors shut, a man dressed in a tattered coat boarded, speaking too stridently to be ignored. "I need help," he said.

I didn't meet his eye as he marched up and down the car. "I need help," he repeated. "I have two kids. Who's going to help me?"

Steely-faced, I kept my eyes down. Most of the passengers ignored him as he repeated his demand for assistance.

He glanced my way, but kept on moving until he found a likelier target: a young girl, carrying what looked like a case for a cello. I saw him zero in on her, moving closer as she gave him an uncertain smile.

"You could help me out," he said. "You look like you can afford it."

With a look of confusion, she glanced around the car, murmuring in a foreign language: Chinese, maybe. *Well, shit,* I thought. From her expression, I deduced she probably didn't understand what was happening. A lot of music students ride the train because there is a conservatory near my neighborhood. A number of them were from China.

"Did you hear me? I said I have two kids."

Shit, shit, shit, I thought as her face crumpled. At that point, the young woman appeared frightened as well as confused. I felt obliged to speak up. It was an inauspicious way to start off the day.

I grumbled inwardly as I prepared to leave my seat, a spot which I knew someone would steal as soon as I stepped away from it, a shabby reward for my noble deed.

But before I could intervene, someone beat me to the punch. Another woman on the train said, "She doesn't understand you."

The panhandler turned to the woman who had spoken; she sat nearby. He said, "I wasn't talking to you."

I froze, halfway out of my seat. The panhandler had turned back to the girl with the cello. "You want to play like you don't get me?" He reached out and gave the cello case a slight shove. The girl clutched it with a protective gesture.

The woman spoke up again. I focused on her, wanting to get a better look. She was on the dark side of fifty with silver in her hair she hadn't bothered to disguise. Her face was in profile, but there was something familiar about it—or maybe I recognized her no-nonsense manner of speaking.

"Quit being an asshole," she said. That caught the young man's attention. He turned away from the musician and fixed a yellowish eye on the older woman.

"Are you talking to me?" he asked, tensing up, his hand curling into a fist. I lurched out of my seat then. Though I didn't relish the prospect of duking it out with the guy, I couldn't let him punch an old lady. My dad raised me better than that.

But before I could enter the fray, the old gal kicked her foot out, connecting with his kneecap. It must have been a forceful blow because he fell back on his butt, gripping his knee and wailing. I stood by, staring down at him in astonishment. How the hell did an ugly scene go down in my presence without me having to play a part in it? It was a novel change of circumstance for me. I wasn't sure how I felt about it.

The train ground to a stop at Columbus Circle, where I needed to switch lines. The car emptied out, and the girl with the cello gave the injured panhandler a wide berth as she hurried away. Like her, I didn't linger, but as I made my way onto the platform, I tried to get a good look at the woman who'd dealt the powerful kick.

Because she looked familiar. I was pretty sure I'd seen her recently, at a support group meeting. In a shuttered, candlelit church in the East Village.

CHAPTER 11

WHEN I ARRIVED at work, I headed straight for Frank's office.

His assistant gave me a cool look as I approached the door. "Do you have an appointment?" she asked.

I wheeled on her. "An appointment? Really?"

She gave a little shrug. I ignored her disapproval as I tapped on Frank's door and pushed it open.

He sat at his desk, toying with his cell phone. When I entered, he looked up in surprise, and as I approached, I sensed my unscheduled visit disconcerted him.

"What do you want?" he said.

My temper began to flicker; Rubenstein was a bullshitter, he'd obviously seen the texts I'd sent the night before. I stepped directly in front of his desk. "Max James. I saw it on the news last night."

Frank shook his head with an expression of regret that struck me as phony. "It's a sad case. Tragic."

"Have you filed the charge yet?"

He set the cell phone on his desk, with the screen down, as if he didn't want me to know what he'd been looking at.

"If only it were so easy." He folded his hands on the desk-top and sighed.

"What's not easy about it? I heard the newscaster. James put his girlfriend in the hospital. The reporter said there were witnesses—eyewitnesses, for God's sake. We've got him this time."

"Not precisely." Frank picked his phone up and tapped the screen with his thumb, probably to signal that our conversation had ended. When I dropped into a chair across from him, his brow wrinkled. "Don't you have somewhere to be? In court, maybe?"

"Nope. My morning case got continued."

"I suggest that you find something constructive to occupy yourself with. I have things to do here."

Like playing with your phone, I thought. He was probably googling himself—again. Edging forward on the seat, I said, "It sounds like an open-and-shut case. So let's open it, Frank."

A long moment ticked by; the silence made me uneasy. My hand twitched; I automatically rubbed it, out of habit. Frank noticed. When he glanced down at my hands, I forced myself to stop, curling them into fists in my lap.

"She won't testify."

That took me back. "You're fucking kidding me."

"I'm not, but I wish you could express yourself with more restraint. How's your therapy going? Have you turned in the form I gave you?"

"It's on my desk." In fact, it was in my pocket. Bearing a single forged signature. Before I showed it to Frank, I wanted to be certain that it didn't resemble my own handwriting too closely.

Frank pushed his chair back and stood: another signal. He wanted me gone. I gripped the arms of my chair, to show him that I wasn't leaving.

"Why do you think she doesn't want to testify?"

"Because that's what she told the police. She was very clear. Definitive, in fact."

I refused to surrender. My mind was buzzing as I tried to divine a strategy. "But there were eyewitnesses to the incident. We'll put them on; they can establish the elements of the offense."

"Seriously? You want to proceed with an assault case without the victim. That's brilliant. He'll get another acquittal, unless the judge directs the verdict in his favor first. You might never make it to the jury. And if you do, you'll lose."

"You don't know that. The girlfriend might come around. We'll work on her. She could make a good witness."

"Oh, she'll be a good witness. For the defense."

Leaning across his desk, he rifled through his inbox. Pulling out a sheaf of papers, he slid it to me over the varnished wood.

"Read the reports for yourself; her statement is in there. I'm not going to let you embark on another fool's errand. There are countless cases for this office to handle, cases with victims who are eager to testify. So I'd appreciate it if you'd get back to your own desk. I have some things I'd like to accomplish this morning."

I picked the reports up from the desk. "Okay if I take this with me? I'd like to read it. Just curious."

"Take it. You can return it to me by office mail. No need to bring it by personally." I ignored the implication, stifling the urge to tell him that the feeling was mutual. With the reports in hand, I made my way to the door.

Before I left, his voice stopped me. "I know you're still troubled by the outcome of the Max James case. It's natural that you'd like another shot. But this is not the case you want. I'm trying to help you, Kate."

Over my shoulder, I gave him a shit-eating grin. "Thanks, Frank."

I walked past his assistant with a fresh sense of determination. Actually, Frank was right. He *had* helped me.

He'd just provided me with all the contact information I needed for Max James's girlfriend. I intended to pay her a visit.

If anyone could turn her around, it was me.

CHAPTER 12

I DIDN'T TELL anyone in the office, not even Bill. I just buckled my trench coat and headed for the elevator.

Bellevue can be a tricky hospital to maneuver, but I had been there before, so I had my bearings. I made my way through the maze and onto the floor where the NYPD had questioned Max James's battered girlfriend. The reports I'd taken gave me the name of the woman I sought, Angelina Piccola. I had to talk my way through multiple barriers; it would have been more difficult without my district attorney identification. It opens a lot of doors.

As I approached the room, a nurse was exiting. She looked me up and down. "Family?"

"District attorney's office," I said, flashing the ID yet again.

She didn't bother to inspect it. "Your timing is good. They'll be transferring her soon."

"Right," I said, like I knew what she meant. "Just for our records, the transfer will be…?"

"To Mount Sinai." The nurse sounded huffy about it, as if

someone had suggested that Bellevue wasn't posh enough to treat the fallout from Max James's brutality. She moved down the hall, and I stepped inside the hospital room, tiptoeing across the threshold. If Angelina was sleeping, I didn't want to startle her.

She lay in the bed, wearing a wrinkled hospital gown. She was alone because the other bed in the room was empty. When I saw her, I winced. Her face was bruised and swollen, her left arm in a cast. Apparently, my shoes made some noise, despite my efforts to be quiet, because she spoke without opening her eyes.

"I told you, I don't want anything to eat."

"No problem," I said as I shut the door behind me. It gave a soft click. "You don't have to eat. How are you feeling?"

She tried to open her eyes, but the bruising around them made it difficult. Looking at me through narrow slits, she made a strangled noise in her throat.

Slowly, I approached the bed, with the same caution I'd use to greet a wounded predator. "Ms. Piccola, let me introduce myself. I'm Kate Stone, with the New York—"

She cut me off. "I know you. What the fuck are you doing in here?" Her mouth twisted as she struggled to sit up.

I held out the photo ID for what seemed like the umpteenth time. "I'm here on behalf of the DA's office. I need to talk to you about the assault. I'd like to hear the circumstances."

Her unbroken arm snaked out, knocking the ID out of my hand. It skittered across the tile floor. "I told the police, I'm not pressing charges. Why can't everyone just leave me alone?"

"Angelina—can I call you Angelina? You are the victim of a despicable crime. Obviously, someone has brutally assaulted you. I want to see the perpetrator held accountable."

"You have no right to bother me. Get out. Nurse!" She said it again, louder, "Nurse!"

Fortunately for me, the overhead TV was on, masking her high-pitched demand for help. Either Angelina couldn't be heard in the hallway or the staff simply ignored it. But I knew the clock was ticking. My time alone with her was running out.

"He's a serial abuser, Angelina. He won't stop. All of the statistics show that. I'd be glad to share some information about domestic violence. I think it would be helpful for you to learn more about it."

"I don't know what you're talking about. No one abused me."

She fumbled with the nurse call button, pushing it repeatedly. Holding the speaker close to her mouth, she called, "Nurse! Help!"

In a fierce whisper, I said, "Angelina, I'm on your side. I want to be your advocate."

"I don't want you on my side. You are my worst nightmare. Get the fuck out."

At this point, she was shrieking. A sound came through the speaker on the device she held. The crackling voice said, "Yes? Do you need something?"

"Get her out of here."

After a pause, the voice said, "Can you repeat that?"

She pressed the speaker against her mouth, screeching. "There's a stalker in here. Call. Security."

I backed away from the bed. The last thing I needed was to get busted at Bellevue. "We can talk later, when you're feeling better," I said, keeping my voice cheery and upbeat. "I have your number."

"OUT!"

Someone gave the door a solid push, banging it against the wall. That was my cue to exit. I strode out into the hallway, ignoring the nurse's startled exclamation as I brushed past her.

I made my way to the elevator at such a brisk clip, I almost didn't see Max James rounding the corner. He carried an enormous stuffed bear with a pink bow circling its neck. The bear had six heart-shaped helium balloons tied to its fuzzy paw.

Either the bear or the swaying balloons must have interfered with James's vision, because he didn't glance my way. I heard his voice as he entered the room of his most recent victim.

"Hey, baby! Look what I got you."

I wouldn't have recognized the voice as his had I not seen him with my own eyes. James sounded sweeter than a cotton candy machine spewing pink sugar onto a paper cone.

People who deal with domestic violence have explained to me that James's apologetic, gift-bearing behavior is a component of the pattern of abusive relationships. The cycle has three basic parts. The abuser threatens, the abuser strikes, and the abuser is really sorry, giving gifts and saying it will never happen again. Rinse and repeat.

My head was so busy counting the many ways that Max James embodied the classic profile of a violent abuser that I failed to realize an important fact. I had left my government ID on the floor of his girlfriend's hospital room.

CHAPTER 13

I SPENT THE afternoon on the phone, trying to chase down the witnesses to the attack on Angelina. It was a fruitless attempt. Two of them couldn't be reached at the phone numbers listed in the police report. When I got through to the third witness, she hung up as soon as I identified myself. And when I called back, she blocked me.

I was out of options. Legitimate options, anyway.

While I spun around in a circle in my battered office chair, I reflected on the offer that I had rejected in the candlelit church, Our Lady of the Forgotten. Maybe I'd been too hasty. I thought of the chance encounter with that fierce, middle-aged woman on the subway. If she was such a force to be reckoned with, what capabilities might the other people in that circle possess?

For the second time in twenty-four hours, I composed a text to Steven Salinas. This time, I played coy and asked him to meet me for dinner. I told him it would be my treat.

He didn't make me wait. Steven texted back within minutes

and accepted my invitation. Looking forward, he said. Not a wildly enthusiastic response, but it would do. I didn't want him to mistake it for a booty call anyway.

Before I left the office, I saw that Frank had emailed me, demanding to know when I intended to return the reports on the Max James assault. He also wanted to see my anger management verification form.

I didn't like the tone of Frank's email. Or the content, for that matter. I thought about ignoring it altogether but decided it would be more fun to reply. Will send your way ASAP.

As I left the building, I thought of the many different ways "ASAP" could be interpreted. *As soon as I get around to it. As soon as I feel like it. As soon as I remember it, tomorrow or the next day.* It was a petty exercise of power, but it gave me a warm feeling of satisfaction.

I had told Steven to meet me at a Chinese restaurant on the Lower East Side. Since I volunteered to pick up the tab, I wanted it to be a tab I could easily afford. Also, the odds of being overheard by anyone who knew Max James were unlikely as long as I was near Chinatown. As I waited for Steven, I sipped a Tsingtao.

Steven arrived before the bottle was empty. As he slid into the diminutive metal chair across from mine, he glanced at the beer. "Drinking again, I see."

"Yes. It's my therapy. The support meetings haven't really worked out." I paused to take another sip before asking, "You want to join me?"

I tried to flag our waitress, but she pointedly ignored me.

He said, "No, thanks anyway. I'll probably order tea."

"Tea? You're gonna be up all night, man. Didn't you order

coffee the last time we went out to a bar? All that caffeine." I gave a faux shudder. "Let me guess. Ambien. Or Halcion."

He glanced away with a rueful expression. "No. Not anymore."

I sensed that I was treading on sensitive ground, but there was no opportunity to lighten the conversation because the waitress finally paused at our table.

"Steamed dumplings, please. And another one of these," I said, lifting the bottle.

Leaning toward Steven, I said, "The pork dumplings are amazing here. You won't be disappointed."

He handed the plastic menu to the waitress. "Vegetable fried rice. No eggs, please."

As she walked off, I said, "Ah. A vegan." I didn't try to keep the deprecation from my voice.

He raised a brow. "And you're a carnivore," he said.

"I guess this means we're not a match made in heaven." I winked at him as I swilled my beer.

"Are you disappointed?"

"Yes. I'm disappointed that you will never know how good those pork dumplings taste."

He leaned forward in his chair as if he didn't want to be overheard. "I could give you a lecture on the horrors of industrial livestock farming."

"You're always trying to lecture me. It makes me want to buy a pack of cigarettes to soothe my nerves. And I can't afford the habit. That's why I bum them from real smokers."

He shook his head in disapproval. "Is this why you invited me out tonight? To try and corrupt me?"

The fresh beer arrived. I took a pull from the bottle before

I answered. "No. I asked you out because I'm ready to let you corrupt me."

My statement caught his attention, and a guarded look crossed his face. "Meaning what?"

"Did you watch the local news last night?"

He shook his head. "I was busy. And I don't watch much television."

Busy with the Batman freaks? popped into my head. I pushed the thought away and said, "He did it again. Another assault."

"Can you be more specific?"

On reflex, I turned in my seat and glanced around. It was an unnecessary precaution. No one in the restaurant was even vaguely interested in our conversation. And the buzz of voices, combined with noises from the kitchen, made eavesdropping impossible anyway.

Nevertheless, I spoke in a near whisper. "Max James. He put his girlfriend in the hospital yesterday. Beat the shit out of her."

As I waited for him to respond, I tried to read his face, but it was a mask. After a long pause, he said, "I guess the DA's office will have another opportunity to put him away."

"That's the problem," I said, my whispers growing strident. "She doesn't want to testify, and it looks like he's already gotten to the witnesses. Paid them off, or shut them up somehow."

His voice was scrupulously polite. "That's unfortunate."

"Hell, yes, it is. Worse than unfortunate; it's unacceptable."

There was an uncomfortable silence. He finally broke it, saying, "What does any of this have to do with me?"

I forgot to whisper. "Jesus Christ, Steven. Quit fucking around."

The waitress appeared at that juncture, interrupting my retort. We sat quietly as she placed the steaming food on the table. When she was out of earshot, I spoke again.

"That's the reason I got in touch. I've reconsidered. About your group, the people I met at the church. I want to hook up with you. So we can do something about Max James."

His forehead wrinkled. "As I recall, you turned us down. Didn't you say something about believing in the justice system?"

My hand tingled. I rubbed the skin under the table, out of sight. "I do believe in it. Just not for this guy. When it comes to Max James, it's not working."

The waitress stopped at a nearby table. Steven flagged her. "Can I have a to-go box, please?"

I felt my face heat up as the anger started to surge. "You won't talk about it. And you won't even eat with me? The food I'm paying for?"

He pulled out his wallet and tossed two twenties on the table. At this place, forty bucks would more than cover our tab. "You called us crazy."

"I just told you, I changed my mind. Do you want a formal apology?"

His dark eyes met mine. "I like you, Kate. And I'm sympathetic to your plight. But you're out of luck. You walked out. They don't give people second chances."

The waitress returned and set a foam box next to his plate. After he scooped the rice into it and secured the lid, he scooted his chair away from the table.

I reached out, grabbing his arm. "Don't go yet."

He looked down at my hand, as if he didn't understand

what it was doing there. I gripped him harder, and said, "You seem like a guy who believes in second chances."

And then I released his arm, and waited. It must have been the right thing to say. He expelled a deep sigh, and then opened his foam box of rice and took a bite.

After he swallowed, he said, "I'll talk to the other people on the team."

My shoulders relaxed; I had been strung tight. "When?"

"Tonight, if I can reach them." He gave me a warning look. "But I can't make any promises. You understand?"

I nodded, but I had a feeling that Steven could bring them around. As my tension eased, my appetite kicked into gear. With my chopsticks, I maneuvered a dumpling into my mouth, and nearly gagged. It was so hot, it burned my tongue.

Maybe I should have taken that as a sign.

CHAPTER 14

I WALKED UP and down the street near my apartment, trolling for a smoker. But foot traffic was light because most people had settled in for the night. Windows were lit in the apartments overhead.

Turning the corner, I headed for Broadway, clutching currency in my fist. A block of restaurants and bars was in reach: prime hunting ground. My eyes lit on a young man wearing an apron, stepping out of a restaurant on break. At the curb, his hand cupped a lighter protectively, to shield it from the breeze.

I strolled up. "Hi. Do you have another cigarette for me?"

He blew the smoke out, giving me the stink eye before he glanced away.

Undeterred, I held up a crumpled one-dollar bill. It was important to be prepared on a mission like this one. "I'm not a bum, see? I'll buy it from you. If you give me a light."

The man gave it a moment's consideration before he reached into his pocket. When I saw him pull out a pack of menthols, I almost rescinded the offer, but decided it was too late to back out. After he lit the cigarette for me, I felt obligated to make some small talk.

"Do you know Nick? He's the bartender at an Italian restaurant on 123rd, Pasticci's. He's a friend of mine."

His face was impassive. "Yeah. I'm personally acquainted with every restaurant employee in upper Manhattan."

Ah, I thought, *a wit*. When he turned his back to me, I mentally composed a retort, something tart, but my phone began to vibrate in my pocket before I had a chance to deliver the quip.

Sucking in menthol, I dug out the phone and checked the screen: Steven.

He had just left me at the Chinese restaurant an hour ago. I pressed the phone to my ear. "Steven. What's up?"

"Where are you?"

He whispered it, like we were exchanging secrets. I walked away from menthol man, pausing a moment before I answered. "I'm on my way to the gym," I said. Because it sounded better than *I'm smoking on the street with a reluctant stranger*.

"We'd like to meet you. Now."

Steven's voice in the phone thrummed with intensity, sending a thrill through me. I took another drag before I answered. "Who's 'we'?"

"The group."

I blew out the smoke. "Really."

He said, "Are you smoking? When you're on the way to work out?"

"Don't be ridiculous." I ashed the cigarette on the pavement. "It's going to take me a little while to get down to that church—Our Lady of the Whatever. But I still have the address."

"We're not at the church."

"Why not?"

He sighed into the phone, as if I had tested his patience. "I thought I told you: The group never meets at the same location twice. It's a security precaution. I'll text you an address."

"Now? You're going to text me now?"

I had to stop and lean against the wall of the nearest building because I was feeling light-headed. Whether it was from the menthol cigarette or Steven's summons, I couldn't say for sure.

"Yeah. As soon as I hang up. Are you listening? This is important."

Annoyed, I stopped myself from saying something I'd regret; what did he think I was doing? "I'm listening."

"The address is for a warehouse in Brooklyn, down by the water. It looks abandoned."

I broke in. "That church I broke into also looked abandoned. Thanks for the warning on that, by the way."

"This warehouse looks dangerous. I'm just telling you so you won't be put off by that."

The memory of the creepy vibe inside the church hadn't faded. If the warehouse was more formidable than the last meeting place I'd encountered, Steven's friends were gluttons for punishment.

But I just said: "Good to know."

"We'll be inside, on the upper floor. It's about eight twenty now, right?"

"Yeah. I think."

"If you're not here in an hour, we walk."

I almost snickered; he sounded so somber. But I kept a straight face. "Twenty after nine. You want me to join you by then. Got it."

His voice deepened. "I'm serious, Kate. This is it. I went out on a limb for you."

"Well, I appreciate that. You're my hero, Steven," I said, trying to lighten the gothic tone of the exchange.

"If you're not here in an hour, I won't pick up the next time you call."

He hung up without waiting for my reply. A moment later, the phone buzzed with a text—he had sent the address.

When I searched it online, I groaned. The directions required me to venture into a dicey block in Brooklyn. The neighborhood wasn't an easy spot to access, and I had been zigzagging across the city all damned day.

As I pulled away from the wall, my hair caught on the rough brick of the exterior, as if it didn't want to let me go. Clutching my hand around the hank of hair, I wrenched it away and headed for the subway. Halfway there, I paused on the sidewalk, thinking: Hadn't I just told him I was hitting the gym? Did I need to go home and change clothes, so he wouldn't catch me in the lie?

But my apartment was blocks away; the subway was straight ahead. "Fuck it," I said, and descended the steps that would take me underneath the city.

CHAPTER 15

I WAS LOST, roaming along blocks of Brooklyn that were just as scary as Steven had described on our phone call. I checked the address again; the information on Google Maps wasn't precisely accurate in this neighborhood.

As I studied my phone, the time jumped out at me. Steven had expressly confined me to a one-hour limit, and it had almost expired.

Gazing around at the cluster of bedraggled buildings, I tried to guess which one was my destination. Several industrial warehouses stood nearby, and all of them looked abandoned. The exteriors bore splashes of bright graffiti on crumbling brick.

I sent a desperate text: Steven! Building description??? Because they all looked deserted and scary to me.

One of the buildings had a maze of razor wire circling the roof. Just below the razor wire, I could just make out faded white letters that had been painted onto the brick decades prior: "Atlas Waste Manufacturing Company."

A voice behind me in the darkness startled me. "You gotta wonder why anyone would want to manufacture waste."

I spun around, my heart pounding. The lighting was dim, and I couldn't find the speaker until I saw a small red glow as a figure emerged from the shadows of the warehouse.

She sauntered toward me and tossed the cigarette butt into the gutter. "You're late, Kate."

I recognized the voice before I could make out her face: it was the woman from the subway.

"I'm having trouble finding the meeting place. Which warehouse is it?"

She smiled; the light from the streetlamp reflected off her teeth and highlighted the silver strands in her hair. "Atlas Waste Manufacturing, of course."

I sounded snappish when I said, "Steven could have saved me a lot of trouble if he'd made that clear an hour ago."

"Maybe he gave you too much credit. You know who Atlas was, right? In mythology? He carried the weight of the world on his shoulders."

Ambling over to the exterior of the building, the woman bent down in front of a battered metal service door and tugged on it. The slats rolled up with a rattle and groan of complaint. I was rattled, too, but wanted to hide my uneasiness; I didn't want to look bashful to the subway warrior.

Following her inside the empty space, I said, "I would have had an easier time if your leader had mentioned Atlas to me."

Without warning, she halted; I nearly bumped into her. "My leader?"

"Yeah. Steven, the leader of your support group."

I couldn't see her face, but I heard her cackle, like she knew a joke that I wasn't in on. Which reminded me of her inter-action with the man who harassed the young Asian woman on the train. "Are you one of those Guardian Angels, who patrol the subway?" Though I'd heard of the group, I'd never actually encountered one. But Guardian Angels purportedly wore red berets, and she did not.

"Nope." She didn't elaborate.

My feeling of apprehension grew as we walked up a dark stairway. When we emerged on the landing, I saw figures gathered on the second floor of the building, seated on the concrete floor.

Without ceremony, the woman announced me: "She's here."

The room was lit with a couple of LED lanterns. I recognized Steven as he stood, brushing the seat of his pants. "Whitney! You found her."

That jogged my recollection. *Whitney*, I thought. *Gambling addict.*

Steven said, "Glad you made it, Kate."

The big guy in the center of the group mumbled something indistinct. I recalled him from the prior meeting; the former Marine who claimed to suffer from PTSD. At the moment, he was suffering from a case of acute annoyance. Judging from the scowl he wore, it didn't look like he shared Steven's enthusiasm. "How long will this take? I've got somewhere I need to be."

Steven said, "Rod, let's at least hear Kate out."

"Sorry for running late. I got turned around." I felt un-comfortable, uncharacteristically shy, like a new kid at school. "I appreciate the fact that you waited."

Most of the group had focused on me, with the exception of the young man with dreads on my right. He bent over his cell phone, playing a mobile game.

Stepping closer, I peered over his shoulder. "Aren't you the one with a gaming addiction?"

He looked up at me for a moment before returning to the screen. "I'm Devon. I guess you could say I'm making negative progress."

Steven said, "Sit down, Kate. I told everyone the basics of our conversation at dinner, but we want more information about Max James."

I sat cross-legged on the gritty floor. "He was found not guilty of assault in my jury trial last week. Steven told you about that, right?"

Several heads nodded.

Without looking up from his phone, Devon said, "We offered to take on the Max James problem at the church. And you turned us down."

I had hoped they wouldn't hold the initial rejection against me, but it sounded like my earlier encounter caused some lingering resentment. My voice urgent, I said, "He's already committed another attack. It was his girlfriend this time. She's in the hospital."

"Which one?" a woman asked. She was Diane, who identified herself as a sex addict at the last meeting.

"She's been transferred to Mount Sinai, but I don't know why her injuries require additional hospitalization. She was originally at Bellevue, but she wouldn't talk to me."

Whitney, the subway warrior, said, "Steven tells us she's not interested in pressing charges against him."

"That's right." As my eyes adjusted to the dim light, I could see that the solemn expressions around the circle showed sincere interest in my plight. So maybe, I thought, they wouldn't hand me an automatic rejection. "That's why I'm reaching out. I need your help."

Steven added, "The DA is dodging it."

The young gamer looked surprised. "Why? What power does Max James have over the district attorney's office?"

I shrugged. "Rubenstein made a gutless call, that's all. James has no personal influence."

"That you know of," Rod grunted.

That took me aback; was it possible that James did have some kind of leverage with Rubenstein? I'd never considered it.

Thinking out loud, I said, "It's a more basic issue. James has economic privilege, the ability to hire lawyers who have connections, and the money to buy his way out of trouble. He's a bully with a lot of resources…and that makes him untouchable."

Steven added, "And he knows how to pick his victims."

I nodded. "Exactly."

The big guy, Rod, chuckled; it had a somber ring, because there was no humor in it. "Nobody's untouchable."

The heads around the circle bobbed in agreement. Just then, the wind whipped through a broken window overhead, sending a chill through the room.

It felt invigorating. I sat up straight, as optimism began to surge in my veins. I was very glad that I had found the Atlas Waste Manufacturing Company.

And then, in the gloom of the warehouse, Whitney spoke up again. "Let's crush him."

CHAPTER 16

WHEN WHITNEY SAID, "crush him," I snickered. Because I assumed she was joking—speaking ironically, in hyperbole. Even when she followed it up, by saying, "We should smash him like an insect," I thought it was a figure of speech. But no one else laughed, not even a chuckle.

I sobered. "Whitney? Your name's Whitney, right?"

"Yeah, it's Whitney. To my friends."

It was dark in there, but I thought I saw her wink at me. It was kind of unsettling.

I gave the woman a nervous grin; under normal lighting, my expression would likely have been revealed as a grimace. "Whitney, you don't know who we're dealing with. Max James works for a major asset management firm. This guy isn't a small fish. If we can lock him up for a year and get a criminal conviction on record, it will be huge. An enormous victory."

Devon shook his head. "You're thinking too small."

An older man agreed; I recalled him as Larry, the alcoholic

from the prior meeting. Scooting closer to the center of the group, he said, "We don't work on a miniature scale."

The youngest woman in the circle flipped a golden braid over her shoulder: Millie, the anxiety addict. "Destroy him or don't fuck with it at all. That's my vote."

I was grateful for the enthusiasm—just unconvinced they could pull it off. "I wish it was that easy."

Several voices chimed in at once, offering a bizarre symphony of suggestions that demonstrated we were absolutely not on the same page. Larry raised his hand for silence. He looked at me, his brow furrowed. "Do you know which is his dominant hand?"

I nodded; it had been established as part of the case when Anna Sung testified that her facial injuries were inflicted by his right fist.

"He's right-handed. Why?"

"Because that gives us a target. We crush the right hand. As an alternative, we could remove some of his fingers. At least three, I'd say."

Diane, the sex addict, spoke up in an eager voice. "So he can't make a fist. Get it? Target his dominant hand, and you have a solution."

My face had frozen into a mask of incredulity. I was struggling to form an adequate response when I heard the gamer murmur over his phone screen.

"Primitive. We can do better."

I breathed out in relief. Rod, the muscle-bound guy, spoke up.

"It seems like an 'eye for an eye' gesture is more appropriate in this situation. We take him to a remote location, tie him to a chair. Give the woman who testified at the trial a baseball bat. She can have at him. Payback."

I'm ashamed to admit that the proposal held a certain appeal. Fortunately, Steven nixed it. "That's a temporary solution, Rod. It provides vengeance for his victim, so it achieves that goal. But it doesn't halt future attacks on his part."

I raised my hand. "I'm with Steven. Physical retribution won't change anything. I don't think that's the direction we're looking for."

Diane turned to Steven and asked: "Isn't this the chick who punched him out on the sidewalk outside the courthouse?"

I let out a nervous cackle. "Yeah. I'm that chick."

A man rose from the far side of the room and walked up to Steven. When he squatted on the floor beside him, I caught a whiff of paint; he was the paint-spattered guy with an anger problem, like mine. In a low voice, he said, "Steven, when you sold us on this project, you didn't say what a negative attitude this lawyer has."

I opened my mouth to protest, but Whitney spoke up. "Max James needs to be incarcerated. That's the only effective prevention. If he's behind bars, he can't attack women."

Whitney scooted across the gritty floor to sit beside me, knee to knee. She put a hand on my shoulder; it felt like a gesture of support. "We will break the pattern when he goes to prison. She's right, we don't need to get physical."

I breathed a sigh of relief, until she added, "Devon can break into James's personal computer and plant a bomb."

Plant a bomb? I envisioned carnage and destruction as a bomb exploded in James's office, bodies flung onto the pavement.

The image of my father's picture in the *New York Post* surfaced in my brain; with an enormous effort, I banished it.

"Won't innocent people get hurt?" I ventured to ask. But my comment was drowned out by the group's general approval of Whitney's proposal.

One member scoffed at it, however. Diane said, "Too easy, Whitney."

"What kind of bomb are you talking about?" I asked.

"Whatever we want. Cyberterrorism, trafficking, mail fraud. How about creating a virtual footprint of bribery of a public official? That would be a piece of cake. And Rubenstein can't overlook that," she said.

Millie, the young blonde, looked confused. "How do we get a judge or some official to go along with it? Bribery is a two-person process."

Whitney explained in a patient voice. "The crime of bribery occurs when the bribe is offered. You see? We don't need a judge to participate in the plan. All that's necessary is for the judge to receive the offer. We can do it all online."

My breath hitched in a gasp. Horrified, I looked around, expecting the group members to veto the proposal. But I saw heads nodding; the others didn't share my revulsion.

In a no-nonsense voice, I said, "No."

But the group members ignored me. Diane, from her seat against the wall, said, "Devon, how much of a challenge would that pose? I don't think we've tried it before."

Devon shrugged as his brow furrowed, considering the question. "I'll have to look into the system his business uses."

"No," I repeated, loud enough to bounce off the walls. "Absolutely not. We need another plan to take him down."

Larry, the older man seated across from me, gave me a weary look. "I don't understand your objection. We thought you were serious about this. Whitney's proposal is a no-brainer, a win-win. Prosecutors don't sweep bribery under the rug. They won't give him a pass on it."

Ready to depart, I stood and brushed the dust off my pants. The conversation was dangerous. "I won't dirty my hands with it."

After I made that declaration, silence fell in the room. Everyone seated in the warehouse stared at me, like they were waiting for something. It was eerie.

Steven spoke up. "Kate, tell us what you're thinking. Help them understand."

"Max James is a serial abuser, a habitual criminal. But I don't want to set him up for something he didn't do. And I don't want to involve a sitting judge. That's just wrong." There was a tremor in my voice; I cleared my throat.

I was getting through to some of them. The blonde, Millie, leaned into Rod and whispered in his ear. He looked at her and nodded. But Devon hadn't quite given up the idea.

"I could create the whole thing virtually. The email exchange detailing the terms of the bribe, making the offer clear. It would be so simple. No one gets hurt in the process, except for the guy you want to convict."

Sinking down again on the dirty floor, I hugged my knees, thinking about Devon's proposal. Though it wouldn't directly victimize any judges, the plan still made me queasy. Having any involvement in the creation of a wrongful conviction was repellent to me.

I couldn't do it. I refused to set up James for some crime

he didn't really commit. I wanted him to pay for his actual wrongdoing. If I set him up for a wrongful conviction, how could I claim a righteous victory? I'd be no better than James or his team of crooked lawyers. In my mind's eye, I saw my father, shaking his head in disapproval.

It was clear that the vigilante radicals and I operated under different sets of principles. But I wasn't quite ready to flee the warehouse. Where else would I find a multitalented group of professionals who were insane enough to attack my nemesis?

I pleaded. "Something else, please? This is obviously a confederation of people who can think outside the box. Isn't there a better way to go after him and bring him down?"

Whitney groaned, stretching out on the concrete. Pillowing her head in her arms, she stared up at the patchy ceiling. "Oh, hell. All right, we'll dig into his business. See where the bodies are buried. Find his personal stash of white-collar crime."

I gaped at her, wondering whether she was kidding. "Can you do that?"

"Yeah. We can do it. It's just a lot more complicated."

Devon grimaced. "A *whole* lot more complicated."

Still hesitant, I said, "How do you know there's anything unethical with the way he conducts his business?"

"A successful financier?" Whitney snorted. "Oh, please. Don't be naïve."

Steven jumped to his feet. "We'll vote. We're overstaying our welcome here; we need to move on out before we're mistaken for burglars or squatters. I don't want to get shot by a trigger-happy security guard."

He held out a hand to me, but I waved it off; I didn't need

his help to stand, for God's sake. I supposed he wanted me to leave, so they could vote in private. "Should I wait downstairs? For your decision?"

"Not necessary. Friends, all those in favor of corrective action against Max James through an attack on his business interests?"

The proposition lacked unanimous support; the ayes were spotty. Whitney waited until others had voted in favor before raising her hand. Deadpan, she said: "Yeah, I'm in."

In the dark, I couldn't count: Did we get a majority? I waited with my nerves on edge as Steven said, "All opposed?"

There were a handful of nays as well. I held my breath until Steven broke into a grin. "Looks like Whitney was the tie-breaker."

She reached for my hand and squeezed it. Her fingers were cold. "It's official now, Kate. Welcome to Justice Anonymous."

CHAPTER 17

BEFORE I LEFT the warehouse that night, I'd pledged solidarity with their overall cause. But it was a ruse. In reality, I had no intention of forging a permanent alliance with Steven and his ragtag group of vigilantes. I still viewed them as a band of outlaws, and suspected some of them were crazy.

And I didn't consider myself an outsider of legitimate law enforcement—not at that point. I still maintained my general loyalty to the justice system, and to my role as a prosecutor. As a rule, I would follow the established, conventional route to respond to criminal activity in New York City.

Max James was the catch; in his case, the system wasn't working. The band of vigilantes could provide a correction to that oversight. Steven's circle was a means to an end. Maybe Bill Parker had a valid point when he suggested I had developed an obsession with Max James. But once we dealt James a blow and eliminated his scourge within the community, I would walk away from Steven and his associates, without a backward look.

That was my intention, anyway.

At the warehouse in Brooklyn, no one indicated when our joint enterprise might commence. I hoped we would jump on it without delay. As long as Max James walked free, the odds of another assault increased.

So I was psyched to receive the summons just a few days later. It was a text from Steven, instructing me to meet him at the Craftsman on Broadway near 125th Street Station.

I didn't need directions. The bar was in my 'hood, just a stone's throw from Grant's Tomb. A string of lightbulbs marked the destination as I approached. I was running early, partly because I was eager to hear their plot. Also, I wanted to snag the booth in back, where we could sit in relative seclusion.

Steven was the first to join me. As he slid into the wooden bench across the table, the server delivered my beverage, a Manhattan on the rocks. Steven gave it a wary glance, which I ignored.

The server turned to him. "I'm Heather. Do you need a menu?"

"No. Just tap water with ice."

She hurried off. The bar was hopping, buzzing with laughter and rowdy conversation. I ducked my head and spoke in a whisper. "So what's the plan?"

He squinted at me. "What? Can't hear you."

"The plan," I said, in a louder voice. "For Max."

He didn't answer because, at that moment, Devon sauntered up. As he sat beside me, I wondered about our choice of meeting place. Was Devon twenty-one? The gamer looked so young it was hard to tell. And he was perusing the beer menu.

When Heather came up to deposit Steven's ice water, Devon pushed the menu away. "Amber ale."

"Fat Tire okay?"

"Yeah."

If the server wasn't worried, neither was I. When she was out of earshot, I directed my attention to Devon. "I'm dying to hear your plan for Max."

He gave me a blank look. "There's no action for him. Not yet."

Steven leaned back against the booth. "You're not ready, Kate. There's a process. You have some skills to learn."

"And we don't trust you yet," Devon added with a nonchalant air. "There's that."

A buzz of anger zipped through my head. If they thought they could play me, I intended to let them know they had picked the wrong woman. But the waitress arrived at that moment to deliver Devon's beer. He tried to flirt with her, even asking for her number. Gulping a swallow of my Manhattan, I waited impatiently for the exchange to end.

As Devon watched the waitress walk away, I focused on Steven. "Is this some kind of game you're playing? Because I don't like it."

Steven was unperturbed. "Not a game at all. But we've got to handle a situation for another member of the group. You'll be part of the solution on that case. After we wrap it up, we'll focus on your guy."

This was not what I had anticipated. The game change pissed me off. I considered bailing on them, walking away from the booth and out the door.

But I had a partially full drink and an unpaid tab. The

process of settling the bill would interfere with my dramatic exit. And there was the Max James situation to consider. The group offered my best shot at him.

"Let's see if I understand the situation." I took another swallow. "You want me to jump through hoops before you will help me."

Devon's face lit up. "Yeah! Think of it as an initiation rite."

I gave him a look. "Really?"

Steven reached out and clasped my wrist. Giving it a gentle squeeze, he said, "This benefits all of us. I think you will be more than willing to lend a hand when you hear the situation."

I wasn't convinced. Nonetheless, I said, "Okay. So tell me."

Devon whispered, "Revenge porn."

I recoiled, snatching my hand from Steven's grasp. "You want me to blackmail someone?"

"No, not like that." Steven shook his head. "One of the associates in our group is the victim. A guy took images with his phone when they were intimate. Now he's using them to manipulate her at work."

They had captured my interest, despite my initial pique. "That's cyber sexual assault. Revenge porn is a crime. Sharing a nude photo of someone without their consent isn't a minor offense; you can get up to a year in jail for it. She should call NYPD."

The men exchanged a look. "It's complicated," Steven said. "She doesn't want to go public. She has a history. And there's a hierarchy at work. Plus, the guy is married. It's problematic."

"It always is. Which associate is it? Who's the victim?"

Steven said, "We don't need to go into specifics. Our group is intended to be anonymous."

But Devon rolled his eyes. "Come on, Kate, who do you think? Millie is a student, she doesn't have a job. Whitney is old so no one is storing cheesecake images of her on their phone. And it's not you. Who does that leave?"

Diane. The sex addict. Steven was right. It was complicated.

But I was sympathetic with her plight. When I worked in the domestic violence division, we wrestled with revenge porn issues. Abusive partners try to hurt their victims in a myriad of ways.

I took another drink, nearly draining the glass. I caught the server's eye and gave her a signal before I announced my decision. "Okay, you've convinced me. I'm in. But I don't have any special abilities in tech. Is that what I have to learn, the new skill you need from me?"

"No, that's my area of expertise," Devon said loftily.

"So what do you want from me? I can outline the legal stuff, civil and criminal remedies. Do you want me to write a brief?"

Steven was grinning, like he knew a joke I wasn't in on. "No. Not a brief."

I was genuinely puzzled. "What am I going to do?"

Heather returned with a fresh Manhattan. Steven waited patiently for her to depart.

And then he said, "Kate, you're going to learn how to be a pickpocket."

CHAPTER 18

MY INSTRUCTION IN larceny started that weekend.

Steven said we would need to meet at my place for privacy reasons. Devon shared an apartment with two roommates in a brownstone on the Upper West Side. I was impressed by his address. Apparently, he was closer to my age than he looked. And his employment at an IT firm paid very well.

And Steven told me he was in a group-living situation. He didn't elaborate, and I picked up a vibe. It felt like he didn't want me to inquire about it.

Before they arrived on Saturday morning, I looked around my studio with misgivings. The seating was limited, just a shabby sofa and the vinyl recliner I had taken from Dad's apartment after he died. I washed the dishes that had accumulated in the sink during the workweek and took a smelly bag of trash to the garbage chute. But I had a quantity of dirty laundry and no place to hide it. I rolled it into a bundle and shoved it into a corner behind the recliner. And I opened the window, hoping that the air outside the apartment was fresher than the air inside.

Shortly after I completed my hasty improvements, I heard a knock. When I peered through the peephole, I saw both of them outside my door. After I unlocked the deadbolts and let them in, Devon looked around, surveying the space with trepidation.

He said, "Do you know that the door to the building doesn't have a lock? Anyone could walk right in."

It wasn't news to me. "Yeah, the landlord says he's gonna fix that soon. Personally, I have my doubts."

Steven took a spot on the sofa and patted the space beside him. I sat.

He asked, "Have you ever been the victim of a pickpocket?"

"No, but my mother had her purse stolen once, a few years ago."

"How did they do it?"

"It was just one guy."

"You think?" He and Devon exchanged a glance, like they shared a private joke. "Tell me what happened."

I took a moment to recall. "It was at the subway. She was going through the turnstile, and some guy shoved in behind her like he wanted to get on without paying for a ride. She was so pissed about him squeezing in there that she didn't realize he'd grabbed her purse until she saw him run off with it."

Devon nodded, intrigued. "That's a good one. A classic."

Leaning back against the sofa, Steven said, "The subway offers a host of opportunities for pickpockets."

While Devon shared his personal experience with theft on the subway, I stared down at the sofa and found a triangle of crust that looked like the corner of an old Pop-Tart. I shoved it between the cushions to get it out of sight.

When Devon wrapped up his tale, I said, "Am I grabbing a purse on the subway? Because I'm not particularly thrilled at this prospect."

"Nothing as unsophisticated as that." Steven stood up, facing me. "Most men carry their wallets in their back pockets, correct?" He turned around to show me.

I made a rueful face. "Why do we need to grab some dude's wallet? Do you need money?"

"We don't. We want the phone." He faced me again, patting his front pocket with his left hand. "He carries it here."

I stared at the front of his worn jeans. My eyes wandered to the faded fly. It was eye level, I couldn't help it. The sight was impressive.

Looking away, I made eye contact. "I'm supposed to grab his phone out of his pocket, and he's not going to catch on?"

"We work together as a team, so that he won't catch on."

He grabbed my hand and pulled me off the sofa. "Okay, here's the setup. The couch is an ice-cream truck. Devon is in line in front of me; you are behind me. I'm the target. Got that?"

"The target?" I repeated, hoping for additional explanation. But Devon stepped over to stand directly in front of Steven. After a moment, I took my place behind him, totally bewildered.

To the empty sofa, Devon said, "I'll have a chocolate-vanilla swirl in a waffle cone with rainbow sprinkles."

I snickered. Steven looked over his shoulder and winked at me. It was starting to feel like a party game.

When Devon stepped away from the couch with his imaginary cone, Steven moved forward and said, "I'll take a cone, a shake, whatever."

Devon jumped back in place, shoving Steven out of the way. "Overcharged, ice cream man! *J'accuse!*" he turned, facing us. "I've been shortchanged!"

And he smashed his imaginary cone into Steven's chest.

I stood by, watching the tableau unfold. Steven cut his eyes at me. "Now," he said.

"Now? Oh! Got it!" I reached in his pants pocket, fumbling for the phone. It took a full minute and a couple of jerks to get it free, but I managed.

I held up Steven's phone, expecting praise.

Devon screeched in falsetto. "Officer! Arrest this woman! She stole my husband's wallet!"

Steven took the phone from me and slid it back into his pocket. "Kate, you'll need to be smoother. Take advantage of the distraction, and when the target is diverted, nick it so fast that he doesn't notice until you're gone."

"Okay. I understand." Unaccountably, I felt embarrassed by my poor performance. Which was ridiculous. I should not regret my minimal experience with stealing the property of others.

Anyway, Steven was encouraging. "You just need practice. It's a physical skill. You will master it. Got to be easier than kickboxing, right? Or karate."

He was right. I could do this. We lined up again. Devon ordered ice cream, Steven followed. Devon accosted him. I plunged my hand in the pocket. It got stuck.

They both laughed at me. "Again," Steven said.

We practiced for an hour, nonstop. My hand hadn't been that close to a guy's crotch for a while. It was unsettling because it gave rise to an involuntary attraction. I had to remind myself that this was simply business. And Steven was not my type.

I was just beginning to get the hang of it when Devon announced he was leaving. He had an engagement downtown. He didn't say what it was, and I didn't ask. We were supposed to be anonymous, after all.

After the door shut behind him, Steven said, "Let's take a break."

It was a welcome suggestion. I stepped over to the kitchenette and opened the door to the fridge, hoping to find a can or two of Coke.

I was disappointed. Looking over my shoulder, I said, "You thirsty? I can offer water."

"Great."

One of my ice cube trays held a half dozen cubes. After I plopped the cubes in two glasses, I should have filled up the tray and placed it in the freezer, but it seemed like a lot of trouble. Leaving it on the counter, I returned to the sofa with the water glasses and handed one to Steven.

"So our target, the man in line at the ice-cream truck. He's the guy who's threatening to post the intimate pictures, is that right?"

"Yeah." Steven took a swallow and set the glass on a battered side table. "That's why we need the phone."

I sat cross-legged on the couch, facing him. "You realize that he could have downloaded the images on another device by now."

"We know that. But possession of the phone will give us power over him. Diane says he's a player, even though he's married. Her pictures won't be the only ones in his photo history. She can threaten to expose him. Tell his wife, maybe."

I didn't really like the sound of that. It was another criminal act prohibited by state and federal law. "Extortion?"

"True." Steven seemed untroubled by the prospect. "But you won't be the blackmailer, so it's not your problem."

"Right. I'm just a thief."

"Exactly." He grinned. Steven had a nice smile, though he didn't display it very often. "Are you feeling like Oliver Twist yet?"

"Kind of." In truth, it was a fairly apt metaphor. "But I remember that Fagin said Oliver was a natural pickpocket. It's taking me some time. I'm more like Eliza Doolittle at her linguistics lessons."

"You're coming along." He patted my knee. "We'll practice as long as you need it. When we're done, it will be second nature to you."

"I can quit my job. Take up a whole new career."

He laughed as he rose from the couch. Reaching for my hand, he gave it a tug. "Come on, Eliza. Back to work."

I groaned as I scrambled off the couch. But I didn't really mind. Sliding a hand in Steven's pocket was pretty fair entertainment for a Saturday afternoon. A question slid through my head, unbidden. *Can opposites really attract?* I tried to suppress it.

"One request: Can we call this guy something other than 'the target'?"

"Sure. Call him whatever you want."

I thought about it for a second before I hit on the right name: the thorn in my side who sent me out into support group madness.

"We'll call him Frank."

CHAPTER 19

TWO WEEKS LATER, I stood across the street from the Museum of Natural History. The ice-cream truck was in place, directly in front of the steps leading up to the museum entrance. Music blared from the truck, a tinny version of "Pop Goes the Weasel," playing over and over at high volume.

My phone hummed. It was Steven. I took a seat on a wooden bench as I answered. "Where are you?"

"In the park. Devon is in the museum lobby, keeping his eyes open and scoping out the sidewalk."

I looked over my shoulder, peering through the trees into Central Park as if I would spot Steven in the hundreds of bodies walking to and fro.

"Does Diane still think this guy is coming?"

"He should be. It's his visitation weekend. And she claims he's a creature of habit. He and his current wife take the kid to the park, hang around for about an hour, get an ice cream."

I shifted on the bench, uncomfortable with the prospect. "What if the kid is standing in line with him? I'm not going to shove a kid."

Because I'm a member of law enforcement in New York, I did not add. Maybe I didn't need to.

Steven's voice was soothing and encouraging. "Just play it out like we rehearsed. It will be fine, gonna go smooth as silk. You are light-fingered after all of our practice."

I gave the sidewalk pedestrians the side-eye, hoping that our target, "Frank," wouldn't come. Glancing at the clouds that threatened overhead, I said, "Looks like rain. Maybe he changed his—"

Steven cut me off. "I see him. Time to cross the street."

Well, damn. It was the moment of truth. I tried to rationalize my actions as I pushed the button on the pole and waited for the walk signal. To hush my inner voice, I rationalized. It's a small crime that I'm committing, to prevent a larger one. And this guy deserves it. Revenge porn is terrible, a misogynistic power play. And I have to do it to get justice for the women that Max James has hurt in the past, and will surely attack in the future. It's the right thing to do, a small price to pay.

An image of my father popped into my head. A look of disappointment was etched on his features. I squeezed the spot by my thumb to make him disappear.

When the light changed, I crossed with a cluster of others heading to the museum. Fake Frank was crossing as well. I could see the top of his head.

Devon had descended the stairs, moving toward the ice-cream truck at a fast clip. We were lucky, the line was short. Maybe the dark clouds overhead discouraged the soft-serve trade.

The target paused on the sidewalk to talk to his wife, and it delayed us for an instant. I stopped on the sidewalk near him, gazing up the steps at the big bronze statue of Teddy Roosevelt as if I'd never seen it before.

I heard the wife say, "I don't want anything. Just get a cone for Charlie before it starts raining."

Charlie tugged on his father's hand. "I want a cherry dip!"

When the boy stepped aside with his stepmother, I breathed out in relief.

Devon slid into line immediately ahead of the target. I stepped up behind him, just as we'd practiced. But some guy with his hair tied back in a ponytail shouldered his way in front of me. I gave him an ugly look.

"Excuse me? I was here first."

He ignored me. I tapped his shoulder. He didn't bother to look back.

This wasn't the plan. The way we had rehearsed it, my position was supposed to be directly behind "Frank." I grew edgy as the line slowly advanced. Devon was moving to the window to order.

I stared at the line-cutter's hank of hair, thinking how easy it would be to grab it and jerk him down onto the pavement. I would enjoy it, in fact.

Easy, Kate. That was the anger impulse, the one that got me into trouble. I needed to suppress it.

When I heard Devon order the chocolate-vanilla with sprinkles, I tapped the ponytail guy's shoulder again.

"Is that your money?"

This time, he responded. "What?"

"I saw a twenty right there on the sidewalk. Did you drop it?"

He stepped out of line to look. *Schmuck*, I thought, as I took a giant step forward. He was scouring the pavement for the fictitious cash while the melody cranked from the speaker inside the truck. *Pop goes the weasel!*

The ice-cream man handed Devon his cone. "Eight dollars."

Devon paid, grabbed his change, and walked away. "Frank" stepped up, started to order the cherry dip. His order was interrupted when Devon charged back to the window.

"You shortchanged me," he shouted.

The ice-cream man shrieked a denial as Devon pushed his way back in front, shouting into the window. "I gave you a twenty!"

The target gave Devon a shove. "You're going to have to wait. There's a line of people here."

Devon pivoted, smashing the cone into the man's chest. My perception of time slowed to a crawl. I saw it play out in slow motion. The soft serve splayed across the guy's white shirt as rainbow sprinkles made a multicolored spray.

And then I made my move. I grabbed his right shoulder with one hand as I slid my left into his pocket. It was just like I'd rehearsed, over and over.

But it didn't work as efficiently in real life. The phone "Frank" carried was bigger than Steven's, and his pocket smaller. I had to remove it with a tug that wasn't as subtle as I'd rehearsed with Steven. And the ice cream on his shirt was apparently an insufficient distraction.

Because he whirled around to face me. "What are you doing?"

Devon dropped his empty waffle cone and trotted off, moving north. The stolen phone was safely in my own back pocket. But instead of walking away undetected, I had to improvise. I stepped backward, looking confused.

"Nothing," I said. "I'm not doing anything. I was trying to help you."

He plunged his hand into his left pocket. In an incredulous voice, he said, "You took my phone."

I continued to back away until I bumped into someone. I hoped it was Steven. If not, I was in a tight spot. "I don't know what you're talking about," I said, sounding injured.

I could feel the phone slip from my back pocket, but I remained focused on the target. Holding out both hands, palms up, I said, "I thought you were going to fall down after that guy bumped you. Hey, I'm just trying to get a cone here."

He wasn't buying it. "Frank" shouted for the police, and we attracted some bystanders. No cops showed up, but a security guard from the museum ran down to see what had transpired. I couldn't escape. I had to hang around and protest my innocence. I even opened my bag for their inspection and pulled out my pockets. When I demonstrated that the phone wasn't in my possession, the guard shrugged it off, and the circle of onlookers drifted away. Pedestrians walked around us on the sidewalk without bothering to look.

A new line had formed at the ice-cream truck. The target's son still wanted his cherry dip, and the boy's high-pitched voice could be heard over the music from the truck. Cursing, "Frank" took his place at the end of the line.

It was time for my exit. Before I left, I said to him, in a voice of righteous indignation, "You owe someone an apology."

I turned on my heel and walked off, satisfied with having the last word. Because I had spoken the truth. He did owe someone an apology.

Not me, obviously.

CHAPTER 20

WE HAD PULLED it off. Steven sent me a congratulatory text, praising my performance. He told me that I had proved myself to everyone's satisfaction. He wasn't exactly clear about who "everyone" was, but it was definitely a green light. He said the group would set their sights on Max James very soon.

So I'd scored a victory of sorts. Still, a thought kept nagging at me after I read the text. What would my dad have said about my escapade outside the Museum of Natural History? If he'd ever caught me taking something that didn't belong to me, there would be hell to pay. I tried to block the self-reproach, to suppress the shame. But that led to the larger issue of what Dad would make of this whole Justice Anonymous enterprise. It was my first thought when I dragged myself out of bed the next day.

It's one thing to resolve to take an action without suffering remorse. Pulling it off totally guilt-free? That would be harder.

That's why I rode the train into New Jersey on Sunday afternoon. I climbed up the slope of the hill, my head ducked against the chilly spring wind. My father's grave lay near the top of the rise, in the newer part of Greenlawn Cemetery. No showy tombstones or marble crypts dotted the landscape, just flat markers pressed into the ground.

It took a few minutes for me to find my dad's stone. A feeling of regret nagged at me as I hunted through the lines of chiseled names. Two years ago, I would have headed straight to his spot because I came to visit the site weekly. When winter came, the time between visits lengthened, but I still paid my respects once a month. After the first year, I grew more accustomed to his absence, and wasn't drawn as strongly to the graveside. On this occasion, I couldn't recall how long it had been since I last made the trek.

I clutched a limp bouquet of flowers, a listless handful of white daisies and yellow mums wrapped in cellophane and tied together with a rubber band. My dad wasn't a hearts-and-flowers kind of guy, but it didn't feel right to come empty-handed after all this time. So I had bought the flowers on impulse, dodging into a bodega before boarding the train that morning. The merchandise was limited, and I had to choose between wilted and ugly.

As I searched for the stone, the wind battered the floral tribute I held, making the cellophane crackle.

At last, I found the spot. His stone still looked new. The unadorned granite rectangle bore his name over the dates of birth and death. A line was chiseled at the bottom in small letters.

INTEGRITY IS DOING THE RIGHT THING, EVEN WHEN NO
ONE IS WATCHING.

I squatted down before the marker, brushing off the dry grass that clung to the stone. Dad always liked that quote. That's why Leo and I picked it for the stone. But the irony was plain. The official reports concluded he'd jumped out of his window. When no one was watching. To avoid doing the right thing.

I didn't believe it.

Running my fingers along the letters of his name, my throat ached with the yearning to see him and talk to him. I needed advice, answers, inspiration, and wisdom.

Feeling just a little foolish, I whispered to the gravestone. "Hey, Dad. I wanted to come see you today. I brought some flowers."

As if I needed to provide proof, I placed the bouquet onto the grass just beneath the marker. The garish color of the orange cellophane seemed to cast an off note; fumbling with the rubber band, I tore off the plastic covering and lay the bare flowers by the stone. They made a pathetic offering.

For a moment, I closed my eyes, trying to conjure the right words. When I spoke again, my whisper was harsh.

"So, I'm not entirely certain about my path right now. I went into the DA's office because I wanted to blaze a trail, strike some blows for justice, aid the injured, that kind of thing. I wanted to be like you. But it's not going so great, Dad."

An image of Frank Rubenstein's face popped into my head. To banish it, I opened my eyes and focused on the landscape.

After clearing my throat, I said, "The guy I work for doesn't seem to be really invested in helping out the underdog. You always said that was the point. Powerful people don't need our help. It's the powerless who could use a hand up."

I paused, searching for words. The wind whipped my hair into my eyes, stinging them, and I tucked the flyaway hair behind my ears before I continued.

"So what if there was an opportunity to do the right thing, in an unconventional way? Even if it's an illegitimate route? Do the ends justify the means? Can that ever work?"

I closed my eyes again, hoping inspiration would come and I would receive guidance, even if I was conjuring it inside my own brain. As I waited, I heard footfalls crunching in the grass behind me. Bowing my head, I waited for the passerby to move on.

When a hand grasped my shoulder, my eyes flew open. Wheeling around, I shoved the intruder away with all my strength, toppling him onto the line of stones. Rolling onto his back, he crab-walked away from me.

"Jesus, Kate. Are you trying to cripple me?"

At the sight of my brother's stricken face, I ran up and offered him a hand. Once he was on his feet, I helped brush grass and dirt off the back of his jacket.

"Leo, you can't sneak up on somebody like that. You're going to get your ass kicked."

His voice cracked as he said, "By my own sister?"

"Yeah, sorry about that." As I studied the hurt look on his face, a suspicion popped into my head. "What are you doing here?"

Because it wasn't beyond belief that Mom would have Leo follow me, just to exercise control and try to tinker with my life.

"I wanted to talk to you, and I knew that you were heading to New Jersey."

"How the hell did you know that?"

He held up his phone. The screen had a blinking button.

"Find My Friends. Remember? You agreed to be my contact."

I had, ages ago. But I wasn't aware that Leo was still keeping tabs on me. "Leo, that's supposed to be for emergencies. I don't want you to use it to follow me around."

With a contrite face, he looked down at our father's gravestone. The bundle of flowers had rolled over in a gust of wind. He nudged them back into place with his shoe.

"It's still weird to think that he's dead, isn't it?"

I nodded silently, a lump forming in my throat.

Still looking down, Leo said, "I would have figured he'd be the last guy in the world to jump out of a window."

When my brother uttered the statement, I jerked away from him as if he had struck me. No one had dared to mention my father's cause of death in years. Not in my presence, anyway.

"We weren't there. We don't know what happened."

Leo looked at me, askance. "Shit, Kate. Everybody knows what happened. He jumped. Because he couldn't face testifying at the murder trial. Couldn't rat out his friends."

The flowers skidded across the stone in another gust. Leo didn't stop them this time.

He said, "He took the easy way out. That's what everybody says."

The criticism brought hot tears to my eyes. I fought against them because I didn't want Leo to see me cry.

Leo's mouth turned down. "You know there's an unwritten code, the brotherhood of police officers, that kind of thing. He just couldn't break it. His partner Victor knew him better than anybody. Even Victor Odom said it, like everybody else."

I wanted to cover my ears, to block out Leo's voice. Instead, I snapped at him. "I don't know who you mean by 'everybody,' but they're wrong. He *never* took the easy way. And he was going to testify at the homicide trial. He told me so, the last time we talked. Right before he…right before it happened."

I'd been the last person to see him before his death. The night before he was set to testify in a manslaughter trial against a fellow NYPD officer, I climbed the five flights of stairs to his apartment to offer support.

I still remembered our last conversation. We sipped beers while he smoked a Marlboro. Sitting in a chair beside the open window, I chose my words with care.

"You're doing the right thing."

Dad said, "I know it. You don't have to tell me that."

"You've been adamant about it: the choke hold, the excessive force. It's illegal, indefensible."

He nodded, somber, as he reached for the ashtray.

I kept talking as if I needed to convince him. "That kid died, despite your efforts to intervene. You're a witness. You've been subpoenaed. You'll be under oath. You have to tell the truth. Simple as that."

His forehead furrowed as he fixed me with a dubious look. Rolling the filter of the cigarette with his thumb and finger, he said, "Come on, Kate. Not so simple."

I knew he was right. For a thirty-year veteran of the NYPD, it wasn't as cut-and-dried as I'd painted it.

My voice grew tight. "Your friends will stand by you," I said.

It was a lie. We both knew it. Break the police code, the fraternal order, and you stand alone.

Before I left, I said, "You'll be great on the stand, Dad. It's going to be fine. Really."

He grinned at me. "Sure it will. I'm looking on the bright side. Maybe I'll make the *New York Post*, after all these years."

I should have stayed with him that night. Shouldn't have left him alone. But I went home.

Because of that, I blamed myself when my dad did make the cover of the *New York Post*. The color photo blocked out his face. But it showed his body, clad in his undershirt and shorts, twisted on the pavement after his five-story free fall. The caption identified him by name, lest there be any doubt: "Morris Stone."

The headline read, "NYPD Witness Takes the Plunge Before Trial."

Staring blindly at my father's grave marker, the headline flashed in my brain like a Times Square news ticker.

Leo broke the reverie when he gave my arm an awkward pat. "I know it was tough on you, hard to accept. You were always his favorite."

My initial impulse was to deny it, to say that he didn't have a favorite. But it was an old argument, and the point was moot. He was dead. No favorites anymore.

I tugged on Leo's arm, ready to leave. He turned and walked alongside me. As we made our way down the hill, I said, "So who's the favorite kid now? You're Mom's number one, Leo."

He laughed, but it had a hollow ring. "I don't know about that. All she talks about is getting you into her law firm."

The suggestion sent a shudder through me. In a voice of absolute certainty, I said, "That will never happen."

The gray sky made a distant rumble, and rain started to fall. We walked faster, to keep from getting drenched. But partway down the hill, I turned around. When I took a final look at dad's graveside, I saw that the yellow and white flowers had blown away. His gravestone was bare, as if I had never been there at all.

So maybe, I thought, that was my answer.

It was a sign: *I'll have to work it out on my own.*

CHAPTER 21

THE GUY HAD me in a headlock. It took me by surprise. I should've anticipated it, should have ducked and blocked his arms.

But he had me in an iron grip, cutting off my air. I aimed a punch at his inner thigh, but it didn't faze him.

My vision was graying out. With my last reserve of energy, I grabbed his wrist and yanked it up, forcing my body upward with my legs. Then I ducked under him, pulling his arm behind his back. I wrapped my arm around his neck and took him to the ground.

Panting as I tried to catch my breath, I shook the sweat from my face before releasing my grip on him.

My opponent stretched out across the mat, moaning. "Shit, Kate. You don't fight like a girl."

I grinned down at Rod. "The hell you say. That's exactly how a girl fights, asshole."

With a show of bravado, I jumped to my feet, offering him a hand up. When he took it, I almost tumbled back on the mat;

Rod was two hundred fifty pounds of solid muscle. Currently employed as a bouncer at a nightclub in Chelsea, Rod had spent a decade in the military before receiving a dishonorable discharge for a trumped-up charge. He was a far more formidable sparring partner than I generally faced. Watching him as he stretched the kinks out of his shoulders, I had a moment of insecure doubt.

"Were you holding back, Rod? You didn't let me take you down, did you?"

He barked out a laugh, wiping his face with a towel. "Nah. I just underestimated you, that's all. That's always a dangerous mistake. I should know better."

Across the gym, a voice rang out. "Kate! My queen!"

Millie's call could be heard a block away. She studied classical voice at a music conservatory in the city. She trotted up, her long blond braids swinging over her shoulders. When she reached us, she gave Rod a playful shove.

"Kate knocked you flat. I got here just in time to witness it. And it was glorious."

She turned to me. Deadpan, she said, "I'm breaking up with him. He's not man enough for me anymore."

When he swept her off her feet, she squealed like a kid. I turned away and began packing my gear in my gym bag. Rod and Millie were prone to flagrant displays of affection. I'm no prude, but sometimes it felt like a peep show.

When they came up for air, I pulled my bag on my shoulder. "I'm heading uptown. Rod, let's do it again soon. I'll give you a fighting chance next time."

He pretended to scowl at me. "I'm onto you. You're used to hitting a target that moves."

That made me laugh. "If you assumed that I've never hit anything scarier than a swinging punching bag, that's your bad."

"Hold on," Millie said, digging in your pocket. "Kate, I've got something for you."

She pulled out a folded sheet of paper, wrinkled from riding in the pocket of her jeans. Beaming, she held it out to me.

Curious, I unfolded it. "Oh my God! This is amazing!"

The sheet of paper was a copy of the original verification form that Frank Rubenstein gave me the day after I decked Max James on the sidewalk in front of the Criminal Courts building. But instead of a series of blank lines, this form contained a series of magnificent signatures with corresponding dates, over the name: Duncan Schmidt, certified counselor.

"Millie, I'm totally in your debt. How did you get this?"

"Edgar did it. Isn't it beautiful?"

"Yeah, it really is." Edgar was the moody artist in our circle.

"Steven told him to attend the anger management group on Forty-Second Street and get the guy to sign. We want your form to look legit. Edgar copied the counselor's signature. He must have liked the meeting. He's carrying a notebook around with him now because Duncan suggested it."

Over the past weeks, I'd learned more about Edgar's anger problem. The primary target of his rage was any artist in the modern school. Also, any museum or gallery that exhibited it. The MoMA had a picture of him at the admissions counter; employees were advised to contact security on sight. He'd been arrested and subsequently convicted for disrupting an exhibition of performance art in which the artist struck a pose on a toilet. Edgar had flung a can of paint at them.

The criminal charges were ultimately reduced to misdemeanor assault, but his career was adversely affected. When I asked him why the performance art had invoked such a violent response, he looked at me like I was crazy. "I'm a realist, Kate."

Looking at the verification form, I was glad that Edgar had trained as a realist. Because it gave him tremendous talent at forgery.

Folding the form, I placed it carefully in my bag and zipped it up. "Please tell Edgar how grateful I am. This form is gonna set me free, make my life so much easier." I envisioned swanning into Frank Rubenstein's office the next morning and dropping it on his desk. Frank had been badgering me about the signatures for the past three weeks.

Millie said, "Tell him yourself."

Baffled, I shook my head. "When?"

"Tonight. While you were giving my man a smackdown, Steven got in touch."

I edged closer to her. In a low voice, I said, "And what did our esteemed leader tell you?"

She cocked her head. "Leader?"

Rod spoke softly. "Do you still think he's our leader?"

I was puzzled. Although Whitney had hinted to me weeks prior about another leader, no one had taken the trouble to fully enlighten me. From my perspective, it looked like Steven was in charge.

Rod nudged Millie. She looked around, as if she feared she'd been overheard. Stepping close to me, she whispered in my ear.

"We're getting together tonight. There's a plan."

"A plan?" I echoed.

"For, you know. A plan for Max James."

My pulse accelerated. This was it, why I'd joined forces with them, what I'd been waiting for.

I backed away from Millie. Her eyes shone with excitement. Rod's face was impassive, his own eyes hooded.

In a whisper, I said, "That's great. When?"

"Eleven o'clock."

"Where?"

She spoke in a bare whisper. "In an alley between a liquor store and a laundromat."

Picturing the meeting place, I shook my head. Did Steven get off on these shady locales?

CHAPTER 22

ONE ADVANTAGE TO the unlikely meeting place in the alleyway: it wasn't difficult to find. I spotted the Green Derby Liquor sign a block away.

My phone vibrated in my pocket. I fumbled for it, half expecting to see that Steven had changed a location again.

But the text wasn't from Steven. My brother had sent an ambiguous message.

Why aren't you at your apartment?

As I stared at the screen, another message appeared.

Need to talk to you. It's about Mom.

My forehead wrinkled in annoyance; I loved my brother, but he always seemed to pick a bad time. And he'd had a tendency to follow in my tracks, ever since we were kids. Decades later, he continued the habit. His reliance on Find My Friends was unsettling; I was still recovering from the surprise appearance at my father's graveside. With a finger poised over my phone, I considered blocking the contact on the app before I relented and let it remain. He was my brother, my only sibling. Neither of us had a wealth of family connections to lean on.

Glancing down the street, I thought I recognized a fellow group member. I kept an eye out as he turned the corner, probably approaching the alley behind the market.

I checked my phone. They took their meeting times pretty seriously and I didn't want to be late to the gathering yet again. I stuffed the phone into my pocket, thinking that I'd let my brother assume I hadn't seen the message. He would never know otherwise.

But I didn't even make it to the traffic light before it occurred to me: it was entirely conceivable Leo would try to hunt me down. I couldn't take a chance that he might crash the meeting in the alleyway. Ducking under the battered awning that sagged over a dry-cleaning business, I pulled the phone out again and hit my brother's contact.

He made me wait until the fourth ring. "Kate?"

"Hey, Leo. I'm not at my apartment. Give me more of a heads-up next time, okay?"

"It's almost eleven. I figured you'd be home by now. Where are you? I'll get an Uber and meet you."

The call was making me antsy; I wanted to find the alley where the group was assembling. Checking the time, I saw that I was running late, again—and this meeting was about my personal target.

"I'm on my way to a meeting right now. Tonight's no good for me."

"Oh, okay." His voice in my ear was mournful, and I phased into my big-sister role. Stifling my impatience with a monumental effort, I heaved a sigh of surrender into the phone.

I said, "What's the matter? Did you say something's up with Mom?"

He groaned into the phone. "Yeah. I really need to talk to you. Some serious shit is going down. She's been acting unbalanced, losing her temper over nothing."

"Steven, that's her standard behavior. She's been like that since we were born."

"I try to avoid saying things that make it worse, but it's impossible. Do you think she's going to fire me?"

The statement was so unlikely, so preposterous, it made me laugh out loud. "Please. You're kidding me."

"It's not funny, Kate. She said it today, right before she left the office."

Turning to face the window of the dry cleaner, I could see the activity on the sidewalk reflected in the glass. I saw Steven pass right behind me. He didn't acknowledge me.

"Leo, Mom's just doing her crazy dance. Hey, I've really got to go. Want to grab a drink this week? I'll take the train, so you don't have to come into the city."

"Yeah. If that's the best you can do."

"I'll text you," I said, adding, "Everything will be all right. I promise."

As I talked, I trailed Steven's footsteps. He ducked into a narrow space between two buildings; I followed several paces after him.

The narrow alleyway plunged into darkness a short distance from the street. I pressed the flashlight on my cell phone and used it to light up the passageway. As I approached shadowy figures, a voice hissed at me in the darkness.

"Turn off the goddamn light. Are you crazy?"

Ignoring the demand, I pointed the light in the direction of the speaker. It was Edgar. He covered his eyes with his hand, as if my light blinded him.

A hand on my shoulder made me jump. Coming out of the shadow, Steven took the phone from my hand and pressed the screen. I snatched his arm, trying to retrieve the phone, but he kept it out of my reach. He said, "A lot of flashlight apps give away information. Your identity, your location. They're not secure."

Larry's voice muttered in the darkness. "How does she not know that? Isn't she law enforcement?"

Millie approached and put a supportive arm around me. "Don't be a dick. Of course she knows. Kate probably has a special app that mutes the information the flashlight gives away."

I was glad for the cover of darkness because it disguised my chagrin. In fact, I didn't know the flashlight was a security leak; who would suspect that such a basic tool could give vital information away?

My eyes adjusted to the darkness. I could see a cluster of shadowy figures in the alleyway. Cautious, I asked, "Who's here?"

Millie's arm left my shoulder. She raised her voice; it echoed as she called down the alley. "Who's down there? Rod and I talked to Devon and Diane. Larry, you're here, right?"

When he didn't answer immediately, her volume increased. "Larry! Speak up!"

At a distance, I saw the red cherry of a lit cigarette and heard a mocking voice. "Really? Is this necessary?"

Steven said, "Whitney is here. Obviously."

A man shrouded in the darkness groused, "This is bullshit. Do you want my contribution or not?"

Millie spoke to me in a whisper—although her voice was so strong, it could be heard at fifty yards away. "That's Edgar. Your anger twin."

The dark figure moved through the narrow space, distributing something. When he approached me, I backed away, to give him room. Glass crunched under my feet. Kicking at the shards, I connected with a moving creature, which scuttled away between my feet. *Rats*, I thought.

When Edgar stood beside me, I could smell the acrid scent of paint or ink. He placed a flat rectangle in my hand, made with thick, high-quality cardstock. I held it up to my face, but couldn't identify it.

"What's this? I can't see a damn thing."

Edgar's voice was comically formal. "You are cordially invited, Ms. Stone."

Millie's laughter echoed through the alley. "We're going to a party!"

Whitney walked out of the darkness, pausing to kick a bag of garbage out of her path. She positioned her cell phone over the envelope in my hand, and the screen provided enough light to make out the print, even without a flashlight.

"We are invited for cocktails on Ian Templeton's yacht. Ooh, very swank," she said, deadpan.

"Bougie," Millie said. "The expression you're looking for is 'bougie.'"

A voice in the dark asked: "Who's Templeton?"

Steven's voice had a ring of satisfaction when he answered. "It's Max James's boss. The head of the asset management firm. Whitney knows Templeton, from her days at a broker-age firm."

"I worked at the firm that was Templeton's rival. So I know him. And I detest him," she said. She lifted the phone so that light from the screen illuminated my face. "Jesus, Kate, why didn't you tell me Max James works for Templeton? You wouldn't have had to work so hard to get my vote."

I stepped away from Whitney to shield my eyes from the phone. "I didn't know his boss's name. And I didn't know you're a broker."

"Was. Was a broker. Before I lost my license."

There was a pause. Before it grew painful, Steven stepped in. "Whitney was a successful player, really sought after. She developed algorithms to predict downturns in the market. She was pretty famous."

"Past tense. Former glory, all of it, thanks to the gambling itch. But in my worst days, I wasn't a crook like Ian and his team."

I inched back to Whitney's side; being blinded by her was a fair trade for hearing the dirt on Max James and his employer. "What kind of crook?"

"Templeton is a hedge fund manager. That alone doesn't make him a crook, of course. A lot of hedge funds can be legitimate, if the investors are sophisticated and understand the risk. But hedge funds are not required to register with the SEC, they don't have the same oversight and reporting rules as mutual funds. So it's easier for hedge fund managers to take advantage of investors."

"And Templeton takes advantage? How?"

"His firm made its money in a Ponzi scheme. They lured

retirees to invest their life savings and 401(k) retirement plans in cryptocurrency. The standard con: they guaranteed an astronomical rate of return."

I wasn't an expert in white-collar crime, but I knew enough to understand the basics. And the scam my mother had bragged about successfully defending last Thanksgiving dinner had involved a Ponzi scheme. She had expounded upon it in painful detail over the turkey and dressing. "Don't those scams eventually fall through?"

"Sure. When his bubbles eventually collapsed, he and his team moved on to find another group of suckers. The kind who were willing to bank on a deal that's too good to be true. They're still at it."

A voice in the darkness muttered, "Whitney's just pissed because she didn't think of it first."

She wheeled around, peering into the alley. "Who said that? Larry?"

Millie's voice sounded, in a soothing tone, "Whitney, I think it's cool that you're onto those Wall Street guys. That's the problem with rich people; nobody makes that kind of money without fucking someone over."

Millie had more to say on the subject, but it went past me. I was pondering the Ponzi scheme. If it was so flagrant, and so widespread, why hadn't anyone stopped him? The US attorney had tremendous resources; this was their kind of case. And my own boss had an entire division of our office devoted to white-collar prosecution. But though Max James was a well-known figure in our office, this was the first time I'd ever heard of Ian Templeton.

As a germ of suspicion began to form, I was distracted

when Whitney brayed with laughter—the sound of someone relishing a delicious moment of schadenfreude.

"We'll cut Templeton's throat at his own soiree. That's golden. I love it," she said. As an aside to me, she added, "I told you we'd bring him down."

She stuffed her invitation into a bag hanging from her shoulder. "The rats are hungry tonight. You know they carry rabies? I'm out of here."

CHAPTER 23

LATER THAT WEEK, when I walked into the DA's office at 1:00 p.m., I was already wiped out. I'd spent the morning at a deposition, doing battle with a defense attorney uptown. His twenty-one-year-old client was charged with the rape of a nineteen-year-old student at a college fraternity party held in a brownstone on 113th Street.

It could have been a problematic case because the rape victim had passed out before the assault, as a result of the grain alcohol–fortified refreshments served at the party. Consent wasn't the issue; an unconscious person can't consent to sex. But she didn't remember the assault, couldn't testify to the details that would provide an evidentiary basis for conviction. However, this case had an evidentiary advantage: the defendant's drunken friends had made a video of the crime and posted it online.

The rape prosecution wasn't originally my case; it was assigned to an attorney in the sex crimes unit. But that attorney was tied up in a jury trial, and the defense attorney refused to reschedule. They sent me in to represent the office at the last minute, as a substitute.

The defense counsel, Eric Shultz, had subpoenaed the teenage victim to conduct out-of-court discovery. He was asking her questions, taking sworn testimony in his office; a court reporter was present to transcribe it. The process was painful to witness—Shultz tried to make the deposition as brutal as possible, asking the girl insinuating questions, pounding on her underage drinking, trying to trap her in an admission that she had "led on" the defendant—even though the girl was incapacitated at the time of the attack and couldn't have consented to it. And because judges aren't present at depositions, there was nobody to rein the guy in. Well, no one except for me.

It was all I could do to contain myself to verbal objections. I almost jumped across the table when the defense attorney asked her to describe the outfit she wore to the frat party. His use of the "short skirts invite rape" tool was inflammatory on its own. But after the girl replied, he gave a low whistle and whispered, so that it was barely audible: "Sexy."

That's when I lost it.

The court reporter was yammering: "Mr. Shultz? I didn't catch that," but I'd caught it, and so had the nineteen-year-old girl beside me at the table. I was on my feet before I realized I'd left my chair.

"You despicable asshole. That is reprehensible." I pointed a finger at the court reporter. "I want it on the record."

She said, "I don't think I heard him right." Frankly, her hearing might have been problematic because the defense attorney was paying her bill.

"I heard him: He whispered 'sexy' at this witness, this young woman who was assaulted by his client." For emphasis, I slapped my file on the table, and papers flew into the air. Scrambling, Shultz pulled out his cell phone and pointed it at me.

"I'm recording this. And the court reporter is a witness, if you come near me. You have a violent reputation, Ms. Stone."

That slowed me down.

Even though I volunteered to sit at the other end of the table, Eric Shultz declined to continue. He said he'd conclude the deposition at a later time, when the DA from the sex crimes unit was available. I was sorry, for the young victim's sake. She'd have to come back a second time, and that was on me.

When I walked across the lobby of the office, my mind was still on the deposition fireworks; I was rerunning the confrontation in my brain, trying to envision a way I could've avoided the bedlam. My outrage with the defense attorney's action had been justified, and I would have failed in my advocacy to ignore it. But why did I have to go over the top? Lost in thought, I wasn't aware of my surroundings, and that's how I ended up in the elevator with Frank Rubenstein.

We stood shoulder to shoulder at the very back of the elevator. I wanted to edge away from him, but couldn't move without reclining against an investigator who wasn't particularly fond of me. So I stood, still as a statue, watching the numbers light up.

As the elevator climbed, Frank gave me the side-eye. "Are you all right, Kate? You look...," he paused, to create dramatic effect, "...angry."

With a rush of air, I expelled the breath I'd been holding. "I subbed for Lindsay Pollack at a deposition this morning. A sex case. It would make the angels weep."

The elevator door opened. "This is my stop," I said, shouldering through the two men who stood in front of me. Before the door could shut all the way, I heard Frank's voice saying: "Hold the door."

I hurried down the hall, hoping I could avoid additional conversation. But when he called my name, my steps slowed.

Turning to face him, I said, "What do you need, Frank?"

"I'd like to see you. In your office."

His tone was neutral, but a wave of dread washed over me as I waited for him to catch up. We walked the short path to the office without speaking.

When I opened the door, Bill Parker sat with his feet on his desk, eating an Italian sub. At the sight of Rubenstein, his mouth fell open, and he dropped the sandwich onto his lap.

"Frank! This is a surprise," Bill said, hastily brushing shreds of lettuce off his shirt front. "Sorry about the mess."

"It's a red-letter day," I said, dragging a battered metal folding chair from the corner of the room and setting it in front of my desk. "I apologize for the seating limitations, Frank; this is all we have to offer."

Without comment, Frank sat in the chair, which tipped at a dangerous angle. He pretended not to notice.

"Bill, I'd like to speak with Kate. In private."

"Right, no problem." Bill hopped out of his chair and headed for the door. As an afterthought, he stepped back and grabbed the sandwich off his desk.

"I'll take this with me, if that's okay."

"Please do." Frank's eyes flitted to the fragrant Italian sub.

I waited for Bill to shut the door before I sat. Easing my chair back, I faked an air of nonchalance.

"You want to hear about the deposition, Frank?"

"I already heard."

Frank tried to cross his knees, but the movement made the chair tip back in the other direction. Setting both feet on the floor, he said, "I received a call from Alfred Goldman."

"I don't even know Goldman. Eric Shultz took the depo."

"Shultz works for Goldman. And Shultz filled him in on your—what shall we call it? Breakdown? Temper tantrum? So Goldman called me as soon as he heard. He thought I'd want to know."

I was contemplating a clever response when Frank went on, saying, "Goldman said I am not to send you back to his office for any reason whatsoever. He believes you are a threat to his personnel and his clients."

I could feel the flush climb up my neck. "That's so interesting. He specializes in sex cases. His clients are rapists. Child abusers. I hope I'm a threat." Tipping back farther in my chair, I tried to laugh. It came out sounding like a cackle.

The laughter was a mistake. Apparently, Frank didn't see the irony.

"I told you to get treatment for your anger problem, Kate. It appears that you ignored my suggestion."

"If we're being accurate, it wasn't just a suggestion."

"That's right, it wasn't. It was an ultimatum—a requirement if you want to remain in my employ."

I tried to keep a poker face as I pulled out the side drawer of my desk and picked up the sheet of paper resting on the top of a messy pile of miscellaneous documents. Sliding the sheet across the desk to Frank, I gave him a *Mona Lisa* smile.

He couldn't disguise the surprise in his eyes as he scanned the verification form.

"It looks like you've attended a lot of meetings."

I was the cat who swallowed the canary; it was difficult, keeping a straight face. "I have. Obviously."

He bent over the sheet of paper, squinting. "Who is this counselor? I can't quite make it out."

I had to stop and think for a moment, searching my recollection for the name.

"Duncan. Duncan Schmidt. He's really great."

Frank's eyes met mine over the paper as he held it aloft.

"Where are the meetings held? Hope it's not too inconvenient for you."

"Midtown." If he pressed me, I'd have to prevaricate; I didn't recall the exact address, and checking my phone history would give me away. "Just off of Ninth."

Deliberately, he folded the paper into a neat rectangle and slid it inside the pocket of his suit jacket. "By the way, you took the office file of that domestic assault, right? Angelina something, can't remember her last name. Did you return it?"

I shifted in my seat as my guard went up. "Yes. Sent it by office mail, weeks ago."

"Okay. That's good. Glad to hear it."

I cleared my throat. This was dangerous territory, but I couldn't stay away from it. "How's the investigation going?"

He fixed me with a look of disbelief. "It's dead in the water. What do you think?"

My blood began to boil; I could feel the flush heating my face. "I think you should charge him with assault."

"We can't proceed with an assault case without a complaining witness. You are perfectly aware of that, Kate. I don't think you're stupid."

As he spoke, he crossed his legs; the movement sent the broken chair out of balance again, nearly spilling him onto the floor. He caught himself and launched out of the seat, shoving the chair against the wall with his foot.

I said, "It's a mistake, Frank. Letting Max James get away with that shit."

"Mistake? You're lecturing me? That's rich."

He headed for the door; as he turned the knob, he said, his voice deliberately casual: "Hey, did I see that you put in a request for a replacement ID?"

"Yeah." My tone was defensive; I wished I sounded nonchalant.

"How did you lose it?" He glanced at me, his face impassive. But the tables had turned. He was the cat; I was the canary.

"Just misplaced it. One of those things…" My voice trailed off.

He pulled the door open. Without looking back, he said, "You can't be careless with those office IDs. Don't want it to end up in the wrong hands."

Frank pulled the door shut behind him. As I listened to his footsteps moving down the hall, I experienced a sinking feeling, like I was falling down a well.

I suspected that Rubenstein knew I had lost the ID at Bellevue. So why wasn't he being straight with me about it?

CHAPTER 24

THE CONVERSATION WITH Frank was unsettling. Every day that week, I was prepared for bad news, expecting a summons from him. When the hammer didn't fall by Friday, I tried to put it out of my head. Because I had other things to think about.

The group members had been busy, doing background work and crafting a plan for our project. Several of us were gathering that night for an update. Millie met me at my apartment as soon as I came home from the office, armed with a small backpack. She went straight to work on me.

"Sit still," Millie said. "You're going to mess me up."

I tried to stop fidgeting, but it required a huge effort. When she swept the brush across my face, it tickled.

"And now," she said, pausing for dramatic effect, "the brow."

She pressed the pencil along my eyebrow, her own brow knitting in concentration. When she moved to the other eye, I felt compelled to speak up.

"I don't see how this can possibly work."

"That's because you know nothing about theater. Everything is an illusion."

She pulled away to inspect me critically, and then went to work again on the left eyebrow.

"But Max James knows me well enough to recognize me, even with a different look."

"This is a makeover, with a new palette," she said.

"And if James sees me at the party, it will blow the entire project."

"Honey, when I'm done with you, your own mother won't recognize you."

She pursed her lips and blew air into my eyes. It made me squint. "Sorry," she said, as she brushed excess powder off my temple.

Millie reached into the pink backpack. Pulling out a tube, she brandished it with a flourish.

"And now: the red lip."

When she was done, she studied me again, assessing her work. "Tonight will be the acid test. If Rod, Steven, and Devon walk by you, fooling Max James will be easy. Because he won't expect to encounter you."

Millie picked up a hand mirror and held it out to me. Feeling a little self-conscious, I took it and checked out the reflection. When I saw the alteration Millie had accomplished, I was seriously impressed. I wasn't quite unrecognizable; it was still me. But a totally different version.

"Do I look kind of slutty?" It seemed like a reasonable question.

Indignant, Millie grabbed the hand mirror away from me. "No. Absolutely not. We are going for a different angle. The kind of woman who responds to the sugar daddies on Seeking Arrangement."

"Oh, Jesus." It was a frightening thought.

She laughed, pulling a hairbrush through my hair so briskly that it hurt. "I'll give you a high pony."

While she worked on my hair, I heard a melancholy note creep into her voice. "This reminds me of the look I had when I joined up with the group. It's eye-catching, you know? I've toned it down a lot since then. Best not to attract too much attention."

With her booming voice, hourglass figure, and mane of golden hair, Millie would always stand out in New York. Even in our crowded urban environment, Millie was striking enough to be noticed.

I said, "People always give you a second look, Millie. I figured you'd aspire to that. Isn't that the point? Don't you want to stand out? That's why you're studying at Juilliard, right?"

"I left Juilliard."

"You're kidding. When?"

"Before I found the group. I'm at a smaller conservatory now, the New York School of Music." She hesitated before adding, "I feel safer there."

After that, she stopped; I didn't press her. Something ugly had happened when Millie left her midwestern roots and came to New York; but it was her story to share. As a trial lawyer with a background in violent crime, I suspected she'd been a victim of a sex offense. And since she had become part of the fabric of a vengeance group, it was unlikely the perpetrator had been convicted of the crime in a court of law.

I wouldn't pry. But I thought she'd be reassured if I let

her know I understood the situation, without the need to press for any painful recounting. I said, "So the person who wronged you escaped justice, without facing consequences for his actions."

The hand holding the hairbrush paused in midair. In a low voice, unlike her ebullient norm, she said, "The rape kit was tampered with, somehow. So he wasn't prosecuted. They said it would be a swearing match without physical evidence, and the guy is highly regarded in the arts."

After another pause, she pulled my hair into an elastic band and tightened it. As she wound a strand of my hair around the elastic, she said, "But he faced consequences. Just not the legal kind."

That statement sent a chill through me. I was torn, between my desire to know the details of the consequences inflicted on Millie's attacker, and my fear that the story she told would put me in an untenable professional position.

Millie prevented me from speaking out; she shook a bottle and engulfed me in a cloud of hairspray. I covered my eyes, too late to protect them from the sting.

"Time to go," she said, her voice cheery again. "No pants tonight, Kate. Wear a dress. Not black."

Turning in the chair, I gaped at her. "Not black? Are you kidding?"

"My opera coach performed at the Met for forty years. She played Delilah and Carmen. She tells me it's imperative that you always perform in a dress. Not black. '*And make sure it moves, darling.*'"

I found a dress in the very back of the closet, something I'd worn to a party back in law school. As I zipped it up, I checked myself out in the full-length mirror that hung inside my closet door. The glass mirror was spotted and fuzzy with age, but the reflection was startling. I had undergone a thorough transformation.

Millie stepped up behind me. "Well?"

I shook my head in wonder. "I don't look like myself. That's for sure."

"Perfect," she said, her voice ringing with self-satisfaction. "Let's go."

The rickety elevator barely had room for the two of us. When the door jerked open on the ground floor, Millie stepped out first.

I heard her laugh as she craned to look through the glass panel in the front door. Turning around, she told me, "Some poor woman is standing outside, pressing the buzzer. Should I tell her it doesn't work?"

The buzzer for my apartment building was still broken. It hadn't been operable in all the time I had lived there.

"Let her figure it out on her own; you're not a doorman," I said, as I followed Millie to the door. But when I caught sight of the woman's profile, my step faltered.

My mother was standing outside the building, jamming the buzzer with her index finger. Even through the door, I heard her muttering curses at the box.

Mom had never been to my apartment in Morningside Heights, although I'd lived there for over three years. And while I had no clue what she was doing here, I knew that the reason for her visit couldn't be good. Sighing, I stepped through the door and watched her, waiting for her to turn around and describe some calamity.

She glanced my way a single time before returning to the inoperable buzzer. Pounding it with the side of her fist, Mom shouted into the speaker. "Kate. Are you there? Answer me, damn it."

The realization washed over me. I skirted past Mom in my red party dress, flipping my ponytail, like I'd seen Millie do. Improbable as it seemed, my new friend had worked a miracle.

My own mother didn't recognize me.

CHAPTER 25

I ELBOWED MY way to the front of the bustling bar at a Marriott on Times Square, where a dozen tourists clamored for the bartender's attention. When I immediately caught his eye, I had to credit Millie's makeover.

I leaned across the bar to ensure he could hear my order over the babble. "Tanqueray and tonic, tall. Two limes."

After paying an exorbitant sum for my cocktail, I shouldered away from the other patrons. Millie had disappeared from view, but when my phone buzzed, her face appeared on the screen.

Impatient, I answered. "Where did you go?"

Her voice whispered through the phone; it was difficult to hear her over the buzz of voices all around me.

It sounded like she said: "They're already here: Rod, Steven, and Devon. I see them at a banquette, by the window."

Doing a one-eighty around the lounge, I asked, "So where are you?"

"Hiding behind the hostess station. I want to see whether they recognize you. Go cruise by their table, just for fun."

This isn't a game, I wanted to say. But I swallowed it back; for Millie, it probably was. I decided to play along with her suggestion when it occurred to me that Millie's ploy might appease my weakness for superstitious signs. If they didn't recognize me, it would be a good omen. Wandering past their table, I watched for their reaction out of the corner of my eye.

Rod gave me a bare glance and looked away; Devon ignored me. I had just sidled up to the window by their table when I heard Steven's voice.

"Kate? You going to join us?"

Feeling a little silly, I wheeled around and slid into the vacant space beside him in the curved booth. Steven regarded me with a hint of a smile.

"Can't fool you," I said grudgingly.

Millie pushed her way through the throng; when she ran up to the table, she sounded a little breathless.

"What do you think? Did you recognize her?"

Rod scooted over to make room for her. With a rueful shake of his head, he said, "I fell for it."

She focused on Devon. He lifted a shoulder and let it drop. "Wasn't paying attention."

I waited to hear Steven gloat, but he just smiled at me. "You look great."

The compliment made me a trifle giddy. To subdue the reaction, I chugged a mouthful of gin. Millie's shoulders slumped.

"You really spotted her?" she demanded. When Steven nodded, she gave a discouraged huff of air. "I'm so bummed. I wanted Kate to go to that party. Now she'll have to stay away, because James could blow her cover."

In an undertone, Devon said, "Max James won't be there."

I was curious to know how Devon could have knowledge of James's personal schedule, but a waitress approached the table. Millie ordered a shot of silver tequila; I raised my half-full glass.

"Tanq and tonic, tall."

When she walked off, Devon gave me a dubious look. In a defensive tone, I said, "This is a bar, right? Where people order drinks. We don't want to attract attention."

Devon raised a brow. Looking prim, he said, "This is a planning session. A pregame."

"No problem. I have a high tolerance." I took a long pull on the straw.

"From lots of practice?" he murmured.

Millie broke in, warding off a spat. "Devon, why didn't Max make the list? What's up with that?"

He looked smug. "He's on the list. But Max just accepted a lucrative offer to speak at an out-of-town investment conference on the date of his boss's yacht party."

A sense of relief washed over me as I absorbed the news. I'd been dreading another face-to-face confrontation. "How'd you find out about that?"

Devon said, "I just hired him. By the time he figures out it's a ruse, he'll be in San Diego, and you'll be on the boat."

"Yacht, not a boat. It's a yacht," Millie said.

We fell silent as the waitress dropped off our drinks. When she was out of earshot, Rod said, "Have you ironed out our roles? I'm ready to hear how this is gonna go down."

I glanced around, nervous. The bar was packed; every table

was occupied. In a hushed voice, I said, "Is it smart to have the conversation here? It's not exactly private."

With an untroubled countenance, Steven reached for my hand, giving it a reassuring squeeze. "We're in a hotel bar in Times Square, Kate, surrounded by visitors to the city. It's just like being invisible."

When he released my hand, I felt strangely bereft, and had to stifle a compulsion to grab him, to recapture the contact. Embarrassed by the impulse—because I was way too old to nurse an unrequited crush—I tucked my hands into my lap and rubbed the spot next to my thumb. But when I caught Steven stealing a glance at my hands, I clutched them into fists, self-conscious about my nervous habit being discovered.

My tone was sharper than I intended when I asked him, "So who's putting his head on the block along with me?"

"Me," Millie said. "And Rod," she added, snuggling up against him as he draped his arm around her.

I gave Steven an inquiring look; he shook his head in response to the unspoken question. "My skill set isn't beneficial for this particular project."

Rod interjected; his manner dry. "If we get the shit kicked out of us, Steven can patch us up afterwards."

A tremor ran down my back. I tried to suppress the shudder, hoping no one caught it. After all, this was my proposal.

But Steven picked up on it apparently. "Kate? Are you okay?"

Putting on my tough-girl face, I squared my shoulders and sat up straight in the booth. "I'm good."

With exaggerated patience, Devon said, "So, the party next

week is on Ian Templeton's private yacht. It's a big event with family, friends, business associates."

"We don't fall into any of those categories."

Millie asked, "Do we just flash the invitations to get onto the boat?"

Devon shook his head. "I hacked into Templeton's system. You'll assume the identity of three actual guests."

Millie's face lit up. "A performance! *My* specialty."

She obviously welcomed the prospect, but Rod looked apprehensive. "What happens when the real guests show up?"

Steven spoke up. "We've got that covered." He and Devon exchanged a look, as if they shared a private joke.

Millie tapped at the screen of her phone, her enthusiasm undampened. "This is going to be so cool. Kate, have you seen the yacht?"

She handed the phone over to me. Color photos illustrated a gushing write-up on Page Six, which described Templeton's yacht as "a modern marvel." In one shot, Templeton stood on the deck dressed in white linen and wearing a self-satisfied smirk as he raised a flute of champagne.

"What a douchebag," I said, as I handed the phone back to Millie. Rod took it from her hand, flipping the screen with his thumb.

He said, "This boat is huge. Did you get the blueprints yet, Devon?"

When Devon nodded, my mouth fell open in disbelief. "The blueprints of the yacht? How?"

He gave me an incredulous look. "How do you think? I hacked the firm that built the boat and downloaded the blueprints."

"Jesus," I muttered. His skills were impressive.

Devon glanced around the room. I followed suit, checking to see whether we could be overheard. No one in the bar was paying attention to our conversation. Still, he lowered his voice to a bare whisper.

"So I did some recon and learned that Templeton keeps a personal computer on the boat, where he stores sensitive business information. The computer is hidden in a safe, in an office in the bowels of the ship."

It sounded like a spy movie with an edge-of-your-seat scene in Templeton's inner sanctum.

Rod rubbed his forehead, as if he'd developed a headache. "How easy is it to access his office?"

Devon and Steven exchanged a glance; Steven grimaced. Looking apologetic, Devon said, "There are some...challenges."

Rod heaved a weary sigh. "Like what?"

"Honestly, it's kind of a labyrinth to get down to the office. Larry went through the blueprints for you. He's worked out the path that you'll need to follow."

I tried to remember who they were talking about. "Larry? The old guy, the alcoholic?" No judgment; I just didn't see what assistance he could provide.

With a shade of righteous indignation, Millie said, "Larry's a structural engineer."

I should have recalled that. Steven had explained that every member of the group possessed a different expertise—medicine, in his case—and each person's skill contributed to the success of their overall mission. He'd rattled off a list of diverse abilities; it was hard to keep them straight. Rod wasn't merely a strongarm man; his military background gave him expertise with firearms. Diane, the sex addict, was a chemist in research and development at a major pharmaceutical laboratory. I knew that Devon was employed at a tech company. Edgar's forgery was well known to me, as were Millie's theatrical gifts. Whitney currently worked as a statistician since she was barred from Wall Street.

Steven hadn't informed me what the vigilantes viewed as my particular talent. Whether they were interested in my legal experience, or my enthusiasm for fistfights, he didn't say. Maybe they liked the fact that I walked around in a state of repressed rage about 90 percent of the time.

Devon continued. "You'll have to get the key card to open the safe. That's crucial."

Rod gave him a flat look. "And where do we find the key card?"

"Templeton keeps it on him. At all times."

Rod made a guttural noise; however, Millie's eyes lit up. "Fun! I love a challenge."

She lifted her shot glass and drained the last drop; following suit, I sucked down my own cocktail. Steven was regarding me with a watchful eye. "You'll have to be careful. If Templeton detects a whiff of trouble, the project is blown. He'll take off and head for international waters."

Millie grabbed Devon's hand and squeezed it. "Devon, I'm so proud of you. This is brilliant. And we get a double score, two birds with one stone: the bougie crook and his woman-beating partner in crime."

Rod frowned; Steven must have noticed it. He said, "Rod, are you comfortable with this? You can opt out."

Rod looked down at Millie. Shaking his head, he said, "If Millie's in, I'm there."

Devon told him, "I know it's complicated, but you'll be prepared. We will anticipate every detail."

Rod still looked glum. Millie playfully prodded his shoulder. "Don't be a buzzkill. It's gonna be great. Piece of cake."

I had my doubts, but I kept thinking: *Just focus on Max James. That's why I'm here.*

Still, the plan had seeded a case of nerves; I automatically rubbed my hand. Again, Steven caught me at it. He bent his head close to my ear.

"Kate? You sure you want to do this?"

I put my hands on the table and wadded my damp cocktail napkins into a ball. With confidence as genuine as the counterfeit bags sold in Times Square, I said, "Absolutely. What could go wrong?"

CHAPTER 26

AS I STROLLED into the bird sanctuary at Riverside Park on Sunday morning, I spotted my brother almost immediately. Leo sat on a park bench, his shoulders hunched, and his head turning from side to side, looking for me. When he spied me, he waved an arm, calling my name.

A moment later, I dropped onto the bench beside him.

"You got something for me?" I asked.

Eagerly, he handed the brown paper bag over to me. Leo knew what I craved. He'd made a special trip to Absolute Bagels, probably standing in a line out the door to make the purchase. Unwrapping a layer of white paper, I found a neatly cut fresh bagel with a thick smear of cream cheese. I tore a hunk of it with my teeth and moaned with pleasure.

"Why didn't you want me to come up to your place?" he asked, sounding a little hurt.

I swallowed before I answered. "You don't want to spend any time in my apartment, believe me. It's a wreck. I haven't cleaned up in ages."

I wasn't exaggerating. My housekeeping was slipshod in the best of times; and lately, I had been way too distracted to worry about it.

"That's okay. I thought you were giving me the brush, that's all."

"No, absolutely not. I've just been crazy busy." I took another wolfish bite of the bagel; we had spent the prior evening at a last-minute planning session for the Templeton caper, rehearsing some tactical moves, and I'd forgotten to eat.

Leo gave me the side-eye while I chewed. "What have you been up to, Kate? What's keeping you so busy?"

I shrugged, trying to look nonchalant. Talking with my mouth full, I said simply: "Stuff."

He glanced away, pretending to look at the scenery. Leo's voice was deceptively casual. "You've been all over town. Every time I check you out, you're in a different spot. Not your own neighborhood, or around the courts building. You're popping up all over the city."

I swallowed again, uncertain of his meaning. Until he went on, making his message clear. "Seems like you are going to some strange places. Mom is worried about it."

Irritated, I tossed the partially consumed bagel onto the crumpled paper sack in my lap, and shifted down the bench, putting more space between us. "Damn it, Leo. It's bad enough to have you following my tracks on your phone. But now you are tattling to Mom? I'm canceling that app. It creeps me out."

I pulled the cell phone from my pocket, ready to make good on my threat. Though I had held off out of consideration for my brother's feelings, he had crossed the line by reporting my whereabouts to our mother. There was no way I was answering to her.

When he grabbed at the phone, he almost knocked the bagel out of my lap. I saved it by shoving it onto the bench beside me while holding my phone out of Leo's reach. With a mournful face, he said, "Don't do it, Kate. Please?"

I tucked the phone behind my back; for a minute, Leo and I wrestled for possession of it, like two kids fighting over a toy. Embarrassed by our display, I gave him a shove. "Stop it, Leo. Jesus."

Leaning back, he dropped his hands onto his knees and gripped them with his fingers. "Sorry, Kate."

Sounding bossy, I said, "Don't do that."

"I won't. I'm sorry." Shamefaced, he added, "It's just that I feel more secure when I know where you are."

I expelled a deep breath. I didn't doubt his sincerity. Since we were kids, Leo had always leaned on me, and that tendency became more pronounced after our father's death. It was an old familial pattern.

"Okay," I said, relenting. "But you've got to keep Mom out of my business."

"Right. I will." He hesitated while we watched a woman pass by, pushing a stroller with a toddler seated inside it. Once she was out of earshot, Leo said, "What if I happen to know that Mom is already in your business?"

My attention jerked away from the retreating figure behind the stroller. "What do you mean?"

"I heard her on the phone this week. Talking to Frank Rubenstein, your boss."

For a moment, I was speechless; why would my mother talk to Rubenstein about me?

Recovering, I said, "What did you hear? Tell me exactly what she said."

"I didn't catch all of it. Just enough to know that she's checking in on you. And his report wasn't, wasn't exactly, well—" Leo paused, parsing his words. He cleared his throat. "Positive."

Seized with a restless impulse, I launched off of the bench. "Let's walk."

Leo stood, stretching his long arms over his head. "Don't you want to finish your bagel? I made sure to get the kind you like: an everything with double smear."

I looked at the gnawed remainder of the bagel, sitting on the bench, atop the white paper bag. A fly had landed on it; it walked daintily across the surface before stopping to rub its legs together. "Nope." I wadded it into the bag and tossed it into the nearest wastebasket. Leo and I walked in silence for a short stretch before I turned to my brother and demanded, "What did you hear?"

He gave me an apprehensive glance. "Rubenstein was talking about something you did at a deposition, and then he and Mom started fighting about Max James. James is the defendant you punched out, right? In front of the courts building? And that's when I walked in. Mom caught me listening and cut off the call."

I shook my head in confusion. It made no sense to hear that my mother was comparing notes about me with Rubenstein. They were on the opposite sides of the fence; he was prosecution, she was defense. And an even greater divide: he was Manhattan, she was New Jersey.

"Anyway, she's been telling people that you are joining the firm, that you'll be coming on board really soon. She doesn't know that I know. But that's why I figured I'm on the way out."

He sounded so despondent I forgot my own irritation about the Rubenstein slam. I reached out to put a hand on Leo's shoulder. Giving him a squeeze, I said, "You don't give yourself enough credit, Leo. Mom appreciates the work you do for her. She has to. Who else could put up with her bullshit?"

We walked along in silence for a while. The sun shone through the trees; if I looked in just the right direction, I could see the light reflecting off the Hudson River.

At length, Leo broke the silence. "Mom knows we're getting together this morning. I'm supposed to make a dinner date for the three of us, this Saturday night. You can ask her about Rubenstein yourself, when we're all together."

I didn't hesitate. "Tell her I'm not available."

It was true. On Saturday night, I would be on Ian Templeton's yacht.

CHAPTER 27

THE NIGHT BEFORE the Templeton party, I couldn't sleep. While I tossed on my lumpy mattress in the wee hours, I envisioned all of the things that could go wrong. Disaster scenarios flitted through my head as the hours dragged by. Most of them ended with a vision of my wrists handcuffed behind me, a cop's hand on my head as I was shoved into the back seat of a patrol car.

When I dragged myself out of bed in the morning, the insomnia reflected on my face. By afternoon, I still looked rough. I could see it in the mirror, but even if I had missed the circles under my eyes, Millie's look of horror when she arrived at the apartment to paint my face served as a vivid reminder.

"Jesus, Kate. You look like shit."

"Wow. Thanks, Millie."

"I'm not kidding. You look like you've been on a three-day toot."

The expression was unfamiliar—one of the homespun phrases she'd dragged to the city when she left the rural countryside. But I didn't miss her meaning; it prompted me to sneak another glimpse of my reflection in the mirror.

When she snatched the cosmetics from her backpack, she wore a dogged look.

"This will be the challenge of my career," she said, approaching my face with the grim determination of an undertaker.

An hour later, she had completed the job, and I opened my closet to pull out the new cocktail dress I planned to wear. Pulling off the price tag made me grimace with shame. The prior weekend, Millie had pronounced every item in my wardrobe unsuitable for the occasion.

"Where do you get your clothes? The vintage places I shop at have much higher quality," she had asked.

"I don't buy vintage stuff. I get my clothes online, cheap. Or sometimes off the clearance rack at Old Navy."

Millie gasped, as if I had fessed up to stealing from a Salvation Army donation bucket. "This is a yacht party, Kate. Get real."

And then she swept me over to the Upper East Side. We shopped along Madison Avenue and shuttled hangers of dresses with prices that made my eyes pop. To pay the tab for mine, Millie pulled out a debit card and slapped it on the counter without batting an eye. I tried to protest, but she waved it off. "Gatsby's got it covered," she said—which made no sense to me. Taking her money rubbed me wrong, but my personal account couldn't have paid for the zipper, much less the whole garment.

Slipping the new dress over my head with care, I stood still as Millie zipped me up in the back. Staring at the ice-blue dress in my spotty mirror gave me a guilty pleasure. I had never worn such a showy frock, even when I lived on my mother's dime, back in my student days.

The dress gave me such a boost that my sense of dread dimmed; and when we walked out of my apartment building to find a limousine waiting at the curb, I didn't feel entirely counterfeit as the driver held the door open. As I slid into the seat, Rod was already inside, waiting for us. Millie scrambled onto the spot next to him.

"Love it. A stretch limo, we are riding in style," she said, planting a kiss on him. After she wiped the red lip print from his mouth, she turned her attention to the control panel, pushing buttons to adjust the music.

Rod leaned over to me. "What do you think, Kate? Pretty sweet ride."

My hand caressed the leather seat. "Rod, who's paying for this?" An anxious thought occurred to me. "Do I owe you money for this rental? I can chip in."

"Don't worry about it. It's taken care of."

He shot me a wink. I didn't inquire further. The group had hinted about a mysterious benefactor who supported the organization and sympathized with their overall mission, but they never went into any detail. Millie had dropped that name at the boutique: Gatsby. When I quizzed Millie about it, I had learned that it was fruitless to press for any details. She just brushed off my questions, changing the subject. But I suspected the benefactor had purchased my dress. There was no way Millie could afford to shop on Madison Avenue.

Millie had pushed the button to open the sunroof. Kicking

off her shoes, she clambered onto the seat in her bare feet and poked her head and upper body through the opening.

"This is great! Kate, get up here. You'll love it."

"I think I'll stay down here, thanks."

Rod gave Millie a rueful look. "Careful, baby."

When she blithely ignored him, Rod moved across the floor of the vehicle and sat beside me.

"Do you have the cloner?"

I opened my clutch bag and showed him the hidden lining that held the key card cloner.

Satisfied, he nodded. After I clicked the bag shut, he said, "We'll need to locate Templeton pretty fast, once we're on board. We don't know how tough it will be to find the safe. It might take more time than Devon anticipated for us. Devon doesn't always take complications into account."

Rod's grim tone was making me nervous again. Especially when he glanced out the window and added, "It's easy for Devon to take an optimistic view of things, since he gets to stay back in the operations arena. He's not exposed, like we will be."

When Millie yelled at some stranger on the street, I gave an involuntary jerk. My nerves were taut. Sliding closer to the window, I stared blindly at the passing street scene while trying to marshal my thoughts.

I needed to get a grip because I was edgy as hell. It wasn't because I didn't have confidence in my fellow vigilantes; and it wasn't because I was inclined to back down from a challenge or a fight. In fact, I was ready to do battle every time I walked into a courtroom. And the hours I spent training for kickboxing and karate tested my mettle for fighting in the physical realm. I liked to fight. I was good at it.

What I was unused to was the organization's way of doing business, through espionage and underground methods. I was accustomed to direct conflict; I got a charge from it, and it followed an established pattern. But playing an underground game, with unfamiliar technology, adopting the identity of other people—that had me thoroughly rattled.

Rod must have read my thoughts. "You need to chill," he said. He reached for my hand; I thought he meant to give me a reassuring squeeze. But he pressed his thumb against the inside of my wrist.

"Your pulse is rapid."

That was no surprise. My heart was pounding out of my chest.

"Do you need to take something? A beta-blocker, something to settle you down? Diane keeps us stocked up on stuff. You don't want to panic when we get on board."

I shook my head. I wanted to be on edge; I needed to be sharp. Moreover, there wasn't a beta-blocker in the pharmaceutical world that could prepare me for the journey I was about to undertake.

It didn't seem like we had been riding long when the limo pulled into a lot near the dock. Millie dropped back onto the seat and shut the sunroof.

"Are we here?" I asked, peering through the tinted windows. Though I searched the area, I couldn't see a yacht. It didn't look like we were close enough to the water.

"Not yet. Check this out."

Rod cracked the window. Peering through it, I saw a familiar man dressed in a brown uniform. He passed in front of our limo without acknowledging us.

Clutching Millie's arm, I whispered, "Is that Edgar?"

"Yeah," Rod said. Although he kept a straight face, his eyes crinkled with humor. "Just listen."

The traffic created a jumble of background noise, but it didn't render Edgar inaudible. We were close enough to hear him as he walked up to the driver's window of a white Ferrari. A silver-haired man rolled his window down.

The man said, "Are you certain? This cannot be the parking for Templeton's party. The dock is blocks away from here."

Edgar said to him, "This is it, sir."

"You expect my wife and me to walk all the way to the dock?"

"No, sir. Mr. Templeton arranged for a shuttle. I'll be driving you right up to the yacht."

Edgar tipped his hat like a character straight out of Dickens as he opened the driver's-side door of the Ferrari.

"If you'll follow me please, Mr. Morrison."

Inside our limo, I turned to Rod. "Morrison? Aren't you and Millie supposed to be the Morrisons tonight?"

Millie knelt on the upholstery of the rear seat and watched out the back windshield. In a loud whisper, she narrated the progress.

"They are doing it. They're climbing into the shuttle." She let out a high squawk of laughter and then covered her mouth with her hand. "Edgar's acting the part of an old-time chauffeur. He is totally in character. I'm so impressed."

Rod rolled the window further down to get a clear look as the shuttle trundled past our vehicle. "There's another rider inside, can you see her? A woman in her forties, sitting a few rows behind the Morrisons. She's got to be yours, Kate."

The tension in my shoulders eased a notch. I was relieved to know that Edgar was absconding with the party guest whose identity I intended to adopt for the evening.

"We're in," I said, my confidence rising.

Millie, still perched on the bench of the rear seat, watched the shuttle's progress down the street. "Edgar's in the turn lane. He's on his way to get caught up in rush hour traffic. He deserves a trophy for best performance for an actor in a featured role."

She plopped back onto her seat, smoothing the skirt of her dress. "We're playing the leads. Obviously." Her face was flushed with excitement as she pushed the speaker button and addressed the limo driver in a prim voice.

"Sir? We're ready to go to the dock now, please."

Rod sat back and watched her with an admiring smile. To me, he said, "Doesn't that woman have the finest manners?"

She pursed her lips to blow him a kiss. "I'm just a sweet midwestern kid. Unless someone crosses me."

Linking her arm through mine, Millie's voice was still light as she added, "And if they do, I'll kick their ass straight to hell."

Funny thing—I believed her. Moreover, I was glad to have her on my side. Millie was a good friend, but it seemed like she could be a formidable enemy, despite her fresh-faced appearance. As the limo rolled up to the yacht, something about the hard glint in her eye was kind of scary.

CHAPTER 28

BOARDING THE YACHT was a breeze for Millie and me. The men on the security detail were far more hesitant about Rod, making him repeat his name and then spell it for them while they checked and double-checked the guest list.

Rod remained unruffled, but Millie's voice could be heard by everyone in earshot as she demanded, "Is there a problem?"

The lead security guy shrugged, keeping his eyes trained on the list. Finally, he looked up and cracked a smile that looked decidedly unfriendly, like a feral baring of teeth.

"Sorry for the inconvenience. Enjoy the evening."

Millie slipped her arm through Rod's as we boarded the main deck. In an undertone, Rod said, "I guess the dudes working security have a hard time believing that Templeton has a Black friend."

"Assholes," Millie whispered. "Who do they think they are, acting like we're not welcome here?"

The irony didn't escape me because, in fact, we weren't

welcome. Templeton's security guards had just admitted three people onto the yacht who intended to bring his empire down and send him to prison.

As we cruised across the teakwood deck, I checked out the other guests. The well-heeled A-listers weren't all unfamiliar. In addition to a smattering of media and entertainment personalities, I spotted well-known government figures. A US senator chatted with a congressman and an appellate judge. I stifled a gasp as another man shouldered his way into their circle. It was Judge Callahan, who presided over the Max James trial and paved the way for James's acquittal. His presence at the party was shocking because it indicated that Callahan was a friend or associate of Max James's employer. Ethically, he should have disqualified himself from hearing the case. My chest tightened with anger.

"You look tense," Millie whispered. "It's a party, Kate. Act like you're having a good time."

When I automatically broke into a wide grin, she shook her head. "Now you look like a psycho. Look around, see everyone else? Try to blend in."

With an effort, I took her advice, trying to relax my facial muscles into something approaching a pleasant expression. This was a new challenge for me, in an arena far different from the courtroom. I decided to dodge over to the bar for a drink. I was pumping so much adrenaline I figured a dose of alcohol could be medicinal.

Strutting up to the bar, I cut in line, disregarding the mutters and pointed looks of the other guests. It didn't bother me to know they were disgruntled with my bad manners. Once the night was over, I would never see these bluebloods again.

The bartender looked up as I wedged my way in. "What can I get for you?"

As I opened my mouth to answer, a man shoved past me. He held a tumbler of whiskey in his hand; I caught a whiff of bourbon. At the sight of him, my throat closed, and my voice went mute.

It couldn't be possible, but there he was, inches away from me. The man holding the whiskey was Max James.

He didn't even mutter an apology as he shouldered past. My heart began to pound as I watched him walk away.

Why the hell was he there? He was supposed to be in San Diego. The sight of him totally unnerved me, and my knees began to tremble. James's presence would blow our cover and possibly bomb the whole enterprise. I wondered what Millie and Rod would say. Surely they'd agree that we should flee the yacht and give up for today.

But maybe, just maybe, he hadn't recognized me. Judge Callahan hadn't given me a second glance. My own mother hadn't seen through the makeover a week ago.

As I stared at him with trepidation, he paused on the deck. Then he wheeled around, staring right at me. Our eyes met.

Oh, shit.

I turned on my heel and plowed through the crowd. The voice in my brain chimed to the beat of my heels on the wooden deck: *He's here, he's here, he's here.*

With Max James on the boat, we were all in peril. I had to steer clear of him. My presence aboard the yacht was no longer anonymous because he looked like he recognized me when he got a second glance. Millie's makeover wasn't foolproof.

As I scurried through the clusters of partygoers on deck, I

kept an eye out for Millie and Rod. For five or six interminable minutes, it seemed that they had disappeared altogether. Growing frantic, I wondered whether they had reconsidered the risk and decided to ditch me. Maybe they'd caught sight of Max James even before I had.

Just as I was becoming desperate, I spotted them on the far side of the deck. At the sight of them, an overwhelming surge of relief rolled over me. Millie smiled and waved at me. I hurried up to the railing to join them.

Pretending I was sharing a delicious secret, I whispered, "Max James is here."

Millie's smile froze. "You're kidding."

"Nope."

"Did he see you?" Rod asked.

"Yeah. I think he knew who I was."

Rod leaned against the railing, looking totally chill. "Then we better move fast. Did you duplicate the key card?"

I shook my head, astounded. "You mean we should still try to do this thing?"

"Sure. Just be smart about it."

Millie hissed, "And stay out of Max's way. You got the key cloner ready?"

I fumbled with my bag. Once I had the cloner in hand, Rod said, "Templeton is standing in a group, straight across the deck. We've been watching him. Cruise over and wait for an opportunity."

I wandered away. When a uniformed caterer approached with a tray of canapés, she paused, holding out the tray. I stood for a moment, pretending to study the appetizers she offered.

It was Diane. She was dressed as a server in a tuxedo shirt and black cummerbund and pants. When I chose an hors d'oeuvre, she smiled and said, "Did you see him?"

I nodded. Didn't need to ask who she meant.

Diane lifted the tray. Before she walked off, she said, "Be careful. Enjoy the mushroom tart."

Nibbling on it as I stepped away, I kept a surreptitious eye on Ian Templeton.

He was in the center of a small cluster of sycophants, surrounded by too many bodies for me to accomplish the feat I had practiced over the past week. While I waited for him to lose the hangers-on, my nerves spiked, and I could feel beads of sweat forming on my upper lip as my eyes darted around the deck, checking to see whether James was nearby.

I wanted desperately to rub that special spot on my hand, thinking it might calm me down, but the key cloner was clutched in my palm and I didn't dare draw attention to it.

I wondered whether I needed to walk away and circle back later. Maybe I looked too obvious, like I was stalking the host. Just as I pivoted to swing back to Rod and Millie, I heard Templeton say, "You need to see the rear deck because we just retrofitted the pool. Promise you'll check it out, I'll want to hear what you think."

It was an exit line. He broke away from the group and walked off. This was my shot. Dabbing the sweat from my lip with a swipe of my hand, I made my move.

Templeton wore his standard yacht uniform: the flowing white linen combo I'd seen in his layout in the *Post*. I could detect the outline of the key card in his pocket. *You can do this,*

I thought, as I swung around in his direction and let my heel skid across the polished deck.

I tumbled against him; he reached out to keep me from falling. While I did my pickpocket magic and cloned the card, I inclined my head close to his, laughing in his face and holding his gaze.

"Ian! I'm so embarrassed."

He kept a hand firmly clutched to my elbow, to steady me. Luckily, he grasped the arm that didn't hold the cloner.

"Are you all right?" Templeton gave me a baffled look, as if trying to place me.

"Too much vodka. I'd better switch to club soda." I pulled away, and as I walked off, called to him over my shoulder. "Great to see you again. Love the yacht."

I experienced a rush of exhilaration as I hurried back to the spot where I'd left my friends. I was buzzing with triumph because I had *done it*. It had gone off just like we rehearsed. No fumbling in this round, unlike the time I pinched the phone at the Museum of Natural History. I was getting better at this game. For the first time in twenty-four hours, I began to believe that we might actually pull this off.

And then I heard shoes pounding on the teakwood deck.

I didn't pause to look but just took off running. My heels weren't ideal footwear for a chase, and the crowd slowed me down. I shouldered through bodies like it was rush hour on the subway.

The cluster of bodies thinned as I made my way closer to the bow of the ship. The wind was so gusty at the bow that it whipped up the skirt of my dress and blew my hair from the loose knot Millie had pinned up earlier. It made sense that the guests abandoned the area to seek out more protected places on the boat.

As I ran to the guardrail on the portside of the bow, my shoe skidded in a slick spot, and I had to grasp the stanchion to keep from falling.

That's when my pursuer caught me. As expected, it was Max James who grabbed me from behind, cinching an arm around my waist. "What the fuck are you doing here?" he said.

My dad's training served me well. Without pausing to think about it, I pivoted, using my elbow to strike him in the jaw.

The hit took him by surprise. He released me, stumbling back a step. I tried to run, but he recovered, grabbing my wrist and pulling me back. "You just can't leave me alone, can you?"

"I don't know what you mean."

When I jerked my arm to escape his hold, he tightened his grip. His eyes narrowed as he said, "I'm going to have to convince you. Isn't that right?"

He was putting so much pressure on the wrist I knew he meant to break it. If he cracked the bone, it would incapacitate me. So I had to act. As he faced me with an ugly smirk, I flexed my free wrist and struck out with the heel of my palm, hitting him in the throat with all the force I could muster.

His head jerked up and back as he staggered away from me. As he clutched his throat, he leaned precariously over the railing. This was my opportunity, a chance to save myself. With both hands, I shoved his chest. Pain shot up my arm from my injured wrist.

He flailed at the metal bar as he lost his balance, but he didn't get a grip on the guardrail. James went over, headfirst.

Leaning over the guardrail, I watched him fall. He made a mighty splash when he hit the water.

I wasn't the only one who heard it. Down the deck, a woman screamed.

My head jerked at the sound, looking for the witness. At a distance, she stood alone in the empty bow. A diminutive figure trying to push silver hair out of her eyes, she shrieked a garbled message about a man overboard. Pointing at the water, she called to me. "Did you see that?"

I gaped at her for a moment, wondering how she could have missed the physical combat that preceded his fall. But she made no reference to the fight as she tottered toward me, clutching her hair. She said, "I'm sure I saw a man in the water! What should we do?"

She was a woman in her sixties, panting with panic. I spoke in a reassuring voice. "I heard something, too. You should find a seat and relax, okay? I'll go get help."

I sprinted away like a woman on a mission to save a drowning man. Once I rejoined the party, I quit running. Because I didn't believe it was my job to help fish my attacker out of the water. I had another task to perform.

Inspecting my wrist, I thought, *He can swim to shore*. It would give us time to execute the plan that would be his undoing.

CHAPTER 29

DIANE WHISKED BY me again, informing me that Millie and Rod were on the rear deck. I found them lounging by the swimming pool. Millie's sandals dangled from her hand while she sat at the edge of the pool, her bare feet submerged in the water.

Back in the thick of the party, I smoothed my hair and shook out my dress. Pulling the shreds of my composure together with a herculean effort, I strolled up to the poolside.

"How's the water?"

Millie kicked her feet, splashing up water like a kid in a wading pool. "Lovely. Wish I could strip down and take a dip."

Under his breath, Rod said, "Sweet Jesus. Reel it in, baby."

I squatted down beside them on my haunches, dipping my throbbing wrist into the pool water.

Millie's feet stopped moving. "You ready? Key card?"

"Yeah," I said, thinking, *Oh my God I hope the fucking thing works*. Because I was still an amateur at the art of undercover espionage, or whatever my new friends called their methods.

She murmured, "What took you so long?"

I pulled my arm out of the water. My wrist was red, already swollen and mottling with a bruise. "I ran into him again."

Millie's breath hitched when she saw the injury.

Rod's eyes checked out the crowd. In a low voice, he asked, "Do I need to get rid of him?"

Gingerly, I dried the wrist on my skirt. "He's gone. I pushed him overboard."

He turned to face me. "You're kidding, right?"

"Not kidding."

He broke into a smile. "That's pretty damn cool. I'm impressed."

Rod stood by the edge of the water and reached down, offering a hand to Millie. As she slipped her shoes back on, he spoke to her in an undertone. "Do you think you can keep everyone's eyes off of us while we go below?"

"No problem." She winked, giving him a cheeky grin.

A string quartet was playing background music on an upper deck of the yacht, one level above us. Staring up at them, I had a mental vision of the musicians on the *Titanic*. I forcibly suppressed the image while Millie strutted up a staircase to waylay them.

We watched as she approached the man strumming the cello and spoke to him. A confused expression crossed his face as the music paused. The violinist shook his head in protest, but Millie was unfazed.

She turned her back to the musicians, stepping in front of them in full view of the guests milling around the main deck. And then she launched into an aria, her voice soaring across the open space.

I shot a look of amazement at Rod, who gazed at her with pride. "That's from *Salome*," he whispered when she paused to draw breath.

As Millie continued, the musicians gradually followed the cue, providing some accompaniment. I checked around, and it appeared that the eyes of the guests were drawn to her. All conversation had stilled, out of necessity. Talking over Millie would be impossible.

Rod put a hand on my elbow and tugged. I nodded. This was our opportunity. While Millie and the band played on, we slipped into the main salon, trying to look like we had a legitimate reason to enter.

Once the glass door closed behind us, it muted Millie's voice. We could communicate without shouting at each other.

"I can't believe her volume. She's not even using a microphone." As I opened my clutch bag, I found the earpiece I carried, and jammed it into my ear canal.

"She was born with it, you know? Like her voice is an instrument. It's part of her natural equipment."

Outside, the aria had wrapped up; I could hear a round of applause. As the clapping faded, Millie launched into another number.

"How long can she keep it up?"

"The girl has got quite a repertoire. And it's not the only trick she has up her sleeve." Rod was adjusting his own earpiece. "Okay, I've got Larry in my head now."

I could hear Larry, too; Devon's voice also chimed in.

"Where you all at?" Larry asked.

"A salon on the main deck. Looks like a big living room."

While Rod filled them in on our location and Larry gave

directions to get us down below, I stared overhead, turning in a circle as I absorbed the surroundings. "Check out that crystal chandelier. It looks like something from a mansion on Fifth Avenue. A chandelier, on a damn boat."

Larry's voice rumbled in my ear. "Quit ogling like a yokel. There's a stairway out the side exit, on the eastern edge. Take it down to the next floor."

We ran down the narrow stairway, pausing on the lower deck. A central hallway led to an exit; three doors lined both sides of the hall.

Larry told us to run for the exit; it would take us to the next level. Before we could reach the end of the hall, I heard footsteps rushing down the stairs we had descended.

Rod turned and twisted the knob of the nearest door; the room was unlocked. We slipped inside and flattened ourselves beside the door, shoulder to shoulder up against the wall. We had taken refuge in a stateroom. The luxurious bedroom inside the yacht put my mother's showy New Jersey home to shame.

I held my breath as we heard footsteps pace up and down the hall. A voice in the hallway muttered something unintelligible as the doors that lined the hallway clicked open and slammed shut, one by one.

I turned my face to Rod. "Bathroom?" I whispered. It was the only hiding place I could think of. The closets were too narrow, and there was no escape route for us. Rod shook his head at my suggestion. "I've got a better idea."

I gasped as he picked me up, tossed me on the bed, and jumped on top of me.

My breath expelled with a whoosh when he landed on me.

Rod tilted his head and covered my mouth with his just as the door flew open.

The guard's voice was loud, with a confrontational edge. "You're not allowed in here."

Rod lifted his head but didn't look around. I could catch a bare glimpse of the intruder: he was a skinny young security guard, and he was alone. I was relieved to see that he wasn't one of those who'd tried to bar us from the party at check-in.

In a tart voice, I said, "Could we have some privacy, please?"

His response was curt. "Party guests are not supposed to be in the staterooms. This is a private area. I'll need to accompany you back to the upper deck."

Rod's voice came out in a rumble. With a breathless groan, he said: "Give us five minutes, man."

I scooted my head to get a better view. The guard had a radio in his belt; I saw him pull it out. As he began to request backup assistance, I shoved at Rod and he rolled off me.

"That's not necessary," I said, scrambling off the mattress and making a grab for the radio that the guard held. "We don't want to make a scene. It will be embarrassing in front of Mr. Templeton. Ian is my dad's good friend."

I got a grip on the device, but the guard wrestled it away from me; he was stronger than he looked. I could hear the response coming through the speaker: "Mitchell? What's going on?"

Mitchell didn't have a chance to answer the question, because I squared off and delivered a punch to the jaw with my good hand. The guard went down and stayed down. A knockout blow.

CHAPTER 30

I TUCKED THE radio under my arm and fumbled for the guard's cell phone; once I had it in hand, Rod dragged him into the restroom. When we didn't respond to radio messages, the phone hummed without ceasing. I stared at the screen, wondering what I should do as Rod shoved the guy into a shower stall and restrained him with his own handcuffs.

Finally, a text appeared on the screen of the guard's phone. Do you need assistance?

I answered quickly. False alarm.

Rod jerked his head in the direction of the stateroom door. I dropped the radio on the floor and chased him out of the room, still clutching the guard's phone.

"Ditch that," Rod said.

"Where?" I whispered. The hallway was empty, just a long row of doors. There was no waste receptacle to be seen. Softly cursing under his breath, Rod grabbed the phone and dropped it on the carpet, crushing it under the heel of his shoe. Then he opened the nearest stateroom door and kicked the phone inside. It disappeared under the bed.

"Bottom deck," he said.

I followed his lead. At this point, it had become painfully obvious to me: I was in way over my head.

Moving stealthily, we made our way down the stairs. I kept my ears tuned, straining to detect any noise overhead, but it seemed that the security detail was nowhere near us. Maybe the phony text I sent had worked. When we reached Templeton's office on the bottom deck, Rod handed me a pair of blue nitrile gloves, like doctors wear during exams. After he donned his gloves, he tried to turn the doorknob.

The door was locked. Unfazed, Rod removed a small black leather pouch from the inside pocket of his jacket. He opened it and selected two slim metal pins.

"Lockpicks?" I whispered. He nodded.

I'd seen lockpicks in a case I tried where a man broke into his ex-wife's apartment. One of the pins Rod held was ridged and the other was curved at the end.

Squatting down to eye level with the lock, he said, "I can do it with a paper clip if I have to. This is quicker."

He inserted the pins into the lock and moved them with meticulous delicacy. In the silent hall, I heard the click when he conquered the lock.

As we ducked inside and pressed the door shut, Larry's voice was in my ear. "Did you make it into the office?"

I responded. "Yeah, but we're leaving a path of destruction behind us. I had to punch a guard out, and Rod—"

Larry cut me off. Apparently he didn't want to hear the details. "I'll turn you over to Devon."

Devon's voice reverberated in my ear canal. He sounded chipper as he asked, "How's the party?"

Devon might be chill, cool as a cucumber. But he wasn't walking in our shoes.

"I want to get out of here," I said.

"You're almost done. You cloned the key card, right? Now use it to get inside the safe."

My hands were shaking so hard, I almost dropped it. So Rod took the key card from my hand and swiped it through the slot in the safe.

We waited. Nothing happened.

Rod tried the card a second time, with the same results.

My voice was shrill as I said, "It doesn't work. What do we do now, Devon? The key card didn't open the safe."

Panicky, I clutched Rod's arm, thinking: *We've come all this way, taken these insane risks for nothing.* My heart was beating dangerously fast.

But Rod just rolled his eyes. "What a paranoid asshole," he muttered. "Templeton put the safe inside another safe."

I stared down at the safe; it looked impenetrable. "Do we have a key for that?"

"No." Rod dug inside his pocket and pulled out two small tubes, then proceeded to insert them in the safe. I peered over his shoulder.

"What are those?"

"Squibs."

That didn't provide an answer; I'd never heard of squibs.

In a whisper, I demanded: "But what are they?"

"Explosives."

With that information, it suddenly registered: they looked like tiny sticks of dynamite. I stepped back and glanced longingly at the door, wondering whether it would be wise to duck out at this point; maybe I should make a run for it. If Rod intended to blow up the office, I didn't want to be a part of the fallout.

"Relax, Kate," he said. "These just have enough power to force the safe open." He cut his eyes at me with a grin. "What, do you think I'm going to blow up the boat, with the three of us still on board?"

I laughed, but the sound was screechy. Because that was precisely what I feared he might do.

The squibs detonated without fanfare. Once Rod was inside the secondary safe, he used the key card I had cloned. This time, it worked like a charm.

Rod and I stood shoulder to shoulder, as we beheld Ian Templeton's personal computer resting inside the inner safe. I couldn't believe we had actually made it this far. I grasped Rod's hand and squeezed it.

Devon buzzed in my ear canal, interrupting my reverie. "Jesus Christ, what's taking so long?"

I inhaled a steadying breath. "We've got it, Devon. The computer."

"Okay. Now you need to insert the Jumpdrive."

I opened my clutch bag and pulled out the special Jumpdrive Devon had provided for me. It would install software into Templeton's computer; the software would enable Devon to hack in.

Devon was quiet. Rod and I waited in silence as I wondered how long the process would take. Minutes passed; our soft breathing made the only sound in the office. As time ticked by, Rod and I exchanged a glance. His brows raised. I lifted my shoulders in a helpless shrug.

After a long interval, Devon whispered, "Shit."

"What?" Rod's brow wrinkled.

"It's a gap computer," Devon said.

A shiver of fear ran up my spine. "You mean we're not connected to the Internet? That kind of gap computer?"

I had never encountered an air-gapped computer. I had only heard of it, when a cybersecurity expert spoke at a law enforcement conference I attended a year prior. He talked about how air-gapped computers were designed to be impenetrable. The expert explained that air gapping is a high security measure used to ensure that a computer is isolated from unsecured networks, like the public Internet. He said that the military uses air-gapped computers to protect classified information. But I hadn't left the conference with any in-depth understanding of the technology because I failed to pay close attention to the guy's presentation. Cybersecurity didn't have much application to the prosecution of domestic violence cases and violent felonies. None at all, in fact.

"Hey, Devon. We're screwed, right?" I said.

Devon said, "I can't hack it remotely. You've got to get past the security system."

My heartbeat revved up once again. Much too late, I realized that Devon should have come in my place. He should be in Templeton's office, dressed in party clothes. I was entirely out of my depth. I wished myself at the bottom of the sea.

Devon sighed into my ear. "We might be able to pull it off. We'll try an electronic network interface. Maybe we can make a security hole."

"I don't know how to do this. It doesn't even make sense to me." I sounded breathless, as if I had been working out.

"I'll walk you through it. Just follow my instructions, I'll tell you what to do."

He proceeded to work with me, taking me step by step. As I followed his instructions, he was patient with me, like he was dictating a "cybersecurity for dummies" course. But I fumbled more than once and had to backtrack, using more precious time.

Rod's phone hummed. When he answered, I heard Millie's voice jump out of the cell phone.

"Where the hell are you?"

Millie had run out of songs, I guessed. But I didn't say it out loud. Devon was still drilling in my ear.

Devon said, "Kate, you're doing fine. We have planted malware, but now we have to get the data out. I can't see that remotely; you are going to have to transfer the stream of data to a nearby device."

"What device? I don't have a device."

Devon told me, "You can use Rod's phone. He has an Android app."

Rod heard him; he handed me the phone. In my ear, Devon told me to set it to airplane mode. While I followed Devon's directions, Rod's head jerked toward the door.

"You hear that? They're coming down the stairs."

Rod was right; I heard the footsteps clambering down the staircase. The prospect of armed guards confronting us in the office sparked my instinct to flee. But the information from Templeton's computer was still uploading onto the phone. If we escaped now, the entire effort would be fruitless, a failure, all for naught. Agitated, I took a step toward the door.

Rod placed a restraining hand on my shoulder. "I'll lead

them away from here. You join Millie on the main deck as soon as you can wrap up."

My head buzzed with questions; in an agitated whisper, I tried to ask how the three of us would manage to unite on deck—but he was gone. In the hallway, I heard the guards shout as they spotted Rod. The sound was followed by heavy footfalls down the hallway. I tensed as they ran past the office door, girding myself to fight, if necessary. But no one disturbed the office.

Minutes ticked by as the binary information in Templeton's computer files uploaded. While I waited in the silence, I had time to ponder some disturbing questions regarding my personal criminal liability in the escapade. In the past hour, we had gone way beyond party-crashing. I wondered how many crimes I had committed, so I ticked them off in my head: criminal trespass, assault, property destruction, cybertheft. I was undoubtedly overlooking some federal crimes.

Finally, Devon told me that the process was complete. He instructed me to hide Rod's phone on my person, so I stuffed it in my bra. He reminded me to leave the scene as clean as possible. My clutch bag held some bleach wipes for that purpose. After wiping the hard surfaces, I returned the computer to the safe and shut it inside. The squibs had scattered some debris, and I had to swipe it up, too.

I scanned the room with a worried eye before I slipped through the door, wiping down the inside and outside knobs before I secured the lock and pulled the door shut. I ripped off the gloves and stuffed them inside my clutch along with the used wipes. Despite my hurried housekeeping job, it felt like we had left far too many signs of our underground operation.

Templeton would surely realize that someone had entered the office and tampered with his computer. I just hoped he wouldn't discover it until we were safely off the yacht.

My nerves were taut, and my body felt like a wire spring stretched out to the max. Perspiration dripped down my forehead, and I wiped the sweat with my bare hand.

I ran up the stairs on tiptoe, trying to move as silently as possible. Approaching the main deck, I braced myself for an attack. But when I emerged from the salon, Diane stood outside the door. No one else was waiting.

She held out the tray. I turned my back to the party and bent over the appetizers, reaching into the neckline of my dress. Only Diane saw me remove the phone from my bra. The handoff was smooth. Diane tucked Rod's phone into her cummerbund as I picked up a canapé and popped it into my mouth.

We turned away from each other, and I crossed the deck. No one took any notice of me. Merging into the crowd, I understood why. All eyes were on Rod.

Pushing through the bodies, I managed to get a partial view of the conflict. The security detail had him surrounded. I stood by helplessly, watching while one of the guards tackled him and took him down.

A woman shrieked right beside my ear. I shoved her out of the way, fighting through the crowd to get a better look.

It took more than one guard to confine Rod. He wrestled the first guy off, flinging him across the varnished deck. After Rod regained his footing, another guard tried to grab him in a neck hold, but Rod shoved that man off, sending the guard into a catering station. I heard the crash of broken glassware.

Two more uniformed guards came for him; one of them held a Taser. The Taser evened the odds.

Rod went down when they tased him. I watched his face freeze in a grimace of pain. The partygoers must have figured the show was over because they stepped back and wandered away, clearing the deck. Only Millie stood nearby, her eyes blinking rapidly. I strolled up to Millie and took her by the hand. We needed to flee, but she resisted when I tried to pull her away.

While we stood on deck, Rod looked up and made eye contact with her. I was astonished to see him smile at Millie, despite the fact that he had to be in agony. He must have given her an unspoken signal because she linked arms with me and whispered, "Okay. Let's head out."

We strolled to the boarding gangway at a casual pace. Stepping down onto the ramp to disembark, I tensed when I heard sirens approach the dock. The noise made me want to dash down the gangway and run to the limo, but I resisted the urge. It was important to look cool. I kept my gaze fixed straight ahead and pretended everything was just fine.

That was an error of judgment. I should have listened to my gut and run like hell.

I didn't spot Max James until I stepped from the ramp onto the dock and turned in the direction of our ride. He was coming for me, and at a glance, I knew I was in trouble. He'd made it back to shore but his wet clothes were plastered to him, and he had a wild look in his eye.

I broke away from Millie and tried to dart out of his path, but there wasn't time. James was on me, grabbing my shoulder and tearing the silk fabric of my dress. When I knocked his hand away, he reached for me again, caught me around the neck, and flung me to the ground.

It was almost a face-plant, but I managed to land on my forearms. When my face hit my hands, the jolt to my wrist was excruciating. The pain slowed my reaction, but I managed to twist to the side, ready to stand and fight.

James kicked me in the ribs before I could rise. I rolled into a ball, clutching my middle as I struggled to breathe. As I gasped on the dirty pavement, two NYPD cars sped up the dock with lights flashing and sirens blaring.

James waved an arm to get their attention. "Police! Detain this woman!"

The NYPD ignored James. Templeton's security officers were dragging Rod over to the police vehicles. The police-men huddled around Rod, talking to the security guards as a patrolman pushed Rod into the back seat of one of the patrol cars.

Max James raised his voice to a shout. "Police!"

His eyes were on the cops so Millie seized the opportunity. She ran up to James, looking like an avenging angel.

And she kneed him squarely in the groin.

He went down with a shriek, curling into a fetal position. Millie grabbed my arm and pulled me off the ground. Leaning on her, I made a stumbling run to the limo. When we made it inside the vehicle, Millie swung the door shut as I collapsed onto the seat.

She didn't bother to push a button for the speaker. Even with the chauffeur's window closed, Millie didn't need an intercom to be heard in the front of the car.

"Drive!" she shouted.

CHAPTER 31

MY FOREARM WAS spurting blood from a gaping wound. I didn't feel it until we were sitting inside the limo.

"How'd that happen?" Millie said.

"I guess I sliced it open when he knocked me down." I grimaced at the blood rolling down my arm.

"You must have landed on something, like broken glass." Millie shimmied out of a nylon slip and wrapped it around the cut. "Put pressure on it," she said.

The limo driver's voice came through the intercom. "Where are we headed?"

"Go to 101 West Eighty-First Street, off Columbus Avenue."

Confused, I whispered, "What for?" Neither Millie nor I lived on the Upper West Side. The address she gave was a high-rent district.

"It's Whitney's place. She lives alone, so we'll have privacy. Steven can patch you up there." Her voice rang out as she shouted at the driver again. "Faster!"

She grabbed her phone from her bag and started texting.

Her face was intent on the screen as she sent the messages. When she looked up, I was adjusting the slip on my arm. The blood had soaked through the layers of the fabric.

"Does it hurt too bad?"

It was pretty bad, but I didn't want to sound like the weak sister. "Yeah, kind of. Funny thing. I didn't feel it when it happened."

"You'll be okay. This stuff happens sometimes. Steven will fix you up. He's really good."

Her phone pinged. As she checked it, she said, "They'll be waiting for us."

I was relieved to hear Steven would check me out. In addition to the gaping wound, my wrist was swelling, and my ribs ached. But I was also worried about the fallout for my fellow team member. I said, "What about Rod? Shouldn't someone see what's happening with him?"

"I let them know Rod's in custody. Steven will make sure he gets bailed out. He knows who to call. Money's not a problem, Gatsby covers that. They'll take care of him. I'll see Rod tomorrow morning, I'm sure of that."

I had misgivings and wanted to ask how she could be so confident that it would be handled successfully. And that name again. Who was Gatsby? I was still being kept in the dark.

"Are you sure Rod will be all right?"

Millie tried to sound upbeat. "Absolutely. This went off just as planned. No major problems, nothing that can't be fixed. Everything's cool."

Millie didn't fool me. One look revealed the crack in her brave facade. Tears welled up in her eyes, smearing her eyeliner. She wiped it with the back of her hand, but rubbing made it worse. "Shit," she whispered.

I wanted to offer comfort, but she turned her back and looked out the window. After a moment, she spoke in a wavering voice. "Rod's tough."

I was quick to agree. "God, yes. Rod can handle himself."

When she didn't respond, I nudged her with my elbow because both hands were bloody. "Is there anything I can do? Wish I could make you feel better."

She shook her head. We sat in silence until we pulled up to an apartment building on Eighty-First.

Whitney was waiting for us. She stood in front of the building with a cigarette, chatting with the doorman. When we emerged from the limo, she dropped the cigarette on the sidewalk. "Look who's here! Come on up, girls."

Although I tried to cover the bloody bandage as I passed the doorman, he gave me an uneasy side-eye. Whitney didn't offer any explanations or excuses. She marched us into the elevator and hit the button for the eighth floor.

When the door closed, she said, "My God, you're a mess. Good thing Steven's waiting for you."

Inside the apartment, he sat on a white brocade sofa. His medical bag rested on a glass coffee table. Though the apartment was spacious and beautifully furnished, it was almost as messy as my place. Piles of folders, periodicals, and miscellaneous stuff were strewn across the room.

Whitney didn't apologize for the disarray. "Steven, Kate's bleeding like a stuck pig. Don't let her sit on my couch."

"Let's work in the kitchen," he said. "I'll examine you in there, Kate."

Inside the kitchen, Millie helped me out of my dress. I stood as she unzipped it. When I stepped out of it, Millie lifted it off the floor and held it up with a rueful expression. Looking at it gave me a pang of lament. The elegant blue dress looked like a Halloween costume. It was torn and blood-spattered with a black smear on the bodice left by James's vicious kick.

Steven glanced over from the sink, where he was scrubbing his hands. "Kate, let's see your arm first."

Sitting in my underwear at the kitchen table, I felt self-conscious, but I tried to shrug off the feeling. Steven was a doctor, and so he regularly saw patients in a state of undress. While he pulled some equipment from his bag, I unwrapped the bloody nylon slip from my arm.

He took a look and said, "You'll need stitches. I'll numb it before I put in the sutures. But I have to clean the wound first, to get out the dirt and debris." He gave me a sympathetic look. "There will be some discomfort."

Steven was right about that. It hurt like hell when he soaped it and cleaned it out under the running tap. He explained that he wanted to be certain no grit or shards of glass remained inside.

After he administered the local anesthetic and stitched me up, he turned his attention to my wrist. His hands were gentle as he examined it. "Is it a stabbing pain or a throbbing pain?"

I winced. "It throbs. But there was a stabbing pain when I broke my fall."

Whitney called to us from the front room. "Devon just sent me the files!"

"That's great, Whitney. You can tell us what you find when we wrap up here," Steven said. He moved to the freezer and filled a bag with ice cubes. "Kate, you'll ice the wrist for twenty to thirty minutes every four hours or so. If it's not better in two or three days, I want you to get an X-ray."

Steven swaddled my wrist in a clean kitchen towel and rested the ice pack on it.

"I'm going to wrap the wrist later. Okay, let's check the ribs." He pressed gently over my ribs, asking me to take deep breaths.

While I breathed in and out, we heard Whitney again, laughing out loud in the next room. "It's a gold mine. This is the evidence we need!"

"Hold off for a minute, Whitney," he said. "We're not done here." He pressed my rib cage again. "I think your ribs are bruised, not fractured or broken."

I exhaled with relief. "Okay, no broken bones. Good to hear."

"You can ice the ribs, too. So, Kate, my official assessment: one laceration requiring sutures, bruised ribs, and a severe sprain to the wrist." Frowning, he removed the ice pack and lifted my wrist, giving it a closer look. His touch was almost tender, and some of my tension eased as he held it.

When he looked up, our eyes met. He gave me a reassuring smile. "You're going to be fine. But it was a hell of a night. Pretty crazy party, am I right?"

I shuddered involuntarily and gave a shaky laugh. "It was memorable, can't lie."

After he wrapped my wrist in a bandage, we sat together for a quiet moment. It soothed me, and I began to feel safe again.

Millie popped in. "They're making Rod's bail. I'm going to meet him over there."

"Millie, that's great. I'm so relieved," I said.

She held up a sweatshirt and yoga pants. "Whitney says you can wear these. I'll give you a hand."

After Millie helped me dress, she left to join Rod. I found Whitney and Steven behind a desk in the corner of the living room, focusing on a laptop.

Whitney looked up and grinned. "We've got his book. Come over here and look."

I stared at the screen. "What is the book, exactly?"

Whitney said, "It's his client listing. It shows the amount he received from each client for investment and the amount that was actually invested. The book shows Templeton only invested a fraction of the amount he was supposed to invest. He kept the spread for himself."

Scanning the numbers on the screen, I tried to make sense of them. "What did he do with the money he kept?"

"It shows here that the money was siphoned off to different accounts, probably in the Caymans, or maybe a Swiss bank."

"That's interesting."

"Right." She clicked the mouse, pulling up another document. "Here's an example. This guy turned five million over to Templeton's firm for investment. They only invested a million. The four million dollar spread is shown as transferred to account number five-four-six-nine. Probably one of the foreign accounts where it's untouchable."

Steven said, "So he's stealing from them outright."

"Oh, yeah. Classic Ponzi scheme. We've got records that his clients receive fabricated reports showing a high rate of return, but it's just blue sky. Nothing is there, he steals it."

I was catching on. "And when the client wants his money, he robs Peter to pay Paul."

"Exactly!" Whitney looked up at me, beaming like a proud schoolteacher. "You've got it. Since the client's money is gone, Templeton has to transfer money from other accounts to meet the demand. Or Max James does. From the records I'm seeing, he is Templeton's senior employee, his fingerprints are all over this."

"So the files incriminate James, just like you predicted." A sense of exhilaration buzzed through me. My injuries felt better already.

"Yep. There's a whole ream of correspondence where they talk about hunting for new investors to cover requests from current clients to cash out. This information will bring both of them down. And the numbers are incredible. The total spread as of the end of the last quarter is over $2.5 billion. Templeton could afford to buy a fleet of those boats you partied on today."

Steven asked, "What's the next step?"

"Devon sets up a blind email account so that we can make an anonymous whistleblower report. We'll send this all over. The SEC, the FBI, the US attorney. We can even send it to your boss, Kate. Straight to the white-collar crime division."

The success made me dizzy, literally. I took unsteady steps to the nearest seat. I might have blacked out, but Steven appeared at my side, supporting me.

As he helped me ease onto the couch, he tucked a cushion behind my head. "You're wiped out. Think you can close your eyes and get some rest?"

I dozed on the damask sofa, but the sleep wasn't restful.

I dreamed of the yacht. Max James and I struggled violently on the deck, but in the dream, he tossed me overboard. The sensation of falling was so real that I screamed.

The scream woke me. Whitney was standing over me, looking concerned. "Nightmare?"

"Yeah. Scary." My heart was pounding, and I wasn't quite back to earth.

She patted my knee. "Get used to it, hon. You joined a scary club."

CHAPTER 32

IN THE DAYS that followed, I waited for a bomb to drop. If Rod and I had been busted as the interlopers in Templeton's private office, someone might be pounding on my door, maybe with a warrant for my arrest. But as the week dragged by, the summons that I dreaded never came. And no headlines appeared indicating that James or Templeton faced criminal liability for the information we had shared illuminating their fraudulent schemes.

I knew that the case wouldn't break immediately. It would take time for the information to make its way through the proper channels, and for an investigation to follow, before charges would be filed. And it was as likely to land with the feds as with the state. I figured the US attorney would ultimately make the announcement. So I was unprepared when my office mate walked into the office, dropped into his chair, and said, "Your nemesis is back in trouble again."

I glanced up from my computer screen, mildly curious. "I have a long list of enemies. Which one are you talking about, Bill?"

"That guy, the one you decked outside of the courthouse. Max James? Isn't that his name?"

My hands froze on the keyboard. "Max James, really? Did you see a press release? What have you heard?"

"Didn't hear anything. I just saw the guy being escorted into court. They're about to arraign him." Bill dug inside his desk drawer and pulled out a Clif Bar. Propping his feet on his desk, he proceeded to tear off the wrapper.

I was on my feet in an instant, looming over him. "Where? Which courtroom?"

"Judge Stark. You know which floor he's on?"

I didn't pause to reply. I flew out of the office and ran through the hallways, dodging the people blocking my path. When I reached Judge Stark's courtroom, I sidled into a seat in the back corner, where I hoped to observe without being seen. I didn't want to draw undue attention to myself.

James stood before the bench, flanked by a lawyer. The defense attorney wasn't familiar. He wasn't using the team who'd represented him at his felony assault trial. He obviously realized he needed a firm that specialized in white-collar crime for this case. Craning my neck, I searched the room for Ian Templeton, but didn't spot him.

As the judge began to read off the charges, Max James's attorney interrupted. "We waive formal reading of the charges and enter a plea of not guilty."

The judge asked the prosecutor to recommend a bond amount. I edged forward in my seat, eager to hear the exchange. Though it was unlikely, I hoped they would set it so high that James would have to remain in jail until trial.

I was so intent on the proceedings at the bench that I didn't notice a woman sliding down the row until she nudged me.

It was my mother.

"What are you doing here?" she asked.

"Shhh!" I scooted away from her, anxious to hear the conversation at the bench.

"Don't shush me, Kate. You haven't talked to me in weeks. Where have you been hiding?"

"Mom, please. I'm trying to hear the judge." Dropping my voice to a bare whisper, I kept my eyes glued to the scene unfolding at the bench. "They're arraigning Max James for fraud."

"I know that. They'll set the bond at two hundred thousand."

What are you, a fortune-teller? I resisted the urge to roll my eyes.

Judge Stark lifted the gavel and parroted my mother. "Bond set at two hundred thousand dollars." He rapped the gavel on the bench. "Next case."

I scrutinized my mother, suspicious of her accurate guess. "What are you doing here, Mom? Why aren't you in New Jersey?"

"I'm meeting a prospective client. But I'll be free by one o'clock, so I can take you out to lunch." She looked down at my sprained wrist, still wrapped in a bandage. "What happened to you? Did you hurt yourself at the gym?"

"Yeah." Mom had provided a logical explanation for the injury. I was glad my stitches were covered by the long sleeve of my shirt.

"We can eat in the neighborhood. Where do you usually go for lunch?"

My mom would not be interested in the hot dog special from the food truck. Squirming in the seat like a kid in school, I hedged, trying to conjure up an acceptable excuse to dodge her lunch invitation. As if on cue, my phone hummed. It was a text from my boss, summoning me to his office.

I heaved a regretful sigh. "Mom, I'd love to, really. But I can't. Frank Rubenstein wants to see me."

She looked nettled. "So when? Later this afternoon?"

"Can't really say." I stood and scooted past her in the row, taking care to avoid stepping on her feet. "I'll be in touch. Tell Leo I said hi, okay?"

I gave her a wave. She glowered at me as I escaped the court-room. Waiting at the elevator, I checked the text from Frank again. It gave no clue to what awaited me in his office. I started to borrow trouble. What was he unhappy about this time? He surely couldn't know that I'd been on Templeton's yacht.

A woman wearing a cloud of Chanel No. 5 walked up, standing in my personal circle of space. I glanced over at her, my nose wrinkling.

It was James's girlfriend, Angelina.

Startled, I took a step back.

She advanced on me, her eyes narrowed to slits. "I don't know how you did it, but you're behind this," she said. "You set him up."

I tensed, ready to fend off an attack. There was no telling what she might do.

But she didn't throw a punch—not even a kick this time. To my surprise, she choked out a strangled laugh. "Better watch your back. You don't know who you're messing with."

CHAPTER 33

THE ELEVATOR DOOR opened, and people poured out of it. Angelina had to step out of the way. As the car emptied out. I shouldered my way inside, hoping she wouldn't follow.

When the doors closed, Angelina wasn't among the bodies crowded inside the elevator. I breathed out in relief. Her words had unnerved me, but as I waited while the elevator stopped on every floor on the way up to Frank's office, it struck me: The girlfriend didn't really know what I'd done. She made a specious, general accusation. And she threw out a wild warning just to keep me off-balance. If she knew what had transpired on that boat, she would have said so.

When I approached his private office, Frank's administrative assistant gave me an expectant look. He must have told her I was coming because she glanced at the door and said, "You can go on back. He's waiting."

I swung the door wide. In a voice of good cheer, I said, "Frank! Exciting day, right?"

He looked up with a somber face. "Is it?"

I pushed down my customary feeling of resentment. Frank Rubenstein was a buzz kill. He had a talent for crushing my spirit. Dropping into the chair that faced his desk, I said, "I'm pretty sure I know why you called me up here."

His eyebrows raised. I noted—not for the first time—they were a different shade from the hair on his head. I'd heard whispers that he colored his hair to cover the gray, because he thinks appearances are important for a man with political ambition. No one in the office mentions it in his presence.

"You do?" he murmured.

Again, the impatience fizzed in my brain. "Yeah. Max James. I just happened to be by Judge Stark's courtroom when he was arraigned, so I slipped in to watch. Investment fraud, right? Multiple counts. What about the guy he worked for— what's his name? Templeton, I think."

Frank didn't answer, didn't respond at all. I knew he didn't like me to fish, but I was an attorney on staff. And once Templeton was charged, it would be a matter of public record, fodder for headlines in the *New York Times* and, of course, the *New York Post*.

I tried to sound like I wasn't particularly interested, but I totally failed. "It's Ian Templeton. He's a big player in hedge funds, I read that somewhere. Of course, that's not illegal, unless they rip people off when they do it. Will Templeton be charged as a codefendant? Is the investigation ongoing?"

Rubenstein's expression changed. His lips pressed together, and his eyes shifted. Was it a covert reaction? But then I wondered whether I just imagined it because he recovered swiftly. Leaning forward in his chair, he folded his hands on the glossy surface of his desk. "Templeton isn't your concern."

Hastily, I backpedaled. "I know that. The white-collar division will be handling it, obviously. But Frank, if I can help with any background, I'm ready to step up. Because I did a lot of digging when I prepped for the Max James assault trial. I could be a resource for the people in white collar."

"You won't be a resource."

My face fell. Frank was such a downer, throwing cold water on my genuine enthusiasm. I was starting to take it personally.

Stubbornly, I persisted. "Who's in charge? I'll talk to them. The DA who's litigating the case against James may see it differently. If it was me, I'd be glad to have any offer of assistance."

He cut me off. "It doesn't matter what you're offering. Or who's handling the prosecution. You won't be a resource for anyone in this office."

I didn't know how to respond to that. We sat in silence for a long minute, engaging in a staring contest.

Frank spoke first. "How's your support group?"

I was so taken aback by the change of topic that it startled me at first, and I didn't know how to answer. The only support group I had joined was my band of misfit outlaws. Could Frank possibly know about it? Because if so, it spelled trouble.

Then I remembered, and caught my breath. He wasn't talking about my new group of associates. Relaxing slightly, I said, "Anger management? I haven't had the chance to make it to a meeting this week, unfortunately. Too busy. But I'm making progress."

Mentally, I made a note to self: *Get Edgar to sign another attendance form.*

"How do you know you're making progress? Did the group leader tell you that?"

A nagging suspicion unfurled in my head. *He's onto you,* I thought. But there was nothing to do about it, other than brazen it out.

"I can just tell. I've been feeling pretty chill. So I attribute it to the therapy. It makes sense."

I gave him what I hoped was a sunny smile. Frank looked away, glancing down as he pulled open a desk drawer. "But you didn't get any words of wisdom from the group leader?"

He pulled a sheet of paper from the drawer. I caught a glimpse of it. It was my verification form. Frank studied it, his mouth turning down in a frown.

"Duncan Schmidt? That's his name, isn't it?" He turned the page around so it dangled from his hand, and I could see the faux signatures. "All these signatures. They are not terribly legible, but they appear to bear Duncan Schmidt's name. Correct?"

"Sure." I tensed in my chair. Something was coming. I wasn't certain exactly what it would be. But a voice whispered in my head: *You're fucked, Kate.*

Frank smoothed the wrinkled form on his desktop before he picked up his remote. Pointing it at the huge screen that hung overhead in his office, I turned to look as he clicked the button.

Duncan Schmidt's bearded face appeared on the screen. The volume was muted. Frank hit the unmute button and bumped up the volume.

Duncan was speaking. "I can't comment on my clients. The matters we discuss in support group are confidential."

A voice could be heard off-camera. I recognized it because it belonged to Patrick Scott, one of the investigators in the DA's office.

"Can you confirm whether Kate Stone has been attending the support group?"

"I can't confirm or deny."

Duncan sounded stubborn, as if they'd already been back and forth on the issue. I was rooting for him, thinking: *Hang tough, Duncan. Don't let him break you down.*

The investigator handed something to Duncan. It looked like a photograph—of me.

"Can you identify this woman? Has she attended an anger management support group that you moderate in Midtown?"

Duncan studied the photo. It was unclear from his expression whether he recognized me or not. But as he handed it back, his tone was adamant.

"I won't confirm or deny. I owe all of my clients confidentiality. It's my professional obligation."

My heart was pounding. Rubenstein wasn't playing the video because it cleared me, that was certain. I realized with a sinking feeling of dread that the "aha" moment on the video recording was coming up.

"I have a sheet of paper, a verification form for Kate Stone, bearing a number of signatures."

Duncan snapped at the investigator. "I've made it clear that I don't intend to reveal the identity of my clients."

The investigator's voice was unperturbed. "I understand

that. But if you will examine these signatures for me…do you recognize them?"

I saw the moment that Duncan turned on me. His bearded face puckered with confusion as he scanned the signature lines. Hesitantly, he said, "My name appears on this form. Repeatedly."

"And it purports to be your signature, Mr. Schmidt. Did you sign that form? On all of those dates?"

As Duncan's eyes darted down the sheet, his head began to shake in the negative. "No. No, I don't recall making any of these signatures."

He looked up in alarm, as if he feared he might be in some kind of trouble.

The investigator pressed him. "Have you ever seen this form before?"

"No, I have not." Duncan shoved the sheet of paper back at the off-camera investigator, behaving as if it had singed his fingers. "Someone signed my name, but it wasn't me."

At that point, Frank clicked off the TV. My eyes remained on the blank screen as I tried to think of a next step, something to bolster my perilous position. Nothing came to mind.

Frank's voice was dry. "Why, Kate. Are you blushing?"

I was mortified to realize that it was true. My face felt hot enough to explode.

When I turned to meet his eye, Frank shook his head in disbelief. "Forgery. Lies. Deception."

He sounded like a preacher, one of those megachurch pastors they have down South. The holier-than-thou tone riled me. I couldn't deny his accusations, but I damned sure didn't intend to admit anything. My jaw locked.

Frank waved his arm in dismissal. "You're fired. Clear out your desk. You have one hour to vacate this office, do you understand that?"

I didn't respond, just rose from the chair and turned my back to him. And before I walked out, I refrained from flinging a parting shot in his direction.

Maybe my anger management training paid off after all.

CHAPTER 34

I HAD JUST popped a beer when Steven knocked on the door.

Earlier that afternoon, I'd invited him to come by, to discuss the day's events. I hadn't seen him in a while, not since he stitched me up at Whitney's apartment. To my surprise, I found I missed his company. I'd grown comfortable with the prospect of talking to him on a regular basis.

When I checked through the peephole, he looked rougher than usual. His hair was tousled, his face sported a couple of days' worth of stubble.

It took a minute to open the row of deadbolt locks and unfasten the chain. As the door creaked open, Steven was leaning against the doorframe.

"Did you know that the security device on the front door of your building is still busted?"

"Yeah," I said. "It's such a friendly, cozy little block. We don't even bother to lock our doors at night. Come on in."

He watched with a wry expression as I shut the door and secured the locks. I had installed three of them myself, the first week I'd moved into the building. It hadn't taken long to realize that my landlord did not intend to respond to my repeated calls and complaints about the front entrance.

Holding up the can of beer, I said, "You want one? I just bought a twelve-pack."

He blinked. "A twelve-pack of Coors Light. Twelve cans."

I took a swallow from the can. "I'm economizing by buying in bulk. I've experienced a downturn in my personal finances."

When Steven didn't accept the offer, I stepped over and sat in my favorite chair: Dad's old recliner. Steven took the spot across from me, on the sofa. The cushion sagged under him. He scooted closer to the middle, where the springs were sturdier.

"So Max James has been charged, right?" he said.

"Multiple counts. I watched the arraignment today, from the back of the room. He's already lawyered up, so I expect he's out on bond now."

A shadow flickered over Steven's face. "That's disappointing. We hoped they would keep him locked up."

"For fraud, white-collar crime? No, that's not how the system works. A guy like James, with financial resources, he wasn't going to remain in jail pending trial. Not unless he's charged with murder."

I guzzled the beer and then squeezed the can to hear it crackle while I vented. "Here's what I can't figure out—what happened to Ian Templeton? Where's the criminal case against him? They're surely not offering immunity to Templeton, to testify against James. Why would they use the major player to nail the lesser criminal? That's not how it's supposed to go down."

I knocked back the very last swallow and crushed the can, tossing it onto the coffee table. Steven followed it with his eyes.

He said, "'Not how it's supposed to go down.' The system, am I right?"

"That's right. It's not." I gave an angry huff as I launched out of the chair. Walking back to the refrigerator, I asked, "Sure you don't want a beer? You won't join me?"

He hesitated before he relented. "What the hell. I'll take one."

I pulled two cans from the cardboard container and handed one to him before I settled back into Dad's battered chair. After he popped the tab, Steven lifted it in a toast.

"Here's to you, Kate. Hell of a job on that yacht. You pulled it off like a pro."

I leaned toward him, holding out my can; we clicked aluminum. After I took a sip, I said, "It was a group effort. I was the weakest link, honestly. I'd really like to thank everybody, if I get the chance to see them again."

"You will." Steven drank from the can, swallowing with a grimace. It struck me as impolite, but I ignored it.

He went on. "The team leader was very impressed with the work you did."

When he paused, I echoed the words. "The team leader?"

"Right. The individual who calls the shots for us. Also serves as a sponsor for our group and provides financial backing when we need it to execute our projects, the cases we take on."

"And this leader. It isn't you, I take it."

"No. No, not me." He shook his head.

Finally, I thought. It was way past time to be straight with me. "Then who the hell is it? Seems like you're the one calling the shots. You set up the meetings, make the contacts."

"Yes, that's my role. I get communications by text, instructions to pass along."

I was genuinely curious, despite my incredulity. I wanted to hear the secret that had been withheld from me thus far. My voice dropped to a whisper when I said, "So who's pulling the strings? Tell me."

"I don't know."

I leaned away from him. The back of my chair reclined. "Liar."

"No lie." He sounded sincere and didn't look like he was conning me. "The messages are encrypted. I don't know an identity. I can't even say whether it's a man or a woman."

I thought of Millie. "Ever hear of someone named Gatsby?"

He gave me a bemused look. "Yeah. He's a character in a novel by F. Scott Fitzgerald. A fictional character, not a real person."

"Come on, Steven. Millie calls the leader Gatsby. Don't bullshit me."

He sounded pragmatic as he said, "When a benefactor wants to remain anonymous, maybe you should let him, her, whatever."

I shivered as a feeling of unreality buzzed in my head. "So you take orders from a stranger. You don't even know his name—or hers. But you acquiesce when this person instructs you to engage in questionable activities. Which constitute criminal activities, to be completely accurate."

Steven gave an apologetic laugh. "The way you put it, it sounds pretty crazy. We generally hook up to take what we view as corrective action, you know that. With the goal of promoting social justice."

I was still skeptical. "Huh."

He shrugged. "Anyway, the leader was really impressed with you. I'm supposed to invite you to join the group as a permanent member. That's why I came here tonight."

That was confusing. "I thought that already happened, weeks ago."

"No."

"It did," I insisted. "Back at the Atlas warehouse, in Brooklyn. 'Kate, welcome to Justice Anonymous.' Those were your words."

"I don't know who said that. Wasn't me."

I needed another beer because the conversation was growing weirder by the minute. When I returned from the fridge, I bypassed the recliner and joined Steven on the couch.

"So what is your story? It occurs to me that you know a lot about my background, but you haven't been particularly forthcoming."

Steven turned to face me, stretching his arm along the back of the ratty sofa.

"It's such a cliché, I'm embarrassed to tell it. I got out of med school, did my residency, got into practice, working in the ER in Queens. I was the first person in my family to graduate from college, did you know that? You'd think I would be the last person on earth to fuck it up."

I listened. Didn't comment.

He sighed before he continued. "The pandemic was part of it, I guess. Seems so long ago, right? And the pandemic is no excuse, everyone at the hospital was buried. But I started taking painkillers, just to get through the shifts, to keep moving. I was desperate to feel good, and opioids can give you that, for a little while. And then I had to take something to fall asleep when I finally got off work. I ended up in a rabbit hole with an addiction. I didn't steal the drugs. I was too noble for that."

"How did you get them? On the street?"

"I wrote scripts for my personal use, and I got caught. They suspended my license."

I should have condemned it. I'd been a prosecutor only a matter of hours prior, sworn to uphold the criminal code. But he looked so mournful that it tugged at my heart. "And now?"

"And now I work at homeless shelters. I'm not there in a professional capacity, obviously. But the men and women at the facilities get some evaluation and advice from an unlicensed professional. Which isn't exactly legal. You could say I'm practicing medicine without a license these days."

I wasn't about to object, or to moralize to him about it. The picture was becoming clearer. Steven was committed to working outside the system. Social justice, rather than law and order.

Looking down at the open beer can as I absorbed his tale, my hair fell in front of my face. Gently, he tucked it behind my ear. In a soft voice, he said, "If this doesn't work for you, I get it. Everyone will understand. You have an inherent conflict, because of your employment. The whole law and order thing. Because you work at the DA's office."

But that was the punch line. I didn't work there, not any longer.

Twenty-four hours earlier, he would have had a valid point. Just one day prior, I was a cog in the machinery of New York City law enforcement. And continuing to join in the group's illicit activities would certainly have raised professional, legal, and ethical quandaries. After our activities on the yacht, I couldn't pretend that they operated in a gray area of legality.

But I wasn't in the DA's office anymore. Frank Rubenstein had freed me up. I could do anything I wanted. I simply needed to decide what that was.

I looked up. Our eyes met. It was good to be at his side again. I had missed it. Oddly, his confessions of his shortcomings weren't off-putting to me. I felt drawn to this new side of him; with his tousled hair and scruffy beard, Steven took on a tremendous appeal. The troubled "outlaw" version of Steven was extremely attractive.

I much preferred this guy to the scrubbed, tofu-eating dude who preached at me about cigarettes. He would never have made it out of the friend zone.

And it gave us even more in common, now that I was an unemployed former prosecutor, fired for submitting a forged document. It made me a member of the outlaw club, too.

I scooted closer on the sagging couch. "We're going to need to talk about this some more. Do you need an answer right now?"

"No, absolutely not. Of course you can think about it."

I intended to think about it. But not just then. I had other plans in mind.

If I lived in a bigger apartment in New York, this would have been the point where I would invite him into my bedroom, to look at a watercolor over the bed, or a view of the fire escape out the window. But I lived in a hovel, a tiny studio.

I gave him a small smile. "Have you ever seen a Murphy bed?"

He wore a poker face. If he knew what was coming next, he didn't let it show. "No. I haven't, actually."

Rising from the sofa, I said, "Let me show you how it works."

CHAPTER 35

THE HOURS SPENT with Steven served as an extremely pleasant distraction, but it could not forestall the approaching storm. At nine-thirty the next morning, I sat in a law office in Bloomfield, New Jersey, thinking: *I swore that I'd never end up in this spot.*

The sad irony wasn't lost on me as I shifted miserably in the leather club chair facing my mother's desk, crossing and uncrossing my legs in some kind of nervous dance. The happy buzz from my budding romance had dried up. It couldn't sustain me in my current situation.

I was sitting in my mother's office, begging for a job.

"So what do you think?" I asked.

I was incapable of injecting any enthusiasm in my voice. I'd already rolled out the scenario. Frank and I were parting ways. I was broke, and needed immediate employment. There was no time to engage in a job hunt, to go through the motions of filling out applications and seeking interviews. The rent was due. In my apartment, my food supply consisted of an empty

213

jar of peanut butter, some ramen noodles, and a half-eaten carton of yogurt. I didn't mention the cans of Coors Light.

Mom made a *hmmm* sound—like she was thinking it over. Her game of playing hard to get was maddening; it made me want to launch out of the chair and curse. She had been badgering me to work with her for years.

Before she could respond, her administrative assistant entered: Ethan, a slim young man whose hair always appeared perfectly groomed, like he'd just run a comb through it. He carried a steaming cappuccino in a dainty porcelain cup and saucer. Mom didn't use coffee mugs—not these days.

Ethan sent an uncertain glance at me as he set the coffee on her desk. "Can I get anything for you, Kate?"

"Nothing for me, thanks." I slumped in the chair, refusing the offer as a stubborn show of indifference.

Mom lifted the cup, blowing gently at the hot brew before she sipped it. I could smell the strong coffee; the aroma made my mouth water. I wanted to take back my rejection of Ethan's offer, but it was too late; he slipped through the door and shut it behind him.

Setting the cup back on the saucer with a quiet click, Mom focused a penetrating gaze on me. "So you need a job. You're currently unemployed."

"I do. And yeah, I am. Unemployed." Sitting before her with my figurative hat in my hands was painful. I turned my head to avoid her scrutiny. The wide bank of windows offered a view of the parking lot. I stared out as if it held a fascination for me.

"And you think you'd like to work here, for my law firm. As my employee."

"Sure." My voice cracked; I coughed, to clear it. "If you need the help."

When I said that, she laughed. Tilting her head to one side, she regarded me with a predator's intensity. "As I recall, you've told me repeatedly, over and over, that you would never work for me. Under any circumstances."

"Never say never." The smell from her coffee wafted over to me. I grabbed the arms of the chair and started to rise. "Okay if I go get some of that coffee?"

"Sit down, Kate."

Instantly, I obeyed. She was doing her no-nonsense-mother persona. It always worked on me.

"Why did you quit the DA's office? You claimed to have a deep commitment to the work."

I hadn't been completely forthcoming about the circumstances of my departure. But as I watched her, I realized: Mom already knew it was a lie. I didn't know how. Maybe she'd heard it through the grapevine. Or maybe she could sense it.

It was time to cut to the chase. "Frank let me go yesterday. I don't want to go into the details. But I'm available to go to work immediately. You know what I was making at the DA's office. You can pay me the same salary, I'll accept that."

It was a paltry salary, by her standards. So I was shocked to see her pull a face.

"Frank paid you the base salary for an assistant DA who has passed the bar exam. But this is New Jersey, and you're not a member of the New Jersey Bar, are you? Does it make sense to pay that amount to an unlicensed attorney who can't appear in court?"

I gaped at her. "Since when do you think my work is

worthless? When you were begging me to come here, you said I could name my own price. Didn't you tell me you'd pay whatever I thought was fair?"

Ignoring the question, she picked up a pen and proceeded to tap it on the desktop with a brisk rhythm. "You need to register for the upcoming bar exam in New Jersey because the New Jersey Bar only grants reciprocity to New York lawyers who have practiced for five years. You don't qualify. And you'll need to study for it; for God's sake, don't follow in your brother's footsteps. Leo has a wealth of study materials. You can use the softcover books and the online course I bought for him the last time he took the exam. And failed it."

Mom tossed the pen and shoved her coffee away, as if it had lost its appeal. She picked up her cell phone and tapped the screen. "Leo? Pull up the test prep materials for the bar exam. The most recent review."

Leo's voice held a note of trepidation as it came through the speaker. "What for, Mom?"

"For your sister." She cut off the call. When she looked up from the phone, I could see triumph reflected in her face. She had me.

"So when do you want me to start, Mom?"

"Today. You'll study for the bar on your own time; I'm not paying for that. While you're in the office, I'll let you do some background preparation on existing files."

She swiveled, turning the back of her chair to me. I saw her sort through stacks of depositions and hard files spread across the credenza behind her desk. Watching her rustle through them made me uneasy.

"Mom, I think we should establish some parameters."

She spun the chair around to face me. A pair of reading glasses hung from a chain around her neck. She perched the glasses on the bridge of her nose and stared at me over the lenses. "What is that supposed to mean?"

I glared back at her, resolute. "I won't participate in certain kinds of criminal cases."

Her mouth twitched with wry amusement. "What cases? Be specific."

"No one accused of sexual offenses. No wife beaters or child abusers."

Her eyes crinkled, like she thought it was funny. "Anything else?"

Her reaction stoked my ire; she wasn't taking it seriously. So I made a blanket pronouncement. "No rich old crooks."

At that, she cackled like a witch from *Macbeth*. Then her face grew serious. "You're in no position to issue ultimatums, Kate. If you don't want to do criminal defense, maybe you can crawl back to Rubenstein."

There was no way to return to Rubenstein—but she knew that. I kept my mouth shut.

"There is one criminal case I'll have to wall you out of: *State of New York v. Max James*."

I almost gasped, but swallowed my reaction just in time. I said: "You're joking."

"Why would I joke about that? His retainer has already been paid. Try to stay out of his way when he comes by the office. It will create tension, even though you didn't convict him in that jury trial."

That stung. I rubbed the spot by my thumb. "You can't represent him, Mom."

217

"Why not? I'm licensed to practice in New York. And I gained a good rep in white-collar defense when I beat the DA's office in that Bitcoin case last year. Don't you remember that? It made the *New York Times*."

I nodded; of course I remembered. Mom didn't shut up about it for weeks, like she was trying to rub my nose in her courtroom exploits. But my mind was elsewhere: I was anxious to hear whether James had a codefendant. My mother might know whether charges against Templeton were forthcoming. I needed to be careful because I didn't want to arouse her suspicions. She had an uncanny knack for reading my mind, and she loved to meddle in my personal business.

Mom held up a file folder. "I'm serious, I want you to steer clear of this. Don't even lay a finger on the file. It would create a conflict."

That much was true. It would create a conflict of such enormity, it would blow her mind. She needed to steer clear of the case, but there was no way to broach the situation without divulging more than I could reveal. I pinched the web of skin on my hand so hard, it would probably leave a bruise.

As I struggled to find an opening, Leo's head popped through the door. "Hey, Mom. I've got the app for that prep course."

"Good. Show it to your sister."

I stood, ready to follow him out of the office and escape my mother's presence. He stepped up and handed me a stack of cards.

"I kept the hard copies of these flash cards, too. You can use them to study, Kate. They're really helpful."

Mom snorted. Leo's ears turned red. The sight kindled

my ire. I wanted to snap at Mom, but she spoke before I had a chance.

"Leo, find a secretary's chair, for Kate. She'll be sharing your office, for now."

He nodded, agreeably; Leo didn't appear to be put out by the imposition of an office mate. We were almost out the door, but before we could escape, Mom called me back. She slid a thick manila file folder across the desk.

"Kate, I want you to review this file and prepare a summary of the witness statements. Point out any inconsistencies."

Wary, I picked it up. "What is it?"

"Don't worry, it's not criminal. It's a civil lawsuit."

I held the file gingerly, afraid to trust that it might not explode. "What kind of case?"

Without looking at me, she picked up her phone and began to tap the screen. "A Title Seven case, alleging sexual harassment. We represent the employer."

She put the phone to her ear and smiled at me. "Since you don't have the stomach for criminal defense, you can be an employment discrimination lawyer."

My mother was so triumphant, it made me want to fling the file against the wall and stomp on the contents. She turned her back to us, reclining in the high-backed executive chair, and started ranting into the phone.

Leo and I walked down the hall together. My shoulders sagged in defeat. He paused to dodge inside an office, where he found a spare chair. As he wheeled the chair down the hallway, I opened the file folder Mom had given me and glanced inside. Scanning the very first page, my heart sank.

"Oh, God," I moaned.

But Leo was upbeat. "I can't believe we're finally working together, Kate. This is going to be fun."

Fun? Really? I locked my jaw so I wouldn't speak the words rocketing through my brain.

I have died and gone to hell.

CHAPTER 36

LEO'S OFFICE WAS a roomy, well-lit space with two windows that let in the afternoon sun. However, there was only one desk. I wondered whether Mom intended for me to sit in the corner, juggling a computer on my lap.

Leo wheeled my chair to the far side of his desk. While I lurked in the doorway, he repositioned his computer monitors and keyboard, clearing part of the desk surface. His skateboard occupied a corner near my newly assigned spot. He carefully moved the skateboard to a far corner, out of harm's way, before returning to the desk.

"Gotta give you some workspace, right? At least until Mom designates a new office for you."

He took one of the flash cards I carried and studied the front and back. As he returned it to me, he said in an eager voice, "If you want me to help you with those flash cards, just say the word."

Flipping through the stack of cards, I relaxed a trifle when I saw questions on evidence and criminal law and procedure.

Those wouldn't pose much of a challenge. As I continued through the stack, my shoulders started to tense up. *Secured transactions. Wills and Estates. Contracts. Sales.*

I groaned involuntarily when the realization struck home. *Oh, God. I would have to brush up on the Uniform Commercial Code—again.*

With his shirtsleeve, Leo dusted off the square of space he had uncovered on his desk. "We have hard copies of the New Jersey BARBRI outline books. They're back in the file room. You want to go look at them?"

"Not this minute. Maybe later."

Leo stole a glance at me as he adjusted the angle of the computer monitors. "It's too bad you didn't practice a little longer in New York. Just another year or so, and you'd have reciprocity with New Jersey. Then you wouldn't have to bother with taking the bar exam all over again."

He was right, and I knew it. But it was too depressing to think about. I dropped into my chair and spun around in a circle. Though Mom may have meant to humble me by providing a clerical seat, it was more comfortable than the broken-down chair I'd inherited in the Manhattan DA's office. I spun a second time, coming to a stop when Leo came back into view.

He leaned against his desk, studying me. "It's a pain to have to do the exam prep again. Nobody knows better than I do. I'm sorry about that. But I'm not sorry you're here. It will be a positive thing."

I nodded, just to be agreeable, expecting him to say that it would be a beneficial change of scene for me.

"It will be good for Mom."

At that, I squawked with a shrill laugh. "Good for Mom in what way? Give her another person to abuse?"

I shouldn't have said it because it felt like kicking a puppy. When Leo turned away, I wanted to take the words back. It had to be unbearably difficult to live with her, at her beck and call. I didn't need to aggravate the wound by rubbing salt into it.

I was considering the best way to placate him when he said, "You and Mom are too much alike. I think that's probably why you can't get along."

That knocked the apology right out of my head. "Where did that come from? Mom and I are total opposites. I'm nothing like her."

Leo grinned at me. "You sounded just like Mom when you said that. See what I mean? You're good in court, like Mom—because you both like to fight—"

I cut him off. "It's not that I like it. It's part of the job."

Acting as if I hadn't interrupted, he went on. "And when you set your sights on something, you can't let it go. Just like Mom."

"I don't know what you mean by that."

"Really? Okay, here's an example: Neither of you can get over Dad's death. It's like a blind spot. Mom doesn't believe it was suicide, doesn't matter what the facts show."

The shock of his words struck me like a physical force; I rocked back in the chair. "What did you say?"

Looking self-conscious, Leo focused on the monitor on his desk. Toying with his mouse he said, "There are stages you're supposed to go through when someone dies. I've read up on it. You and Mom are stuck in the denial stage. That's what I think."

I raised my voice, to get his attention. "No, Leo. Tell me what you meant about Mom not thinking it was a suicide? This is the first I've ever heard about that."

He craned his neck to look out the open door of the office, before walking over to push it closed. "Sometimes she goes off on a rant about it. Raves about how he wasn't the personality type. That it went against his nature to kill himself. She thinks the conclusion in the police investigation was wrong."

The admission was so astounding, I couldn't respond. Shaking my head, I tried to absorb the revelation.

At length, I whispered to him: "But she's never mentioned that to me, Leo. Not once, in the past three years."

"You're never around to talk to her, Kate."

"But why didn't you say anything?"

"Why would I want to talk about it? I hate it. She goes off on the subject when she's drinking. You ought to hear her when she's downed a bottle of wine. She swears somebody must have pushed him out the window. Then she starts crying, and there's nothing I can do."

The recollection bothered him, it was clear; his shoulders shook.

I rose from the chair and walked over to stare blindly out the window. It had never crossed my mind that my mother shared my reservations regarding my father's cause of death. As I turned it over in my head, it struck me that my mother's opinion reinforced my suspicions. If my mom thought there was cause for doubt, it strengthened my resolve. She knew Dad better than almost anyone. Better than I did, maybe.

The possibilities swarmed in my head. My thoughts were

interrupted when I heard a hum on my phone. Absently, I pulled it out to see that I had received a text. From Steven.

When I saw his name, I smiled. Opening it, I expected a morning-after greeting. Something sweet, maybe suggestive. A request for another round.

I was wrong. No personal note appeared. The screen displayed a terse announcement.

Meeting tonight @ Freedom Tunnel

Riverside Park at 125th St.

10:00

Looking at the text, inspiration struck.

I checked the time again before I slipped the phone into my pocket. There was no way I'd permit myself to be late to the meeting tonight. I had a proposition for the group.

I left the flash cards and my mother's case file on Leo's desk, while I pulled the chair to face the window and began to marshal my thoughts. I had to prepare my pitch.

CHAPTER 37

I FIGURED IT would be easy to locate the meeting inside the Freedom Tunnel. For once, Steven had chosen a location in my own neighborhood, at a place convenient to me.

At 125th Street, I walked beneath the bridge until I reached the overpass. Following the directions Steven sent to the group, I found the old railroad tracks and followed them to the tunnel.

Once inside, I wished Steven had scheduled the meeting earlier in the day, before the sun had set. The interior of the tunnel was eerie. Picking my way along the tracks, I flashed the beam of my cell phone to light a path inside. The walls were covered in graffiti written in fluorescent paint that evoked recollections of the scary funhouse ride I screamed through at an amusement park in my childhood. I'd been told my flashlight created a security risk, but I kept flashing the beam. I didn't care whether the phone gave away information regarding my whereabouts, I refused to stumble through the tunnel in total darkness.

As I walked the tracks, I kept my ears open, as well as my eyes. I knew enough about the Freedom Tunnel to recall its history as a shantytown. After 1980, when freight trains no longer ran through the tunnel, the two-mile structure had been populated by the homeless. The railroad cleared them out over twenty years ago, but I had heard that some stragglers still occupied it, and I had no intention of disturbing them.

I'd made my way through a long stretch of the tunnel—past a mile, it seemed—before I heard voices. I still couldn't see anyone in the darkness. I came to a full stop, prepared to turn and run, if necessary. And then, I heard Millie's distinctive laugh.

Breathing out in relief, my muscles relaxed. I only had to walk along the tracks another fifty yards before I finally saw them. Someone held an LED lantern.

I called out. "Hey! It's Kate. I meant to be early this time, honestly."

They obviously heard me because someone hooted derisively.

When I reached them, I managed to take a head count of the shadowy figures. All eight of the other members were already gathered in the tunnel. I was the ninth to arrive, yet again.

Millie ran up to me, clutching me in a tight hug. When she released me, she said, "Congrats, Kate! You did it."

I didn't respond. I wasn't entirely certain what Millie was referring to, until Steven spoke.

He said, "I told them about the charges against Max James."

"Aren't you excited?" Millie said. She was grinning like the Cheshire cat. Her teeth gleamed in the dim light.

"Yeah, I'm glad he's been charged." Briefly, I considered confiding to the group that my own mother had joined the defense team. But I thought better of it; it might interfere with my goal for the evening.

Holding up her flashlight, Millie studied my face. "Are you bummed? Is it because they haven't nailed his boss yet? You know, Kate, there are things we just can't control. Sometimes we have to be satisfied with a partial victory."

I heard Devon say, "Max James was the original target, anyway. Not Templeton."

In the darkness, Whitney's voice snarled. "Templeton. Such a dick."

I gathered my thoughts, preparing to introduce my new proposal. "I think we did an incredible job together. And I have another project to suggest. Something that's really important to me."

"Hold up, Kate. Stop right there."

Diane had spoken. Steven lifted the lamp to illuminate her face. She wore an expression of frustration.

"I have an idea for the next case," she said. "Something I've given a lot of thought. And I had just started talking about it when you stumbled in late. Again."

In the dark tunnel, I rubbed the spot by my thumb. Of the band of outlaws, Diane was the one individual I did not particularly like. We hadn't managed to forge a connection.

She said, "I've been cruising the antique stores, and I'm positive that one of them is selling illegal elephant ivory. When I asked them about it, they were super evasive. The state Department of Environmental Conservation was supposed to shut this guy down, but he's slippery. Everyone knows what he's doing, but no one who has oversight is stopping it. I think we should take him out."

Rod blew a slow whistle. "You want us to take a dude out? Because he's selling ivory? You are talking about elephant tusks, right?"

Steven's voice was thoughtful. He said, "Selling illegal ivory is a crime. It's an international issue."

"Man, I've never even seen an elephant before. I'm not going to jail for a damn elephant." Rod shook his head derisively.

Diane stepped up to Rod, her fists clenched. In a confrontational tone, she said, "Conservation is my passion."

"You're in my face," Rod said.

Steven said, "Let's all back off. We can have a civil discussion about it. Diane, how do you want to shut the dealer down?"

Steven's interest appeared to appease her. In a calmer voice, she said, "I was thinking ransomware attacks. We hack the dealer's account and hold their IT system hostage."

The group watched her in silence until Devon asked: "And then?"

"And then we make a demand. For a ransom payment, or an ultimatum. Order them to get out of the ivory business, or we'll freeze the IT indefinitely. Or both."

Larry said, "Where did you come up with this?"

"I read an article about it. And since we're engaging in cyber warfare now, it made sense. Devon can do it for us."

Devon's voice was weary. "Again? I'm carrying the load? For your target?"

I saw Diane tense up; she clearly didn't appreciate the response she had received from the group.

Steven took a step away from her as he said, "Diane, maybe you should do some more background work on this. It sounds like you don't have conclusive evidence of the dealer's guilt. Not yet, anyway."

That was the break I needed; I seized the opportunity.

"While Diane is doing her background, we can work on my case. I'd like a chance to present it to you tonight. It's personal to me."

Whitney said, "We don't do personal cases, Kate." I couldn't see her until a Bic lighter flared. "Taking on a personal case just makes people unbalanced, which increases the risk for all of us."

"Please, Whitney, hear me out. It's about my dad."

Whitney's cigarette glowed. I could just make out her eyes. "Your dad? I thought your father was dead."

The stark statement felt like a blow, but I didn't let the impact show. "He is. Dad died three years ago. The police concluded that it was suicide, that he jumped out the window of his apartment. But I've never believed that. I have always thought my dad was murdered."

My throat closed up. I had never before said the words aloud. To share my private suspicion was painful. The word "murder" stuck, closing my windpipe; I clutched my neck involuntarily.

Larry had been standing on the outskirts of the group. He took a step in, closer to the light. To my dismay, he looked skeptical.

"That's a pretty wild accusation. What evidence do you have that makes you think that, Kate?"

My throat was still tight. It was hard to get the word out.

"None."

Larry shook his head. "Sorry, kid. This is why we don't do the personal cases. There's no point in chasing our tails for nothing."

I felt Millie clasp my hand. She sounded indignant when she said: "For nothing? We're talking about Kate's father. Show some respect, Larry."

Rod stepped in. "Yeah, Larry, that's pretty cold."

I looked at the others, trying to assess their response. Devon rubbed his neck, looking uncomfortable. "Kate, this sounds like a purely emotional reaction to a personal tragedy. What do you think, Edgar? Have you even been listening?"

Edgar stood at the edge of the circle with his back to us, facing the wall of the tunnel. He had his phone focused on the graffiti painted across the wall.

He aimed the lamp at the graffiti. "This painting is fascinating."

The light from his phone flashed along the tunnel wall, illuminating a picture painted in garish fluorescent colors. The graffiti depicted a human skull. Under the image, someone had spray-painted the words in capital letters: "DEATH WISH."

The sight triggered a sensation of dread. Though I tried to suppress it, a paranoid voice whispered inside my head, *That's a really bad sign.*

I shook off the superstitious reaction. Finding my voice, I said, "Can't we just join forces to look into it? I never had the opportunity to review the police file. If Devon can get the reports, we might find details to support my theory, that the death wasn't accidental. The timing is suspect, for one thing. Dad was due to testify in a manslaughter case against an

NYPD coworker the very next day. We should delve into that case, too, to see whether he made enemies who might want to silence him permanently."

"That's reasonable," Rod said. "She's just asking for an investigation. If we look into it, and the facts don't support Kate's belief, then we can drop it."

Diane's voice rose. "What about the ivory?"

"Fuck the ivory, Diane. We're talking about a human life." Millie's voice rang in the tunnel. She still held my hand, squeezing it in a tight grip.

Steven lifted the lamp. His head turned as he studied the faces in the group. "It doesn't look like we can reach a consensus on this."

Devon said, "Let's vote, then. I want to get out of here. This place is creepy, the walls are closing in on me."

On my right, the beam of Edgar's light swung from side to side, illuminating more graffiti. His face was lit with admiration. "It's like a gallery in here. I need to come back in the daytime, when I can see it more clearly. So primitive, yet inspired. Some of these painters were realists, actually."

Whitney moaned, grinding a cigarette butt under her shoe. "Edgar, leave the graffiti and get over here so we can make a decision. I'm with Devon, I'd like to wrap this up and get out of here."

Steven called for the vote. Some voices chimed yea, but it sounded like there were as many nays. I was grateful to have Millie's hand to hold on to. And glad for the darkness, so that no one could see me clinging to her like a scared kid.

Steven said: "It's too close for me to call in the dark. We will have to do an individual voice vote. I'll call the names."

I held my breath as they voted. Millie, Rod, and I voted in favor of the investigation. When Larry, Devon, Edgar, and Diane all voted against it, my anxiety ratcheted up.

It was Whitney's turn. She leaned against the wall, her head cocked to one side. I felt like Whitney always liked to torture me by making me wait for the ultimate call. Finally, she said, "What the hell. Sure, let's look into it."

Four to four: we were tied. Steven would cast the deciding vote.

I focused on him, expecting a speedy resolution in my favor. When he hesitated, anger and resentment spiked in my chest. It required a wealth of self-control to remain quiet, and to keep from lashing out.

Finally, he spoke. "Yes. I think we should pursue this, for Kate."

My tension released so suddenly that I was in danger of losing my balance. Millie propped me up, whispering in my ear, "We've got your back, Rod and me."

Several feet away, Diane was bitching about the outcome. I heard her demand that Steven notify the mysterious, nameless leader. She insisted the leader was entitled to know, because it was a close call, and a violation of the ironclad policy regarding personal cases.

Steven nodded, pulling out his phone. His head bent over the screen, as he started tapping on it with his thumbs.

The group began to disperse, but Edgar lingered. He remained close to the wall, walking along the tracks and shining light on the unsettling image of the skull. My eyes were drawn to it, despite my revulsion. It looked like something out of a nightmare. When I dragged my gaze from the skull, I read again the letters, spray-painted in black: "DEATH WISH."

If I was inclined to be superstitious, I might think it sounded like a warning.

CHAPTER 38

THE FOLLOWING DAY was spent in my mother's law office. My first stop when I arrived was her private office; I wanted to talk to her about Dad. Though I certainly didn't intend to reveal my plan to unearth the circumstances of his death, I was curious to learn her take on it. It felt like a logical first step into the investigation. But the office was empty.

When she didn't arrive by midmorning, I asked her assistant when she was expected to appear. He was scrupulously polite, but claimed to have no clue as to her whereabouts. A large calendar served as his desk pad; the dates had notations scribbled in ink. When I bent over the calendar to check the notes for that day, he quickly covered it with his hand.

Frustrated, I took my space at the far end of Leo's desk. As I delved into the Title VII sexual harassment file Mom had assigned to me, Leo and I wrangled. I sympathized with the allegations of the wronged employee. He reminded me we were representing the other side, and that I should focus on

235

shielding the employer from liability. Eventually, I closed the file and tossed it onto the corner of the desk.

As the day progressed, I prowled the office, hunting for my mom. But she was out until midafternoon, and when she finally arrived, she closed herself in the office. When I tried the knob, it was locked.

I rapped on the door. "Mom! I need to talk to you."

She didn't respond. I could hear her murmuring. Maybe she was on the phone.

But I'd been waiting all day, and I really wanted to broach the subject. "Mom!"

"I'm busy!" Her tone was not encouraging.

"When can we talk? It's important."

"Go. Away."

I turned in a huff and stalked back to Leo's office. As I passed Ethan's desk, I cut my eyes at him. He stared at the computer monitor with a placid expression, his hands busy on the keyboard.

The door to her office was still firmly shut when I left for the day. I couldn't wait her out because Rod and I were meeting at the gym. And it wasn't like I'd never run into her again; I'd be back in New Jersey again the next day. And the day after that.

The knowledge was depressing.

But as I commuted out of New Jersey and then traveled under the streets of New York, my spirits bounced back. It would be good therapy to go a few rounds with Rod at the gym. Between plotting and executing the yacht heist and recovering afterward, I hadn't worked out in weeks. Rod was initially reluctant to schedule a session because of my sprained wrist, but I promised him I'd protect it. Maybe, I thought, Millie might tag along, and we could go out afterward. She invariably put me in a good mood.

The subway car rumbled down the track, nearing my destination. It jerked to a stop on 116th Street. The next stop was mine.

I pulled out my phone when it hummed: Devon had sent a new email. My pulse thrummed when I saw the subject line: Father.

I skimmed the email lightning fast. Devon said he had managed to locate the investigative file on Dad's death but didn't want to divulge how he'd accomplished it. He said he had glanced through the summary, and from his swift review, it looked like one of the individuals named in the report agreed with my opinion. It was Dad's longtime partner, Victor Odom. The reports were attached.

I hit the attachment to open it.

The email disappeared.

I stared at the phone, unable to comprehend what I had just seen. The email was gone, as if I had imagined it.

I checked my inbox. Not there. I wondered whether I had deleted it accidentally. So I looked at the trash folder. I found over a hundred deleted emails, but Devon's wasn't among them. Then I looked in my junk folder, but didn't discover it there.

Frowning at the phone, I tried to devise a fix, a remedy. Sometimes, when the phone was glitchy, it was best to turn it off and let it rest for a minute. I pressed the buttons on the side and swept my thumb across the screen.

The subway car stopped and the doors slid open. I pocketed

the phone and exited the train, pondering Devon's message. If Dad's old partner believed that suicide was an unlikely explanation for his death, it reinforced my theory and strengthened my resolve. Because that made three of us: Dad's partner, his ex-wife, and his daughter. And all three of us had insight into my father's personality and behavior. We were in a position to judge what he was capable of doing.

I was eager to read the paragraphs in the investigative report that contained Victor's statement, so that I could learn about his take on the cause of death. When I climbed out of the subway station and emerged on the street, I turned the phone back on.

The email was still missing.

My phone rang. It was a call from Steven.

I didn't waste time on preliminaries. "Hey, Steven. Did you get an email from Devon? Because something is weird with my account."

Steven didn't answer the question. "Kate, we need to meet. Where are you? You want to get a beer?"

"You mean right now?" I kept walking, moving along with the crowd down the sidewalk. "I can't. I'm meeting Rod at the gym."

"Is there a restaurant near the gym? Or a café, a bar?"

"Yeah. A little Irish pub, just two doors down."

"How soon can you be there?"

"I'm five minutes away. But I told you, I'm meeting Rod at the gym."

"Tell Rod you'll be late. I'll be waiting for you at the bar."

As I walked the remaining blocks to the gym, I waged an internal debate. On one hand, Steven's high-handed demand for my presence rankled. One tumble in the bedsheets did not give him any kind of dictatorial power over me; I needed to make that clear to him. The direct method to send that message would be to ignore his call and meet Rod, as I had planned. That would be the smart decision.

But as I neared the gym, the blinking neon light of the little pub beckoned. From the phone call, it sounded like Steven was wound up tight about something, and it probably related to the investigation into Dad's death. If so, I wanted to hear what he had to say.

When I reached the pub, I dipped under the awning and sent Rod a quick text. Then I pulled open the door.

There Steven sat, as promised. His head was bowed over the bar. Both hands grasped a mug of coffee. When the door swung shut, he looked up and saw me. He set the coffee down.

I slid onto the barstool next to his. As he turned to meet my eye, it was clear that he had news to convey: bad news.

"What?" I asked.

He didn't respond immediately. My impatience spiked; I wanted to pound my fist on the bar and shout, *Just tell me!* I had to clench my teeth and lock my jaw to remain silent.

Finally, he said, "You'll recall that last night, Diane wanted me to notify the person who gives oversight to our group. She was insistent that I report the outcome."

"Yeah. To the leader," I said. My voice was sarcastic when I added, "Gatsby, right?"

His eyes darted away, always a bad sign in my experience. "Right. I texted the leader last night. Got a response later. A demand for more information."

"Which you supplied, I'm guessing."

The bartender approached us. I shook my head, and she walked away.

"So I sent back a pretty thorough rundown. What you had proposed. That the vote was split. What we ultimately decided to do: commence the investigation, to determine whether it supports your gut instinct."

He paused, and took a deep breath. Steven looked down the length of the bar before he spoke again, as if eavesdroppers might be lurking.

In a murmur, he said to me, "The leader shut it down. Effective immediately."

I should have been prepared for the ill tidings, but it came as a blow, nonetheless. My fighting instinct came galloping to the rescue. My hand involuntarily clenched into a fist on the top of the bar.

"So we'll go ahead and do it anyway."

Steven sounded adamant when he said, "We can't. It's non-negotiable. That's what I was told."

"Nonnegotiable? Who the hell is this invisible tyrant? We don't even know a real name, don't have a clue to the person's identity. But this individual wields absolute power over us? That's ridiculous."

When I stated my objections, my voice grew louder. The bartender gave me a leery glance. Steven placed his hand over my fist. Leaning in, he spoke in a whisper. "I received a very definitive message, Kate. If we don't comply, we'll lose our funding. And the group will be disbanded."

I shook my head, incapable of absorbing his meaning. It didn't make sense to me that Steven would calmly accept such arbitrary orders.

"The fuck? The group will be disbanded—says who? What are they going to do, tear down all the creepy churches and warehouses and tunnels so we can't meet anymore?"

Steven shook his head, staring down at the wooden bar. I interpreted it as a total capitulation. He was waving the white flag, just as the mystery leader demanded.

But I wasn't about to surrender. I intended to fight.

Scooting off the barstool, I said, "This is probably for the best, actually. Because I wouldn't have lasted very long in your little club if I'd known I had to be a toady to an invisible bully. If anyone wants to know my membership status, you can tell them for me, I quit."

CHAPTER 39

THE BURST OF fury that fired me up when Steven announced the shutdown of my project began to ebb after I stormed out, tore down the block, and entered the gym. A quick search of the building didn't reveal a familiar face. When I didn't find Rod on the gymnasium floor, it occurred to me that he might not show. Maybe Steven had gotten to him, too.

After I changed clothes in the locker room, I checked my phone. There was no text from Rod. On my email account, I scanned the inbox again, nursing an improbable hope that Devon's email might have magically reappeared. However, the only new message was an announcement from Instagram: See what's new.

Discouraged, my shoulders slumped. I picked up my bag and pushed the locker room door open. My energy was flagging. I wanted to go home, because I wasn't up for a solo round with a punching bag. If I had to engage in a one-woman activity that night, it felt like the occasion called for drinking alone.

I had barely made it through the door when I saw Millie

charging across the floor toward me. When she grabbed me around the neck, I had to brace myself to keep from falling to the floor.

Millie hugged my neck tight. Her booming voice echoed off the gymnasium walls. "Those assholes!"

In a muffled voice, I asked, "How did you hear?" My face was smashed against her shoulder. When she released me, I stepped back, to catch my breath.

"Did you talk to Steven? Has he been in touch?" I asked again.

Rod walked up to us, with his phone in hand. He held it up. "Group text. From Steven."

Curious, I checked my phone again, but there was no text for me. That made sense. I was no longer part of the group: hence, no group text.

"But why?" Millie's face was flushed with indignation. "We had a vote last night. How can Steven just pull the plug like that? Did Diane do something? I can't stand her. She gives off a real sneaky vibe."

I shook my head. "It was the top cat."

They looked at me without comprehension. Rod squinted. He said, "What's that?"

"You know, 'the leader.' You call him Gatsby, right? Gatsby said it's off. Or else. So I quit."

Rod eyed me curiously. "Really, Kate? You up and quit, that's it? So what are you going to do?"

I hadn't had any time to consider next steps. But when Rod asked the question, it came to me like a knee-jerk response. "I'm going to look into it on my own. I'll have plenty of time to devote to it. I got fired from the DA's office.

So I'm going to focus on resolving the questions I've been struggling with, to figure out for myself whether Dad really jumped, or was shoved out that window."

Rod sounded contemplative. "Do you think that's smart?"

The question caused me to dig my heels in further. "I'm a contrary person; it's my nature. When someone says I can't do something, it generally increases my determination. This is about my father, I should have done it a long time ago."

Shuffling up close to me, Millie started sniffling. When I saw her blink back tears, my throat tightened. Self-conscious, I rubbed it. "I'm going to miss you two."

Millie grabbed my shoulder and squeezed it, hard. I winced.

"You aren't going to have the chance to miss us because we're not going anywhere. We're in. Right, Rod?"

Rod gave her an inquiring look. Quietly, he asked, "We are?"

"Absolutely. No question."

Maybe I should have called it off, right then. It was my obligation to see it through, but Millie and Rod had no reason to shoulder the load. It was selfish of me to involve them; I should have turned Millie down flat. Told her I was going it alone.

But I didn't. Because it felt incredibly good to share the burden. So I ignored the nagging voice in my head when it told me I should let them off the hook. I joined Rod on the gymnasium floor. As a reward for his generosity, I let him take me down twice.

Of course, I blamed my poor performance on the injured wrist.

CHAPTER 40

I WAS PHYSICALLY spent when I got off the elevator of my apartment building—that "tired in a good way" feeling that comes after a long workout session. My muscles were relaxed. But when I stepped into the hall and saw a shadowy figure leaning outside my door, I tensed up immediately.

"Where have you been? I've been waiting for you."

She emerged from the shadow. Under the flickering overhead light I saw her: Whitney.

I turned the key in the lock. "Didn't you get the message? Deal's off."

"Yeah, I got the message. I was just curious to know if you did."

I lifted my shoulder in a shrug. "What's that supposed to mean?"

The door swung open. After a moment of hesitation, I said: "You want to come in?"

She sashayed through the doorway with a proprietary air. You'd have thought she was chipping in on rent. She even stretched out in my favorite chair, the vinyl recliner I had inherited from Dad's apartment.

I dropped my bag in the corner. Sneaking a covert glance, I wondered whether I could ask her to sit on the couch. I was bone-tired, had been looking forward to the recliner all the way home. But it didn't seem very polite.

When I dropped onto the sofa, I saw her smirk as she glanced around the room.

"I feel right at home in your apartment, Kate. Maybe it's because you're such a terrible housekeeper."

I frowned when she pulled a pack of Marlboros from her pocket. As she lit one, I tried to assert myself.

"This is a studio, Whitney. If you smoke in here, I'll smell it for days."

"So open the window. Or light a candle."

She took her second drag. I scooted forward on the couch and used my tough-talking voice. "I'm serious, Whitney. Throw it in the toilet. Now."

"Don't you want to talk about Devon's email?" She took another hit, blowing the smoke up to the ceiling.

That put an abrupt stop to my objections.

I couldn't light a scented candle, because I didn't own one—not since I lit one in my bedroom in high school and forgot about it. Mom left the scorched wall unrepaired for six months, to serve as a reminder.

So I tried to open the window, to let the smoke escape. The window in my apartment was stubborn; it stuck in the frame, but I managed to crack it open. I dragged a lopsided ottoman under the window, so that I could have a whiff of fresh air.

"So you got the email from Devon? The one with attachments of reports about my father?"

Whitney casually flicked her ash into a coffee cup I had left on the side table that morning. "I got it, for a minute. I was looking at it when it disappeared."

My adrenaline started pumping. "How much did you read? In the body of the email, Devon said that there was a witness who didn't think the death was suicide. My dad's partner on the force. Did you see that?"

"I think so. I was just scanning it."

I groaned in frustration. "How can an email disappear like that? You can't unsend an email."

"Can't you?"

She was playing coy; the conversation made me edgy. I jumped off the ottoman and walked to the kitchen sink. "You want anything?"

"I'd take some ice water."

I poured two glasses from the tap. When I checked my freezer, I discovered that I had failed to refill either of my two plastic ice cube trays.

With a sheepish grimace, I handed a glass to Whitney. "Not cold. Just wet."

She took a sip. With a straight face, she set the glass on the table.

"Delicious."

I laughed and took a swallow from my own tumbler. The temperature of the water was tepid.

"What do you mean about the email? I've never unsent one, didn't even know that was a thing."

"But you're not Devon. When the email disappeared, I

called him. He'd just learned that the case was canceled, so he canceled the email."

I sat cross-legged on the floor in front of the recliner. "The investigation may be dead in the water for Devon, but not for me. I'm just getting started."

"We've been instructed to shut down, sweetheart."

I bristled. "No one gets to shut me down. The first thing I'm going to do is run down Victor Odom, and talk to him. I don't need Devon's email to find out what Victor knows."

She looked impressed. "I see. So you're a bloodhound."

I sat up a little straighter, buoyed by her praise. "I had to do some of that in the DA's office; it was part of the job. My cases weren't big enough to merit a piece of the office investigators' time. I had to do a lot of my own legwork."

"Cool." She shook another cigarette from the pack and offered it to me. "Join me?"

I only hesitated a moment before I took one. Maybe it was the manner in which she presented the offer: as if it was a membership rite, to be admitted into her good graces.

"Just one," I said, as she flicked the lighter for me.

We smoked in silence while I puzzled over the mystery of the missing email. I wished Devon hadn't defected from the task; he had an impressive skill set, one I didn't share. If he could wave a magic virtual wand to make information drop into my lap, it would save a ton of effort on my part. But ultimately, it was my job to shoulder the hunt. And nothing about it would be easy—including the possibility that I might discover things I'd rather not know.

Whitney reached out with the dirty coffee cup in hand, so that I could ash into it.

"Well? What are you thinking?" she asked.

Giving my head a rueful shake, I gazed up at her. "I'm thinking that it will be a tough road, uncovering the truth about his death. But I can't just leave it where it currently stands. People who know him still believe that he was too much of a coward to testify. Some even suspect he supported the excessive force, and that's why he would rather die than testify. It's just not possible. I honestly believe my hunt for information can exonerate Dad. I want to clear his name, remove the tarnish from his reputation."

She blew out a smoke ring. My eyes followed it.

"So that's what this is. A heroic exercise to restore the dignity of a dead man."

Her tone of voice sounded like she was making light of my endeavor. I said, "Dead or not, he's my dad. I want to understand his motivation."

"And yet?"

"And yet." I took another hit of the cigarette, to take a moment to clarify my thoughts. "If it wasn't suicide, then what? He was murdered? Is that better? I'm afraid of what I may uncover. That it will reveal something I'd be happier not knowing."

Whitney dropped her butt into the cup. Some stale coffee must have remained at the bottom; I heard a sizzle.

Leaning toward me in the chair, she grasped my free hand and squeezed it, then let it drop.

"That reminds me of an old story of mine. Want to hear it?"

I shrugged, and she took the gesture as encouragement. With a dry cackle, she continued. "When I was a kid, my mom gave me a doll for my birthday. It was one of those Betsy-Wetsy dolls, you know?"

I didn't know. She must have seen my blank expression.

"It came with a little bottle. You filled it with water, poked it into a hole in her mouth, then you squeezed her stomach to burp it. She would pee her pants."

The childhood story was bizarre. I had no clue why a kid would want to engage with a doll like that; moreover, it had no bearing on my current situation.

But I nursed a hope that Whitney might lean toward helping me, so I kept my mouth shut.

"One day, I decided to give the doll milk instead of water. Seemed more authentic to me. And kinder. My motives were pure."

I was starting to catch on. I nodded. I could see where the story was headed.

"The milk spoiled inside the doll, right? Even after she peed, there was a residue that was rotten. And after that, every time I squeezed her stomach, she let out the most hideous stink you can imagine. Right through that little hole in her mouth."

Though I wanted Whitney to get to the point, I tried to sound sympathetic. "So you had to get rid of it, to throw the doll away."

Her eyes glittered. "No. That's what I'm trying to tell you, the point of the tale. I kept the doll tucked away in my closet. Because I had this compulsion, I guess I'd call it. I would go to the closet and drag that doll out and burp it. Just so I could smell that terrible stench."

She paused expectantly. We stared at each other in a protracted silence.

I blinked first. "What's that got to do with me?"

She threw her head back and laughed. "We're just alike, honey. You are digging up a corpse. It will stink to high heaven, and you know it. But you can't stop yourself."

She patted my head, like I was a child, or possibly a dog, and smiled down fondly.

"We are two peas in a pod. I feel like we're family, you and me. Not the kind you're born into, but the family you choose. That's why I'm going to give you a hand with this. I'll help you find out what happened to your old man."

CHAPTER 41

RIDING THE TRAIN to work the next day, I resolved to get into action.

When I pulled out my phone, I saw that Steven had sent two texts overnight. I deleted them without a glance and placed a call to Dad's old precinct: the Twentieth, on West Eighty-Second Street. After a couple of false starts, I managed to reach a woman who could provide me with information. But when I told her I needed to get in touch with Victor Odom, my late father's partner, she delivered a setback. I was informed that Victor had retired shortly after Dad died. And yes, they knew his current whereabouts. But no, she couldn't pass along his address or phone number.

It was an obstruction, but I refused to be discouraged. As I walked into Mom's office, I was still feeling more positive than I had since Rubenstein gave me the axe. It was exhilarating to have a solid aim in mind: I was determined to find answers to the unresolved questions about my father's death, and clear the stain from his name. And the knowledge that I had collaborators gave me an added boost. Millie, Rod, and Whitney genuinely wanted to assist. Whitney even said we were like family. The support made me uncharacteristically upbeat.

Ethan looked up in surprise when I strolled through the lobby. "You're early."

"Good morning, Ethan." I walked directly to Mom's office and tugged on the door, but it wouldn't open.

"She'll be in later. Closer to ten o'clock, she said."

My mother's inaccessibility dampened my good spirits, but I recovered quickly.

"Fine. I'll see her at ten."

Ethan's voice followed me down the hall. "She has an appointment with a client at ten o'clock."

Leo already sat behind his desk. A glimpse at his computer monitor showed he was playing *The Sims*. He swiftly closed the window, his face flushed with guilt. He said, "I didn't think you'd be here so early."

"It's a new day, Leo, and I'm making a fresh start. Did you tell me the New Jersey BARBRI books are in the file room?"

"Yeah. Want me to get them for you?"

"No, don't bother. I'll just go back there and dig around."

Leo pushed back his chair and stood. "I'll show you. It's pretty packed back there, because Mom never throws anything away. She saves all her hard files. She's still hanging on to files from twenty or thirty years ago."

That was encouraging news for me. We walked to the far corner of the office complex, into the room that had formerly held the law library. The library had been converted to a huge filing room, since the lawbooks Mom used decades before had become obsolete. Metal file cabinets stood in rows inside the space. The bookshelves lining the walls held a hodgepodge of legal publications and continuing legal education folders in black binders.

I glanced around, unsure where I should begin my hunt.

"Does she have a system?"

"For filing? Yeah, the cabinets are designated by year, and the contents inside are alphabetical." Leo strode to a nearby shelf, pulling down a half dozen thick paperback volumes. "But this is what you need for the bar exam."

The bar exam study guides were not the object of my interest. I itched to dig into the metal cabinets, but Leo would undoubtedly want to peer over my shoulder and ask questions I couldn't answer.

"Take those back to the office for me, okay? I'm going to get my bearings in here."

Leo took a step toward the door, but paused to look back. "You won't be doing any filing on the job, Kate. Mom has a clerical worker for that. And the new cases that she handles are mostly online, anyway."

"I know." I didn't offer additional explanation as I began to inspect the cabinets. Leo finally deserted me, leaving me free to pull open the metal drawers and riffle through the contents.

I needed to go back three years.

It didn't take long to find it. Mom had her faults, but a lack of organization was not among them. She was a meticulous record keeper.

The cabinet holding files from the year of Dad's death had what I sought under the letter *S*: a folder marked "Stone, Morris." I pulled out the manila folder Mom had made after Dad's death. Flipping it open, I saw a copy of the death certificate, his last will and testament, an insurance policy. When I reached the clipping from the *New York Post*, I recoiled. My stomach flopped and I snapped the file shut.

It reminded me of what Whitney had said the night before, when she told her bizarre childhood story. Digging into the circumstances created a perverse, self-inflicted agony, like squeezing the doll with the knowledge it breathed rotten milk.

But I gripped the file and carried it back to Leo's office. When I entered, he gave the file a curious look and started to speak. "What are you doing with that—"

Leo broke off the question when footsteps pounded down the hallway in our direction. I heard Ethan's voice, raised in indignation.

"That is not Ms. Stone's office, sir. She won't be in until later this morning."

When I stepped to the door and looked out, I was confronted by a familiar figure bearing down on me.

It was Max James.

I backed into the office, but he followed me. Leo jumped out of his chair.

"Are you looking for my mom, Mr. James? Her office is the other way, up in front."

James didn't glance Leo's way. His eyes were fixed on me.

He said, "What were you doing there?"

My pulse had begun to race when he entered the room, but I tried to keep a cool facade. "Leo, tell Ethan to call security."

It was a bogus move. I didn't know whether my mother had a security firm under contract. But Leo took the hint, and bolted out of the office.

James advanced on me. The events of the past week had taken a toll on him. His eyes were bloodshot, and his clothes were rumpled and wrinkled, looking as if he had slept in them.

"How the hell did you get onto his yacht?"

I took the easy path, opting for denial. "I don't know what you're talking about."

"Don't fuck around with me. You weren't alone, either. You came with that big blond girl. You think you can lie your way out of this? I have proof."

James held up a large manila envelope, swinging it back like he intended to strike me with it.

I edged away from him. He couldn't inflict much injury with a paper envelope, but if he hit me, I intended to punch back. And though I was prepared to fight, it would be preferable to avoid a physical conflict in my mother's office.

I said, "I don't know what you mean, but this is a private office. You need to leave."

James tore open the envelope, pulling out two 8x10 color photos. When he tossed them onto Leo's desk I looked down, giving the photos a quick glance. They were taken on Templeton's yacht as Millie and I approached the gangplank to make our exit.

James snatched the pictures off the desk and held them

in front of my face. He was breathing hard, and his breath smelled like stale booze.

"So tell me: Who set me up for this? Was it Templeton? Is he in on it with Rubenstein? And why did Templeton drag your fucking mother in as my lawyer? Maybe this scam is something you cooked up with her. Is that why you were at the party?"

I tried to wrap my head around the rapid-fire accusations. Stepping closer, James shoved the photos at my face, nearly brushing my nose.

The pictures were unquestionably damning. How could we have overlooked this possibility? I'd seen a professional photographer at the party, snapping candid shots. But she was primarily interested in photographing Templeton and the VIPs, and I'd thought we managed to stay out of her way. It was a foolish supposition. We should have anticipated that we would be captured on film.

Ethan appeared outside the doorway, looking distraught. "Mr. James, I just spoke with Ms. Stone. She says you can wait for her in the lobby. But if you persist in making a disturbance, I have been instructed to dial 911."

James didn't look at Ethan, but he must have registered the threat. He picked up the torn envelope and tried to shove the crumpled photos back inside. When the photos wouldn't fit, he flung them onto the floor.

Taking a step back, James said, "Don't think I'm going down. Not unless I take a lot of people with me."

The words sent a jolt of fear through me. After he uttered them, James left Leo's office and disappeared down the hall.

I couldn't let him fling that threat and walk away. Without stopping to think it through, I ran after him. "Hey! James!"

He was out the door, slamming it with such force that it rattled in the frame. When I followed him outside, he was heading to his car. I stood in front of my mom's office and shouted at him from the sidewalk. "You're finished! Done! Your friends won't keep you out of prison this time!"

James was halfway across the street, but he whirled around and started toward me. I didn't flinch. It was way past time to deliver the final smackdown. *Use your good wrist*, a voice whispered in my head.

Getting into position, I widened my stance. I was ready to take a swing and make it count.

But James slowed, like he was rethinking the fight. Instead of launching an attack, he stopped right in the middle of the street.

"You really think you can put me away? You don't have a clue what I'm capable of doing to you. But you're gonna find out."

He sounded like he meant it. But I kept my game face and choked out a laugh. "Really?"

Turning his back to me, he jogged to his car. It was a shiny Mercedes sedan, parallel parked on the other side of the street, directly by a sign that read "Reserved for Customers of Vogue Dry Cleaning."

I felt compelled to respond because I couldn't let him think that he intimidated me. I called out, "Hey, James—bring it. I've never been afraid of you."

Clearly, the jab galled him. After he jerked open the driver's door of the car, he paused with his right hand on the top trim and his left on the window frame. Instead of sliding into the driver's seat, he turned to get the last word.

"Watch your back. Someone is coming after you to fuck you up. And I'm going to be there when it happens."

That's when the speeding van struck him, tossing James and the Mercedes door up into the air.

CHAPTER 42

I LEAPED OUT of the way to avoid Max James and the flying door. Shards of metal and glass showered the pavement as I ended up doing a duck-and-cover under the awning outside my mother's office. Huddled on the sidewalk, I heard the thump of metal, screeching tires, and horns blaring.

I was so focused on self-preservation that I never even tried to see the driver or the license plate of the van. The police responded quickly. They arrived at the scene shortly after I picked myself off the pavement and brushed glass from my clothes. A nice young officer questioned me about the incident. I tried to be helpful but I could only describe the vehicle in general terms.

It was a white van, moving fast. The patrolman pressed me for details as they loaded James into an ambulance. It was embarrassing to offer such limited information. My father taught me to keep my eyes open and my senses alert. But it was a shock, witnessing an event like that. Even though I hated the victim of the wreck, it was a tough thing to see.

After I gave my statement, I stood in the lobby of Mom's office with Leo and Ethan. We peered through the glass at the emergency vehicles and EMS workers swarming around the scene of the hit-and-run. The ambulance departed, its siren blaring as it sped off with James inside.

Minutes later, when my mother stormed into the building, all three of us backed away from her. She was wearing her crazy face, a formidable sight to behold.

Her voice was shrill. "Outside, they said there was a collision involving someone from my office. What the hell happened?"

Leo and I stayed mum because she directed the question to Ethan. He edged away, increasing the distance between them.

"Yeah, Max James. It was a hit-and-run. They've just taken him away in the ambulance."

"Is he dead?"

He winced. "I don't think so. They didn't cover his head or put him in a bag. I don't know how extensive the injuries are. I didn't see it happen, but Kate did."

I was shaken by the incident, but I didn't confide that. "He was about to get into his car. A van hit him. The injuries have to be bad. The collision threw him and his car door into the air."

She squinted as she shook her head. "I don't need an accident report. I want to know what he was doing in my office. Why was he here an hour early? Ethan, you called and told me there was a confrontation. What was going on?"

Ethan raked his fingers through his hair, mussing his carefully sculpted coiffure. "I told him he was early. Offered him a coffee while he waited. He ignored me, charged down the hall to Leo's office."

Leo blanched as she swung around to face him and demanded: "Your office? That doesn't make any sense. What did he want with you?"

Leo's voice held a familiar defensive note. "Mom, I tried to settle him down. But he was yelling at Kate. She told me to go call the police."

Her eyes narrowed. It was my turn. "Damn it, Kate. I told you to stay out of his way."

I attempted to avoid sounding like a whiny kid, but it was difficult. "I tried. Leo and I were back in his office, minding our own business. I didn't initiate anything."

She scrutinized me closely. My clothes were still dusty from my roll on the sidewalk. I knew her bullshit detector was operating at maximum power. I couldn't tell her about the photographs, which were currently tucked inside my bag. And I was reluctant to reveal that I had chased him out of the office to participate in a shouting match in the street. But it was apparent that she was waiting for further explanation. I settled on a partial truth.

"He said someone set him up on the fraud case. It was crazy talk. You're not going to believe this. James accused us of colluding against him."

She gaped at me. "*Us?*"

Emboldened, I said, "The two of us, you and me. That we cooked up a scheme together. He implied that we planted false evidence, and you're serving as his attorney to make sure he's ruined."

It was news to her, I could tell. She looked bewildered,

and was silenced by the revelation. After a pause, she gave her head a brisk shake and pulled out her key ring. After she unlocked her personal office, I followed her inside, shutting the door behind me.

"So Mom, I've gotta ask. Why did James agree to let you be part of his defense team if he doesn't trust you?"

She bent over her briefcase, sorting through the contents. Without looking up, she said, "Why are you in here? Haven't you caused enough trouble for one day?"

She couldn't dismiss me that easily. "I thought it was weird that he asked you to represent him, even before this happened. I tried to put him in prison for assault. You're my mother. Seems like you'd be the last person he'd choose."

"Well, you don't know everything, do you?"

She pulled her calendar up on the computer screen. After glancing over it, she went on. "What you don't know could fill volumes. Speaking of volumes, why don't you go study for the bar exam? Brush up on New Jersey law. I changed my mind, I'll let you do it on office time."

She swiveled to face me. Her eyes lit up, as if a thought had struck her.

"Have you given any thought to moving here? You're wasting hours on that commute. When does your lease expire?"

"Oh hell no." My heart started to hammer in my chest. The suggestion should not have taken me by surprise. I knew she wanted to exert control—over my employment, my residence, my activities. It was a battle we had waged for years. "I'm not leaving the city."

"You live in a hellhole. Not that you've ever invited me inside. But I've seen your apartment building. It's frightening.

There are lovely residential neighborhoods near my office. You could have a house here, in New Jersey. I'll help with the down payment."

Recalling the sight of my mother shouting into the broken buzzer of my building, I suppressed a smile. "I like the apartment, Mom. It suits me."

She closed her eyes, heaving a deep sigh before she muttered, "Just like your father."

Her remark provided the opening I needed. I focused on my dad, pushing Max James out of my head. I sat in the chair facing her, hoping for a breakthrough with my mother. In my eagerness, the words tumbled out. "Mom, I actually want to talk to you about Dad. I've been thinking a lot about his death, and I've got some reservations. We've never really discussed it, but I need to do that. I think it's time."

"Kate, there's no point. He's dead and buried."

"But it's the way he died, that's the point. Don't you have a problem with that?"

"No." Her voice was flat. "Your father stopped being my problem long before his death."

"That's not what Leo says."

When I ratted Leo out, her face grew wary. "Well, that's ridiculous."

"Leo says that you agree with me. That Dad would never have willingly jumped."

She recovered swiftly. Her voice was smooth as she jerked the files from her briefcase and spread them across her desk. Flipping through pages, she said, "Leo is just telling you what he thinks you want to hear. He's done that since you were children. Now run along and let me get to work."

Discouraged, I rose from the chair and stepped toward the door. But a stubborn resolve prompted me to speak. I wouldn't let her have the last word.

"I'm going to look into it, Mom. Do some digging, talk to people."

Her hand froze on the papers she held. "You most certainly will not."

I met her eye. "I've made up my mind."

"You will not go digging into your father's past. It's a stupid idea, a waste of time and effort."

She wasn't just disapproving—she was shaken. I was surprised to see it. But I was adamant. "Well, it's my time. So I can waste it however I want to."

When she pounded her clenched fist on the desktop, I jumped. "Absolutely not, I forbid it. Do you hear me? Why do you have to be so bullheaded?"

The reaction was over the top, even for Mom. I leaned against the door, trying to read her expression.

"Why are you so flipped out by this? Give me one reason."

She glared at me. I didn't flinch. Her voice was dead serious when she spoke. "Okay, here's one. A good one. It's dangerous. Extremely dangerous."

I hadn't expected that, so I didn't have a ready response to it.

She had the last word, after all.

CHAPTER 43

THE ATMOSPHERE IN the office was stifling that day, and the dramatic events of the morning had left everyone on edge. Though I tried to suppress it, the image of the impact and Max James hurtling into the air repeatedly popped into my head. My mother's presence in the workplace heightened the tension, because she refused to remain closeted inside her office. She would spring out the door at unexpected moments, charging into our space like a scary jack-in-the-box.

I longed to delve into the file I had filched from her cabinet before the James incident, but there was no opportunity. Someone's eyes were fixed on me at all times: Mom's, or Leo's, or Ethan's. By midafternoon, I couldn't bear the strain any longer. Without offering an explanation or a farewell, I gave myself the rest of the day off, and bailed.

Safely aboard the New Jersey Transit train, I settled into a window seat. I checked my phone: another text from Steven. I swiftly deleted it and pulled out the pilfered file from Mom's office. It required more courage than I possessed to read through the collection of newspaper clippings, so I turned them over, averting my eyes. I scanned through my father's last will and testament. It was a standard document, naming Leo and me as his sole beneficiaries, and leaving his modest estate to be divided evenly between us. Dad designated my mom as the executor of the estate. In retrospect, it made sense to me. He knew she'd do the right thing. And when he died, I was in no shape to shoulder the burden. At twenty-five, I was crippled with grief at his loss. Maneuvering the probate process would have been a wretched task.

When I set the will aside, I saw that another document had been clipped to the back. Removing the paper clip, I found a cover letter stapled to a report. It was printed on the business letterhead of a private investigator in Manhattan and addressed to my mom.

She had never mentioned she'd hired a PI to conduct an independent inquiry into the circumstances of my dad's death. With a buzz of excitement at the discovery, I swiftly scanned through the multipage report. The PI had been thorough. He attached witness statements, a diagram of the apartment, photos of the interior, with a close shot of the window. There was also a picture of the sidewalk outside his apartment where small flags marked the position of Dad's body on the pavement. The sight made me tear up. Blinking rapidly, I moved onto the statement summaries in the body of the investigative report and pored over them.

He had talked to a number of people: Dad's fifth-floor neighbors, the doorman of a neighboring apartment building, the employees of a diner that sat directly across the street. Briefly, I wondered why he hadn't questioned me. I was one of the last people to talk to Dad. Wouldn't my perspective be important in an investigation? I had some insight into his state of mind that day.

Though I read with a critical eye, I couldn't spot any earthshaking revelations. The investigator devoted a page to Dad's upcoming testimony, outlining the facts of the manslaughter trial, but it contained no new facts. It was a retread of information I already knew. On that page, the PI referenced Dad's longtime partner, Victor Odom, as another trial witness. I flipped through the report, hoping to see a statement from Odom but didn't find one. And the only contact info the report provided on Odom was the address and phone listing from the Twentieth Precinct on Eighty-Second Street.

One thing that was apparent from looking at the report was that my mother had done a close reading of it. It was her longstanding practice to mark up reports, and she'd used plenty of yellow highlighter and red ink on this one. The PI's summary looked like an angry schoolmarm had corrected it. Sentences had been scratched out, and the margins were filled with her handwritten exclamation points and question marks.

The investigator's conclusion was contained on the final page. He wrote that the results of his investigation were consistent with the findings of the NYPD, and that in his opinion, their deduction was accurate, in light of the facts. He agreed with the medical examiner's ruling that my father had committed suicide.

The conclusory paragraph bore the mark of my mother's pen. She had drawn a bright red *X* across it. The inked symbol of her judgment sent a chill across my shoulders.

I carefully tucked the report back into the file and pulled out the final document, the death certificate. It was the standard form, laying out my dad's demise in brief, cold language.

For the manner of death, the state of New York checked the suicide box, leaving "natural causes," "accident," and "homicide" blank. The immediate cause of his death was described as "blunt force trauma," but there were additional lines beneath it identifying the underlying causes. The official report said he had died as a consequence of jumping from a building.

But Mom weighed in on the death certificate, too. Under the "jumping" description, she filled in another line for an underlying cause, writing in bold capital letters: "HUBRIS."

I shook my head, baffled, thinking she must have been crazy to alter and deface the official document. And how did hubris play a part?

I did a quick dictionary search, just to make sure I fully understood the term. The definition said "hubris" was excessive pride or self-confidence; arrogance, conceit. Did that sound like my dad? I wasn't sure.

So the definition didn't provide any clarity. But overall, I was psyched by the discovery of the file. It gave me a starting point. I could retrace the steps of the private investigator, see what he had missed. And it was energizing to know that my mom thought his conclusion was bullshit. Maybe my own efforts would reap different results.

I pulled out my phone and sent a group text to my new splinter band of outlaws: Millie, Rod, and Whitney.

Anyone free to meet tonight?

Millie responded immediately, saying that Rod was working at the club in Chelsea. Reading it, I felt deflated; I was eager to hash out my discovery. My mood instantly rebounded when Millie sent a follow-up text, saying we could meet at the nightclub, around seven o'clock.

I was busily texting back when the train ground to a stop. Hastily, I sent my message before gathering up the documents, returning them to the file, and stuffing it into my bag. I exited the train in such a rush, I almost ran straight into him.

Someone was waiting for me at Penn Station.

It was Steven.

CHAPTER 44

WHEN I SAW Steven within arm's length of me, my initial reaction was ridiculously juvenile. I beamed at him, and started to lift my hand in a friendly wave.

And then I remembered. He was the naysayer who threw cold water on my hard-won project on behalf of my father. Letting my hand drop, I executed a half-turn and walked away from him.

Steven caught up with me in a flash. He sounded testy as he asked, "You weren't going to tell me about getting fired?"

"Who says I got fired?"

It was a dodge, but I didn't owe him any explanation. It's not like the single night we spent together created a relationship built on mutual trust.

I picked up the pace, intending to leave him in the dust. But he matched my stride, saying, "When you ignored my texts, I called the DA's office to speak to you. They said you were no longer employed there."

As I continued to shoulder my way through the congested

271

concourse, I refused to respond. Steven remained right on my heels until we emerged on Seventh Avenue.

Clearly, he wouldn't be brushed off easily. I swung around to face him. "Why are you following me around?"

"I want to talk to you. We left on the wrong note last night. I want to fix that."

Frustrated, I shook my head as I tried to read his turnaround. While I lingered, someone rammed into me from behind. I had to catch myself to keep from stumbling off the curb and into the street.

Steven grabbed my elbow, steadying me. "Let's go somewhere and talk."

I nodded in resignation. I had the time, because it was way too early to meet up at the club with the group. Steven and I wandered down the street, but the area didn't offer many tempting venues. The nearby Starbucks was packed, without a single vacant seat. As I dodged the travelers streaming out of Penn Station, we took refuge in a small Korean takeout spot on Thirtieth Street.

While I grabbed the window seat, Steven headed to the counter, returning shortly with bottled water and a steaming bowl.

"It's stew," he said with a shrug. "I felt like I had to order something, if we're taking up space."

He offered a plastic spoon, but I shook my head. As he tucked in to the dish, he said, "You want to talk about it?"

I didn't, so I kept it short. "I got busted for my support group verification form. Rubenstein found out that the signatures were fake. It cost me my job."

He gave me a sympathetic grimace. "I know the work was

important to you. But now you have a chance to do some real good on the defense side, now that you work for your mother."

I had tipped the water back for a swallow. I choked on it, and had to catch my breath before I could respond.

"How did you know I'm working for my mom?"

"Millie told me. She can't keep a secret, by the way. I'm surprised you haven't observed that yet. Didn't you wonder how I knew that you would be on that train?"

I had been so intent on avoiding him, that I hadn't stopped to ponder what he was doing at Penn Station or how he happened to know I would be there.

"So Millie ratted me out, told you where you could run into me. Seems like it would have been simpler for you to meet up with us in Chelsea."

His brow furrowed. "Millie said I couldn't come to the meeting unless you okayed it first. She was serious, believe me. She swore that Rod would tell the bouncers to throw me out."

His words created a mental image that brought a smile. When I covered my mouth to hide it, Steven shot me a rueful look.

"Right, it's funny."

I polished off the water and screwed the cap onto the empty bottle. "Why would you even want to attend our little gathering tonight? You made it very clear that you have no interest in our goal."

He looked at the plate-glass storefront with a somber expression. I studied his profile, wondering if he'd had a change of heart, and why.

When he met my eye, there was an intensity in his gaze. "I've given our conversation a lot of thought in the past twenty-four hours. And I realized that you were right."

He had spoken my favorite words. Maybe that's why he totally won me over. In my head, the velvet rope at the nightclub door magically lifted to admit him to the club.

But I played coy, just for fun. "I don't know. You were pretty committed to following orders from your boss, the invisible ruler."

He reached for his phone and tapped it. "What if I give you something? To prove my commitment to the cause?"

I bent over the table, to try and read the screen, but he tilted it at an angle, to shield it from my view. In a moment, my phone pinged.

Curious, I checked it. A new email from Steven appeared. When I opened the email, my face lit up as I read the message.

"Steven! You found Victor Odom!"

My forehead wrinkled as a thought occurred to me. "How did you know I was looking for him?"

"Whitney told me."

"Whitney? Is everyone talking about me behind my back?"

He didn't answer, just smiled, his eyes glinting with humor. I sighed out with a huff of resignation. "When I called Odom's precinct for information, they refused to tell me anything. And you can't find a cop's home address on the Internet. How'd you get it?"

"Devon taught me a thing or two over the past couple of years. I have some of the search engines he uses."

My eyes dropped to the phone screen, to make sure it hadn't disappeared.

There it was, the contact information for Dad's partner at Elfinwood Senior Living in Hoboken, New Jersey. I would be able to see what Victor Odom had to say. I already had a jump on the PI my mother had hired.

"What's Elfindale Manor? A condominium or something like that?"

He said, "I think it's one of those assisted living places. For retired people. He's pretty old, right?"

I nodded. After a moment's pause, Steven asked: "Am I in?"

He looked so eager that it won me over. Suddenly, I was able to remember the things I had liked about Steven, just a short time ago.

Reaching under the table, I squeezed his thigh and told him, "You are officially a card-carrying member."

He scooted his chair closer to mine as he leaned in to whisper in my ear. The words made me blush like a high school girl.

My day was definitely looking up.

CHAPTER 45

WHEN WE WERE ushered into a VIP booth on the second level of the nightclub in Chelsea, I grew apprehensive. Turning to Steven, I whispered, "Are we paying for bottle service? Because it's going to cost a fortune."

Millie was already there, cozied up in the corner of the booth, with her bare feet stretched out across the white leather upholstery. She must have overheard because she said, "Don't worry about it, Kate. Rod is tight with the hostess. They are letting us sit here for a while, because it's dead in here, it's so early."

It was early, just past seven o'clock. The club was scantily populated, and the dance floor was empty.

Once I knew the VIP experience was free of charge, I relaxed, sinking into the cushions with a guilty sense of pleasure. Running a finger across the white leather, I said, "No wonder everyone's obsessed with money. There are some definite perks to being rich."

When I looked up, Millie was giving Steven the side-eye. She said to him, "So I guess you decided to join us."

"Yeah." He looked sheepish. "It took me a day to see it. But I'm definitely in."

I left the booth and leaned over the brass railing, checking out the activity on the lower level. A woman sitting at the far end of the bar looked familiar, though she was facing the other direction.

I turned to Millie. "I think Diane is downstairs. Did you see her?"

She gawked at me. "Are you kidding? It can't be. She never comes to clubs, it's a trigger for her sex addiction. You must be mistaken."

When I looked down at the bar again, the woman was walking away, so I couldn't see her face. I shrugged it off. Maybe Millie was right, and I mistook her for someone else.

"Is Rod coming up here to join us?" I asked.

Millie shook her head. "He's on the clock."

She might have said more, but the bottle girl walked up, assessing us with an expert eye. "Millie, do your friends want anything?"

"No, Nicole, thanks anyway. We're just going to chat for a while."

With a look that said she'd already pegged us as free-loaders, Nicole stalked off to hunt for customers with deeper pockets.

Millie watched her go. "I feel kinda guilty about using one of her tables. When I was a Denny's waitress back home, I hated people who parked at a table and didn't tip. But we'll leave before the place starts to fill up."

I slid back into the booth. "Denny's? No wonder you left Missouri to beat a path to New York."

I thought she'd laugh, and agree with me. But she looked away, with a melancholy air. "I've been feeling homesick lately. Sometimes I don't feel safe in the city. Like this morning when I left the apartment—"

I waited for her to finish the thought. She started to say more, then appeared to change her mind. Turning away with a moody expression, she fell silent.

When she didn't elaborate, Steven caught my eye, raising his brow with an inquiring look. But I couldn't provide an explanation.

If Millie didn't want to confide, I wouldn't press her. We had business to discuss. Opening my backpack, I pulled out the battered envelope and placed the 8x10 photos on the table.

"Here's a new development," I said.

Steven and Millie studied the photos. In a terse voice, he asked, "Where did you get these?"

"Max James came by my mom's office this morning. He basically flung them at me."

Millie shook her head in confusion. "Why would he be in your mother's office?"

The picture of the van hitting James popped in my head, but I suppressed it. "It's complicated. Mom was brought in on his defense team. I think he had an appointment with her this morning. But he came in early, looking for a fight. With me."

I paused before adding, "After he left the office, he was in a hit-and-run. He's in the hospital."

Steven said, "A car wreck?"

"No, a car smacked into him while he stood on the street, and it kept going."

He gave me a searching look. "Pretty weird coincidence."

Gingerly, Millie picked up one of the photographs. Her eyes widened with anxiety as she examined it. "Does this mean we're in trouble? Rod hasn't been formally charged yet, but he's sweating it. Did they turn these over to the police?"

Steven stared at the photos with a somber face. "Max James wouldn't be sharing anything with the police. Not unless his attorneys know about it." He looked up. "What does your mother think, Kate?"

I choked out a laugh. Did he really think I could talk about it with my mother? I would need to explain my family dynamics to Steven.

Millie tossed the picture back onto the table. "It's too bad you're not with the DA's office anymore. You could do some recon, find out whether they are looking at us."

Steven said, "Is there anyone you can turn to who is on staff? Someone you trust?"

There was only one person I could look to for help at that office: Bill Parker.

"I think so, yeah."

"Well, do it," Millie urged.

"I will. I'll contact him tomorrow."

Millie huffed out an anxious breath, tucking her bare feet under her. My first impulse was to offer support, but when I smiled and gave her arm a gentle squeeze, she jerked it away. To make her more comfortable, I scooted over, to put some distance between us. Though she'd made no secret of her struggle with anxiety, I had never seen her in the clutches of a panic attack before. It was painful to witness.

A voice called out to us as Whitney approached the table. "It's a celebration! We need champagne!"

She trotted up to the booth, bouncing onto the upholstered seat. Steven and I scooted together to make room for her.

She raised her hand to flag down the waitress. Nicole returned, looking dubious.

"We'll have a bottle of Veuve Clicquot, with four glasses."

When I started to protest, Whitney waved away my objection.

"It's on me. This is a red-letter day for you, Kate."

I had no clue what she meant. Nicole reappeared in a flash, with a bottle of champagne and four flutes. A young waiter followed, with a bucket of ice.

Whitney snorted. "You can take the bucket away. We won't give the wine a chance to get warm, not at this table."

When the glasses were filled, Whitney waited for Nicole to walk off before lifting her flute in a toast.

"To Max James, may he rest in peace. Not."

I had lifted my glass, ready to clink it against hers. But when I heard her words, I was startled. I set my glass back on the table.

"What do you mean?" I asked.

"Max James. He's dead, I just saw it on social media." As she made the announcement, Whitney flashed a wide grin. She lifted her glass higher in the air.

"Congratulations, Kate! You wanted your revenge, and you got it. To the winner!"

I watched Whitney take a swallow of the wine. Millie downed the glass. Steven gave me a searching look; maybe he could read my mind.

Max James was my enemy—probably the enemy of every

woman he encountered. But did that mean I would dance on his grave?

Clearly, I had thrown in my lot with some cold fish. It was disconcerting to sit in a circle of people who toasted to vehicular crashes and accidental death. But what they lacked in empathy, they made up for in skill. My splinter group of troubled souls would help me find out about Dad.

They were all staring at me, waiting. Could I drink to James's death? And then I recalled the last thing he'd told me, that someone would fuck me up and he'd be there to watch it. I lifted the flute.

"Cheers," I said, before I took a sip.

CHAPTER 46

I DON'T KNOW exactly what I expected when the Uber driver dropped me off at the entrance of Elfindale Manor, where I hoped to speak with Victor Odom. I had very little experience with retirement communities. Based on my recollections of Victor back in the day when he and my dad were on the prowl, I'd envisioned Victor living in one of those swinging fifty-five-plus condominiums that have cocktail parties and golf courses, and where residents need to be tested regularly for STDs. But that wasn't what I saw when I stepped out of the car.

Elfindale looked like a sad nursing home.

I pushed the buzzer outside the front door. Through the security glass, I saw a magenta-haired woman seated at the front desk.

A voice rasped through the intercom. "Who are you here to visit?"

I spoke directly into the box. "Victor Odom."

"Are you on Victor's visitor's list?"

That took me aback because I certainly wasn't. The

obstacle required quick action on my part. I slapped my DA's identification against the glass. Rubenstein had been in such a rush to get rid of me that he hadn't bothered to relieve me of it. It was inauthentic at that point, but the woman at reception wouldn't know that.

"I'm Kate Stone from the Manhattan district attorney's office. Victor Odom is NYPD, retired. This is official business, relating to a cold case." *Liar*, my brain whispered, but I ignored it. The statement was almost true.

The receptionist reacted promptly. I was relieved when the door mechanism clicked, unlocking for me. Pushing through it, I asked the woman for directions.

She told me Victor lived in suite 122 and directed an orderly to walk me through the labyrinth of hallways. When I reached Victor's room, I paused outside the door to take a breath.

The orderly gave me a questioning look. "He's awake, right now. If you wait around until later, there're no guarantees."

I took the hint. After a moment's hesitation, I pushed the door open, steeling myself when my senses were assaulted by the smell of urine and disinfectant.

Victor's name was scrawled outside the door to Room 122 in erasable marker; I'd checked it before I entered. But at first glance, I thought there must be a mistake, because a withered old man occupied the bed inside the room. I took a step back, fearing I'd stumbled into the wrong place. But when he roused, looking up at me with a bemused expression, I recognized Victor in the shrunken figure on the bed.

He said, "You don't work here."

I stepped closer. "Hi, Victor. I'm Morris's daughter, Kate Stone. I haven't seen you in a while, not since Dad died."

I could see the point at which recollection struck for him. His face creased with a grimace that passed for a smile. "You've grown up, girl. What are you doing here?"

His arm was attached to an IV, and a bedside monitor beeped as his heart rate and vital signs bounced across the screen. This wasn't the man I remembered. Victor was always hearty and ruddy-faced, a barrel-chested man with a loud laugh. But everything had changed in the past three years.

His chest rasped when he repeated the question. "What are you doing here? Why are you coming to see a sick man?"

When I tried to answer, the words caught in my throat. I had to cough to clear it. "Victor, we need to talk. About Dad, and about his death. I'm trying to figure some things out, to put the pieces together."

His breath rattled as he pierced me with rheumy eyes. Victor didn't respond, did not appear to be willing to answer.

The silence made me edgy. But I was determined to proceed. "Victor, did you know that I saw Dad on the night he died?"

He gusted out a rattling breath with the help of his oxygen tank. "Did you now?"

"Yeah. And he didn't act like a guy who planned to jump through a window."

"So you're an expert on that? You can spot a jumper just by looking?"

Impatience made me bolt out of the chair and step directly to the side of his bed. "Victor, we both knew him. When I saw Dad that night, he didn't say goodbye, didn't make any of those statements that the experts claim are part of the suicide profile. I know you were around him right before he died. Weren't you?"

The oxygen tank hissed and a tube fed the oxygen through Victor's nose. The oxygen saturation monitor beeped as he struggled to breathe. I recalled that Victor had been a classic chain-smoker, lighting one cigarette off the end of another anytime I'd been in his presence. It sent a warning message to me: *Quit toying with nicotine.* I should reconsider my habit of hunting down smokers in the street.

"How much did you talk to your dad before he died?"

Stringing that many words together took an effort on Victor's part, I could tell. Recalling my last conversation with Dad, I said, "I was there for thirty minutes, maybe. It was in the early evening, late afternoon."

Victor rolled his eyes in frustration. It hurt to watch the movement. The membranes of his eyes were red with inflammation. "That's not what I mean. I'm talking about the weeks and months before he died."

I shrugged my shoulders, trying to recall. "I don't know. Once in a while. We were in touch."

"Did you know what he was up to?"

The rheumy eyes were bright. It sent a chill through me. Especially since I wasn't sure what he meant.

"I knew he was going to testify. He was adamant about that. You were subpoenaed in the trial, too, weren't you? How bad was it, the pressure inside NYPD? I know that he thought that his friends would turn on him."

"I'm not talking about the manslaughter. Did you know he was digging into corruption in the city? Looking at big money. Dark money, influencing the courts and local government. Did he tell you that?"

I was stupefied. I had been working for the district

attorney's office at the time. If Dad suspected corruption, why hadn't he mentioned it to me? Victor's hand twitched on the crocheted afghan that covered his legs. I recalled he'd been married multiple times. Maybe one of his former wives knew how to crochet.

"He got paranoid, didn't he? Wouldn't talk about it, especially over the phone. Do you remember that?" Victor asked.

I didn't have a clue what Victor was referring to, but I wanted to hear more. I nodded, keeping silent, to encourage the flow of words.

"Your mother was furious. Cussed him out about it, called him an idiot. Told him to back off. She was always a hothead, I can swear to that."

Victor's face contorted. It was impossible to tell whether he was smiling or grimacing; it looked like the rictus grin of a skull. His gaunt face reminded me of something I couldn't quite place. A shiver creeped up my back when I made the connection. He resembled the painting in the Freedom Tunnel. My brain whispered the words painted beneath it: "Death Wish."

He tried to lean forward in the hospital bed, but it was a struggle. He pushed the control button with a thin hand, to elevate the head of the bed. And then he waved his spotted hand, inviting me near. I leaned close to him when he began to whisper. When he whispered, I could smell his breath. It was foul, like something inside him was already decaying.

He said, "He told me he was being tailed. Wouldn't say who was doing it. Who do you think it was that was after him?"

Victor paused, as if he expected me to provide an answer. I stared at him, distraught. What information did he believe I could provide?

Victor looked unbalanced, the image of a man approaching his death. When a nurse entered, I was impatient with the interruption. She pushed a button attached to his IV.

After she left, I saw him relax. His eyes fluttered, and the hard creases around his mouth eased. I wondered what the miracle drug had been.

After a few minutes, Victor focused on me and lifted his chin. Smiling at me, he said, "Look who's here. You're Morris's girl, Kate, aren't you? How's your mother, hon?"

I reeled, trying to absorb the abrupt turnabout. "Mom is fine. She said to tell you hello," I lied.

Victor's eyes grew shifty. "I know what she'd tell us, if she was sitting here. She'd say, remember the good times, Victor. Just block out the rest. Life is short."

"What else would my mom say, Victor?"

I asked the question in a hushed voice. Maybe he didn't hear me. He turned his head away and closed his eyes. Within moments, his breathing grew more regular. It looked like he had fallen asleep.

I slipped out of the room, leaving him to his morphine dreams. Walking down the hallway, I had to dodge past sad figures, ancient men and women drooping in wheelchairs. I barely registered it though, because my mind was running a question over and over in my head.

What dark money was Victor talking about? What corruption had Dad uncovered?

And what was my mother's involvement in this tangled scenario?

CHAPTER 47

ON FRIDAY, I nursed a hope that I might find some clarity on the questions that plagued me. I had a lunch date with my old friend from work, Bill.

I had contacted Bill after the meeting at the nightclub in Chelsea, because I wanted to set Millie's mind at ease. She was flipped out about the incriminating photos from the yacht. When I called Bill, I told him I needed to see him, to beg a favor. We agreed to meet for lunch at the end of the week. He said he'd try to unearth some information on my behalf.

I looked forward to the lunch date, and not just because I was eager for information. I missed seeing Bill on a daily basis. As I took my station by the food trucks outside the court-house, I kept a sharp eye on the Criminal Courts building. I spotted Bill as he exited, his head bent down as he descended the stairs.

As he approached, I waved at him, puzzled when he didn't smile or wave in return. He seemed to show no sign of recognition whatsoever. It hurt my feelings—I didn't think

Bill would ditch me as a friend because my circumstances had changed. I shoved my hands into my pockets and walked to meet him.

When we met on the sidewalk, Bill didn't stop to greet me. He kept moving down the pavement, saying, "Can't talk here. We'll go to Columbus Park."

He walked so fast, I had to trot to keep up. Though I tried to make small talk, Bill didn't respond. He behaved as if he didn't know I was there.

He hurried through the wrought iron gate into the playground, where small children clambered on the playground equipment. A bench on the far side of the pavement sat in a spot shaded by trees.

When Bill claimed a seat on a bench and slumped against it, he sighed out in relief. "I don't think anyone from the office saw us. Pretty sure, anyway."

His face was so flushed, he looked feverish. I asked, "So what if they did? Why are you acting so weird?"

"I don't want my head to be next on the chopping block."

Surreptitiously, he looked around before adding: "There's a weird vibe in the office these days."

I wasn't sure how to respond to that. In my experience, the vibe in the office had always been weird. But since Bill was so skittish, I thought I had best cut to the chase in case he got scared and ran out on me.

"Did you talk to your buddy? The guy in white collar?"

"Yes. That's when I started to pick up on it." A woman walked past us, pushing a baby stroller. He waited for her to pass before he continued.

"When you wanted me to ask around about Max James,

I agreed to do it because I didn't think anyone would mind talking about it. Hell, it's academic anyway. The case is moot, the defendant is dead."

"They can't prosecute a dead man," I agreed.

"So Charlie is my contact in the white-collar division. We met at Whiskey Tavern, had a couple of drinks, and I asked him for the deets. He clammed up on me, got real paranoid."

I was surprised to hear it. But I nodded, to keep Bill talking.

He said, "Maybe I should have backed off. But it kind of piqued my own interest, you know? Because I figured that white collar should be the division of the office that doesn't make the DAs on staff crazy. So I was determined to make him talk about it."

I was encouraged to hear that Bill had forged ahead. "How did you do it?"

"We vaped some medical marijuana in a restroom stall. You owe me, by the way. Charlie sucked up half of my monthly supply."

I snorted out a chuckle. Bill frowned on recreational use of the green leaf, but he was a card-carrying, certified patient of medical cannabis. He took his drug seriously, didn't share, didn't vape for fun. Bill must have been genuinely motivated to get information out of Charlie.

"So did you get him high? Relaxed and chatty?"

"Yeah, it loosened his tongue, and he started opening up about James. He said it was a big surprise when the case landed in his division because Max James was always insulated."

After making the statement, Bill's head twisted around to look in all directions. He was seriously worried about being overheard.

I had been entertained by the mental picture of Bill and Charlie passing the pipe in the men's room at Whiskey Tavern, but the statement about James gave me a jolt. "What do you mean, he was insulated?"

Bill's eyes shifted again to survey the surroundings. He whispered, "It's like you always expected. Didn't you try to tell me that? There are people who are off-limits, people they don't touch."

Questions started going off in my head, exploding like a strip of firecrackers.

"But in this instance, that doesn't make sense. Because Max James *wasn't* off-limits. I prosecuted him for felony assault, remember?"

"Yeah, Charlie mentioned that. He said you were like a bull in a china shop."

Offended, I squawked out loud. "That's a quote? Really?"

"It's a quote, but they weren't Charlie's words. He was quoting the head of the division."

I fell silent. Staring down at the pavement, I ruminated over the unflattering description.

Bill sighed. "So that's about it. Everyone was shocked when Rubenstein handed off the investigative reports in white collar and said to work up charges on James. The lawyers were real antsy, the case was like a hot potato. Now that he's dead, Charlie thought the atmosphere would ease up. Instead, people are more on edge than they were before."

He paused, turning to meet my eye. When he didn't continue, I said, "So that's it, end of story? What about a codefendant? When will they file against his boss, Ian Templeton?"

Bill squinted at me in confusion. "Templeton? Who said anything about charging Templeton?"

"He's the other bad actor." I was in danger of saying too much, but I couldn't hold myself back. "The information that condemns James also indicts Templeton as a coplayer."

He shook his head. "Sounds like your mom was coming up with a desperate defense theory, trying to cast blame elsewhere, to exculpate her client. It wouldn't have worked, Kate. Templeton is the one who fingered James. All the information for the criminal case came directly from Templeton. He let us know he had a crooked employee who was stealing from his clients and from the business."

I was so stupefied, I could barely think. The information regarding Templeton's illegal scheme had come from his personal computer, but he hadn't turned it over. I knew that I had unleashed it, with the assistance of my anonymous cohorts. How could Ian Templeton have coordinated a plot to point the finger at James without revealing his own misdeeds?

"This was a bad idea," Bill said, sounding fretful. "You can't put me in this position again, Kate. I know we've been through a lot together, but a real friend wouldn't push me into doing something like this. No more asking for the inside scoop, you understand?"

He was right, I knew that. But I couldn't let Bill get away, not yet. Millie needed to know about our personal liability, whether gate-crashing Templeton's boat was going to bite us in the ass.

My voice was almost syrupy as I said, "Bill, you're the best—and after today, no more digging, I swear. But wasn't there some kind of dustup at a party Ian Templeton hosted recently? Something that happened on his yacht? Will charges be filed from that?"

"A party?" Bill stood, brushing off the seat of his pants. "What kind of criminal case would originate from a party hosted by Templeton? Don't you get it, Kate? Templeton is one of those people the law can't touch. He has so much money and power, he's immune. He's got friends in high places."

Before Bill walked off, a look of apprehension crossed his face. "Hey, Kate. If something happened to somebody on Templeton's yacht, I don't want to hear it. A rape, or an assault, or a dead body thrown overboard? Just don't tell me about it." His hand slipped under his tie, pressing against his chest. "I'm feeling an anxiety spike, and I'm low on my meds, thanks to Charlie. Well, thanks to Charlie and you."

He turned his back to me then. I felt sad as I saw Bill lope away with a hand on his sternum, his shoulders hunched. It felt like the end of our friendship.

If I had known what was in store, I would have chased after him, talked him into a gyro sandwich. But I didn't, so I let him go.

I pulled out my phone and sent a group text, to my remaining four friends. Asked whether anyone wanted to meet for an update. Two responses popped up, Millie first and then Whitney.

Looked like a girls' night out.

CHAPTER **48**

I WAS PSYCHED about meeting up with Whitney and Millie. I had a progress report to make, and I wanted to do it in person, to pick their brains about my meeting with Victor at the nursing home and Bill's take on Max James and Ian Templeton. I was so anxious to meet, I invited Whitney to pick the spot. If I'd known she would drag me out to a casino near JFK airport, I would have reconsidered giving her the option.

I walked into the casino from the valet parking entrance. The slot machines assaulted my ears with relentless dinging, an audible sign that gamblers were being duped into believing luck was on their side.

I spotted Whitney at the bar, sitting at a table that held a bright blue drink in a footed fishbowl glass. I slid into the banquette booth and asked, "What the hell is that?"

"They call it an 'AMF,' in polite company. The *A* stands for 'adios.' You can probably figure out the rest." She raised a brow as she sipped from the straw.

I glanced around, restless. "I'm curious, Whitney. Why did

you pick this spot? Meeting in a casino when you've sworn off gambling?"

"I still like the atmosphere."

Whitney gave me a slow blink, lifting her shoulders in a careless shrug. She seemed chill, giving no hint she was tempted by the metallic music sounding from nearby slot machines. The card tables were located at a distance, but her eyes didn't stray in that direction. Maybe she had beaten the addiction; she certainly didn't seem distracted by the gambling activity. By contrast, I found the relentless noise and activity unnerving. But I tried to mimic her aloof attitude.

A cocktail waitress dressed in a corset and fishnet stockings ambled up in high-heeled shoes and asked for my order.

"Water. With a slice of lemon."

As the young woman walked off, Whitney lifted her fishbowl and gave me a rueful glance over the rim. "I'm disappointed."

"Excuse me?"

"That girl will think you don't expect to tip her."

"Oh, hell." Of course I intended to tip. Service personnel rely on tips to pay the rent; my dad taught me that when I was a kid. And the casino waitress should be compensated for having to wear that embarrassing costume. I decided Whitney was right.

"I guess I should order a drink. We'll be here for a while because I've got new information. I saw Victor Odom, and he supports my theory. I got a little insight on James and Templeton, too. But I don't want to get too much of a buzz. We need to be sharp," I said, directing a significant look at her jumbo blue beverage.

A flurry of movement prevented Whitney from responding. Millie stormed up to the table and dropped into the booth, breathing hard. With a shaking hand, she smoothed stray wisps of hair from her damp forehead.

Whitney's brow wrinkled. "What's the matter with you?"

"I think I saw Larry."

Both of us stared at her, uncomprehending. Whitney broke the silence. "Why would you be bothered by spotting Larry?"

"He's stalking me."

Millie reached out and grabbed the stem of Whitney's glass, slugging down half of the garish blue liquid. After she set it back down on the table, she checked out the casino, looking over both shoulders.

With a possessive gesture, Whitney grabbed the fishbowl glass and pulled it close to her. At a nearby slot machine, people started to scream. Millie jolted at the sound, though it was merely a celebration of a person's good fortune.

Millie wiped her mouth with the back of her hand, smearing her red lipstick. I picked up Whitney's damp cocktail napkin and handed it to her.

"We're here, Millie. It's going to be okay. Tell me what's scaring you."

She pulled a compact from her bag and swiped at the red smear with a hand that still trembled. "This shit's out of control, and it's freaking me out. What about those pictures? Did you find anything out about them?"

I glanced around to be sure no one was listening. "Millie, my friend at the DA's office says there's been no mention of charges coming from the yacht party. That's good, right?"

I hoped my conversation with Bill would reassure her, but

Millie acted like my words didn't register, that she hadn't even heard me. Her face crumpled as if she was about to cry.

Whitney said, "So what's Larry doing, exactly?"

Millie whispered, "I thought it was a coincidence at first. When he kept popping up, I wondered whether my imagination was playing tricks on me. I mean, Larry's kind of nondescript. Graying, glasses, sort of flabby. Maybe all middle-aged men look alike to me."

Whitney and I exchanged a look. She shook her head with a helpless expression.

So I said, "Millie, did you try to confront him? He's not a stranger. Why don't you ask him what's going on?"

"I tried." She repeated the words, the pitch of her voice rising. "I tried, twice. He disappeared."

Another woman strapped into a corset appeared, but she wore sheer black hose, rather than fishnets. She carried a huge goblet of blue liquid, identical to the one Whitney had consumed. As she placed it in front of Millie, the waitress said, "A guy at the bar sent this over."

I glanced over at the bar. It was packed with a variety of men of all ages. But no one seemed to be looking our way. And no one looked remotely like Larry.

"Oh, to be young again. That never happens to me," Whitney said.

"Happens to me all the time," Millie muttered as she lifted the glass and drank.

The waitress started to walk away. I called to her. "Ma'am? Could you bring me a Stella?"

She didn't give me a glance. "This isn't my section. Your waitress will be by in a minute."

I sank back against the booth. Whitney scooted closer to Millie, eyeing her with concern.

"What does Rod think?" she asked.

"He thought I was crazy, at first. That it was just the anxiety. When it kept happening, he got pissed off. He knew I couldn't be mistaken time after time. He tried to call Larry, to ask him what the fuck was going on. But the number wasn't in service."

That revelation was troubling. "That's weird."

She took another blue swallow before she went on. "And so he went to the place where Larry works, out in Brooklyn. He was going to confront him. But Larry refused to talk to him, wouldn't even see him. Security threatened to call the cops if Rod didn't leave. He had to back off. Rod's still out on bail from that arrest on the yacht, for third-degree assault. We're in limbo, waiting to see whether they plan to file a charge against him."

When Millie stopped to take a breath, she stared down into her cocktail glass. "What is this drink?"

Whitney said, "It's an AMF. Kind of like a Long Island iced tea. Except blue."

Millie gave her head a shake, as if trying to clear it. "It's strong."

"Don't chug it. It's not beer." Whitney's voice was dry. She turned to me as she reached into her bag and pulled out her phone. "I've done some background work on your father's death. I tried to locate the people who witnessed the jump from the window."

"He didn't jump," I snapped.

"Right—that's what we're trying to determine. The building

298

across the street from his apartment was under renovation at the time. The exterior was covered with scaffolding."

I shook my head. "I don't think so. Seems like I would have remembered that."

"Really? From three years back? It's so commonplace in the city, I don't even notice it."

I tried to recall. Had I seen scaffolding across from Dad's apartment? Walked under it? It didn't ring a bell, but in the aftermath of his death, my grief had made everything foggy for weeks on end.

Whitney said, "It's a reasonable explanation, explains why the cops didn't unearth any witnesses who saw it happen at eye level. So there's no one who can state whether he went through the window voluntarily."

She had a point. But I wanted to follow through on it. We needed to be thorough.

Doggedly, I said, "We'll talk to Dad's neighbors. People who lived on the fifth floor, and in the apartment below his."

Whitney nodded. "Right. Because if there was a fight, a disturbance, shouting, that bolsters your theory."

She tapped the phone with her thumbs. "I've talked to the guy who manages the building. He gave me five names. I'm sending you the contact info right now."

My jaw dropped. Literally. I stared at her for a moment before admitting, "I'm seriously impressed."

"Thank you."

"How'd you do that?"

"Get the contacts? I bribed the guy." She winked at me. "We won't have any trouble getting access to the building."

That shut me up. I didn't ask the amount because I couldn't

afford to repay it. And a whisper of guilt floated through my head. *Not legal, not ethical.*

I shook my head to silence it.

Whitney's voice was brisk. "We can go together, split them up, see what they say. Then we can figure next steps."

I nodded. "Great. When?"

"How about now?"

The immediacy of the plan heartened me. I turned to Millie, who was drooping in the banquette.

"Millie, are you up for this? Want to go talk to my dad's neighbors? It's on our way home, not that far from your place."

She looked up, attempting to focus, but her eyes were glazed. Her speech slurred as she said, "I'm not feeling so great."

I picked up the fish bowl and gave it a sniff. "What's in this drink?"

Whitney frowned. "A lot of things, some of this and that. But she only had one."

"A big one. And half of yours." I set the jumbo glass back on the table, giving Millie an uneasy glance.

Whitney's hand snaked around Millie's upper arm. "Hey, girl. Buck up! Do we need to wheel you out of here?"

Millie's head tilted to the side as she gave Whitney a glazed look. "I wanna go home."

I stared down into the fishbowl. "Do you think someone tampered with this? She's acting like she's been roofied or slipped Special K."

In the DA's office, I'd heard many tales of young women who had been rendered unconscious after consuming drinks spiked with Rohypnol or ketamine.

Millie's eyelids were drooping. When Whitney tapped her cheek, she didn't respond. Whitney looked over at me with a grim expression. "We're out of here. You hold up her left side, I'll get the right."

It was a slow process, but we managed to stumble out of the casino and onto a bench at valet parking, where we waited for them to bring Whitney's car around.

Our exit created a scene, and dozens of eyes were on us as we dragged Millie across the floor. When a casino manager tried to intercede, Whitney waved him off, shouting that his server had drugged our friend. She said we weren't interested in any "help" he intended to offer.

The slog through the casino was tough. I didn't have the chance to scope out the faces at the slots and card tables.

So maybe I was mistaken—it's not like I could swear to it. But I thought I caught a glimpse of Devon at a craps table, watching us stagger toward the door.

CHAPTER 49

THE NEXT MORNING, I was dragging—again. We'd had a nightmarish ride back to the city. After Millie vomited on the floor of the car, I advised Whitney to pull over, but she didn't oblige. Instead, she pushed the button to roll down the passenger window and ordered Millie to hang her head out the side. Millie's long hair whipped through the air while Whitney drove like a madwoman, speeding past the traffic, laying on the horn.

We had another fight after we crossed the bridge. I thought we should go straight to the hospital to have Millie's stomach pumped. Whitney observed that the contents of her stomach had already emptied out, inside the car and onto the pavement outside. And Millie begged to go home. She wanted to be with Rod, and nothing else would appease her.

Millie's pleas were impossible to ignore. When we pulled in front of her building, Rod was waiting outside. After piercing us with an accusing glare, he wordlessly lifted her out of the car and carried her into the building. He made me feel like a frat boy who had let a freshman get wiped out on grain alcohol punch.

While Whitney drove off, muttering about the cost and trouble the cleanup would entail, I sat in the back seat with my nose stuck in the crook of my arm. She complained about the mess for such a protracted length of time that I offered to wipe it up, but she declined. A nobler friend might have insisted on helping, but I took the coward's way out, bailing from the car when she hit the brakes near my neighborhood.

It was a rough night.

So the next morning, I was relieved to find my mom's office quiet, nearly unoccupied. The office was always open on Saturdays until noon to accommodate clients who couldn't meet during the regular work week. Ethan was there, but Mom and Leo weren't around. Since no one was there to spy on me, I did some sleuthing in Mom's files. When I found what I wanted, I sat on the floor of Mom's former law library, hidden behind a solid row of storage units. My back rested against the side of a metal file cabinet while I pored over a file I had pulled from one of the most current drawers, under the letter *J*.

I didn't feel guilty about reading through the Max James criminal file, even though my mother had warned me against touching it. With his death, he couldn't be harmed by the intrusion.

And I was like Nancy Drew with the key to the old clock. After my conversation with Bill, I knew there was something fishy about the case, and I was determined to uncover it.

The district attorney was required by rules of criminal procedure to let the defendant know the particulars of the evidence they have against him. To comply with the rule, they must turn over the contents of their investigation to counsel for the defendant. Rubenstein's office had provided discovery to the defense attorneys after James was arraigned for the felony counts of fraud. The file was thick, with a wealth of reports and attachments.

As I combed through the pages of reports, I saw that Bill Parker was right. The file contained no damning evidence against Ian Templeton. Nothing in the sheaf of papers indicated Templeton was involved in the illegal scheme. The only mention of Templeton came at the beginning of the investigation. According to the reports, he contacted the DA's office claiming that he had received information from an anonymous source, and disclosing that one of his employees was running a Ponzi scheme, working through his company to defraud his clients.

The startling realization was that it appeared I was the anonymous source. The material Templeton was credited for sending to law enforcement was the evidence we had downloaded on his boat. As far as I could make out, Templeton had intercepted the leak, scrubbed his own wrongdoing, and sent it to the DA.

Max James had been set up. But not only by my circle of outlaws. He was Templeton's patsy.

I heard a buzz of voices from the front of the office. I jerked out a drawer and replaced the James file before leaving the storage room.

Leo and Mom stood in the reception area. They were dressed in funereal black attire. Leo winced as my mother adjusted his necktie. "Not so tight, Mom!"

She jerked the knot to the center of Leo's white shirt collar as she rattled off instructions to Ethan. "It's a graveside service at the Scharpf Cemetery. I don't think we'll make it back to the office this afternoon. We'll need to stay through the entire thing so people will notice that we made an appearance."

"What's up?" I asked.

Leo stepped away from Mom, tugging at his collar to loosen it. "It's the Max James funeral. Mom thinks we should drop by to pay our respects. Gotta represent the family."

I snorted because the idea of Max James meriting my family's respect was absurd, whether he was dead or alive.

Mom's face got a pinched look. "Don't make that ugly noise through your nose, Kate. This is business. I need to be seen, as his defense counsel."

"Really? Seen by who?"

"Whom. By whom." She gave an impatient shrug under a black silk jacket. "He moved in some influential circles. Max James had friends in high places."

As I envisioned the likely mourners, I had an inspiration. "Do you think his girlfriend will be there?"

"How would I know?" Mom said, rummaging through a black leather handbag. "I've never met the woman."

I had met her on several occasions, all of which ended unhappily. But it struck me that she might be privy to information that could illuminate the puzzle of his case.

But I hesitated. "What about Templeton?"

"What about him?"

"Will he be there?"

Mom's voice was snappish. "Do you think I've got a list of people attending the damned thing?"

I wasn't eager for a run-in with Ian Templeton. The

revelations about his manipulation of the white-collar crime division were alarming. But I let my curiosity override my uncertainty. "I'll go with you," I said, keeping my tone deliberately casual.

They both turned to stare. My brother's brow wrinkled, while Mom's eyes narrowed as she studied me. "You? Why would you bother?"

"Just curious."

She looked me up and down. "You're not dressed for it."

I tugged at the hem of my shirt. "I'm wearing black."

She glanced out the storefront window, appearing to consider the proposition. A sign painter was working on the street side of the glass. She had hired him to paint "Stone and Stone, Attorneys-at-Law" on the window. Maybe the sight of the glossy black letters convinced her.

"Oh, all right. Wear a mask, so no one will recognize you. Ethan, do we still have some of those surgical masks?"

After searching through a storage closet, he found an old box that was still half full. I reached in and plucked out the blue paper mask.

"Mom, is this really necessary?"

"Put it on. When people see it, they'll think you have a health issue, and they'll stay away from you. On this occasion, that will be for the best."

I decided she was right. There might be people in attendance I didn't want to encounter. I looped the elastic bands over my ears and followed Mom and Leo out of the office.

CHAPTER 50

MAX JAMES'S GRAVESIDE service was a major event. My mom had to park a long distance from the burial site. There were strings of cars lining both sides of the narrow cemetery path: limos, Bentleys, Mercedes, Teslas. Her BMW looked humble in the line of vehicles. As Mom, Leo, and I trudged along the uneven ground to the grave site, I realized that she was right about two things.

As she predicted, I was not appropriately dressed for the occasion. Wearing all black wasn't enough to make me fit in with the crowd. The other mourners in black were dressed to the nines in well-cut suits and designer garb.

But the paper surgical mask she'd instructed me to bring worked its magic. People avoided me like the plague. They shot me sideways looks and gave me a wide berth, moving hastily out of the way of my germs.

The snubs didn't bother me because I wasn't there to rub shoulders. Out of consideration for the mourners' comfort, I backed off and lurked on the outskirts of the gathering. I was amazed by the number of people in attendance. Who knew a shithead like Max James would have so many friends?

Then it struck me. Maybe some of the people present for the occasion wanted to be sure he was good and dead. For reassurance, they needed to see his casket descend into the grave and be covered up with dirt.

I didn't have a bird's-eye view of the proceedings from my vantage point at the fringes of the crowd. In the midst of banks of extravagant floral arrangements, I could just make out the closed casket near the gaping hole dug into the ground. Facing the casket, a dozen chairs sat in two rows under a canvas tent. The chairs were occupied by immediate family, I assumed. The tent seemed unnecessary, because the weather was pleasant, with just a few fluffy clouds overhead in the sky.

The service began right on time—too early, perhaps. When the soloist began to sing, people were still gathering. I saw a black SUV buzz by, parking at an angle in a spot that did not accommodate the car's size. Curious, I sidestepped to check out the latecomer, and gawked behind my mask when he emerged from the back seat.

It was Judge Callahan, who had presided over Max's assault trial. Who had shaken his hand after the not guilty verdict.

A door slammed on the passenger side of the vehicle, and a familiar profile appeared. I wiped my eyes, as if they might deceive me, when I saw Frank Rubenstein make his way toward the service.

I wanted to hunt my mother down, to demand an explanation about what was going on. Why would a New York State judge be paying respects? Why would Callahan and Rubenstein dirty their hands with the corpse of Max James?

I crept along the side of the gathering, hunting for more familiar faces. Scoping out the mourners, I expected to find Ian Templeton, but I didn't spot him. My mother was in the midst of the group, her hand resting in the crook of Leo's arm. She was wearing a huge pair of black sunglasses so I couldn't read her face.

Though I wanted to tug on my mother's sleeve and ask her about Callahan, there was no opportunity. The singer had wrapped up the last notes of "How Great Thou Art" and stepped back. A man in a preacher's clerical collar stood, taking her place.

He didn't wear a microphone, but his voice carried through the crowd like an instrument, as Millie would say. "Friends, we gather here today to lay Maxwell Alfred James to eternal rest."

Though I continued to scan the crowd, I didn't spy any more familiar faces among the Wall Street–types in attendance. A few of them glanced my way, but most remained focused on the pastor. He gave a brief bio of James's life, naming his virtues. Predictably, the remarks were brief because the list was short. He launched into the twenty-third psalm, which my dad used to like. When he came to the verse about the Lord preparing a table before Max in the presence of his enemies, I snorted at the irony. Heads turned my way, and I stepped to the back again.

As the pastor wrapped up his remarks, he asked everyone present to join him in prayer. Heads immediately bowed. I bowed my head, too, as a reflex. My parents had taken us to church for a while when Leo and I were kids. The religious instruction phase of our upbringing didn't last long, but when a preacher says to pray, I still lower my head and close my eyes.

So I was unprepared when a hand clutched my arm and jerked me around.

It was Angelina. She wore black widow's weeds, with a floppy hat obscuring her face, but I recognized her.

She said in a harsh whisper, "Who sent you here?"

I looked over my shoulder, but no one was watching us. "No one sent me. I'm here with my mother. She represented Max."

"I know who she is. They murdered him outside her office. Do you get it? The trouble I'm in now? If they would put out a hit on Max, they'll kill me, too."

I glanced over my shoulder again. The prayer was long, heads were still bowed. Turning back to her, I whispered, "Who wants to kill you?"

Her voice was urgent as she said, "Gatsby."

It was jarring to hear her utter that name. If the invisible leader was a familiar figure to James's girlfriend, his reach was far more extensive than I had assumed. It made me fear that I had an extremely deficient understanding of the vigilantes' connections.

I said, "Who is Gatsby? What's his full name?"

She gave me an impatient grimace. "Don't be stupid. It's not a person's name. It's a group."

That sent a panicky chill through me, as I wondered: *Is it my group?* My heart rate increased, but my voice sounded deceptively calm. "What are you talking about? You need to be more specific if you want me to help you."

She took a backward step. The preacher droned on:

"Dear Lord, accept the spirit of your faithful servant, Max James."

Angelina whispered, "Dark money. Gatsby's a star chamber."

The S in the word "star" came out like a cat's hiss, but I still did not comprehend her meaning. "What?"

She took more steps away. As I followed, she said, "You know what dark money is, right?"

"Yeah," I whispered. I did have a general understanding of the term. Politicians used dark money from big donors, usually corporations. It was even used to affect judicial appointments. Victor had referred to it when he said Dad was looking into dark money that influenced local government.

Her eyes bored into mine. "And you know what a star chamber is?"

"Sure. I think so." I was bluffing because my mind was racing. Exactly what was a star chamber? Was it a movie I had seen, something on TV where a bunch of old men did a power play?

I was about to ask for more details when a sharp voice interrupted us. "What's going on here? Why are you bothering my daughter?"

My mother pushed me behind her, shielding me from Angelina. Angelina's chest heaved as she said in a choked voice, "This is all her fault. Everything that happened. It's on her, because of her."

Mom ripped off her sunglasses. Her voice dropped to a low rumble. "Get. Away. From us."

My mother's face must have been scary to behold. Angelina took one look at Mom and bolted, tearing across the graveyard, darting past the tombstones.

Mom whirled around, donning the dark glasses and adjusting them on the bridge of her nose. "Let's go. We have to find Leo."

She moved across the bumpy ground at a brisk pace. I followed her, trying to understand the encounter. "Mom, what did she mean? Why is it my fault?"

She didn't look at me. Her voice was clipped as she said, "Nothing's your fault. I see Leo by the car. Hurry, so we can beat the other drivers."

I agreed with her answer. I hadn't ended Max James's miserable life. Mom was right, nothing was my fault.

So why did I feel guilty?

CHAPTER 51

AS MY MOM stormed off in the direction of the parked car, I followed. She moved so fast that I tripped over the stone markers that dotted the landscape as I tried to keep up.

When we reached the car, Leo sidled up and elbowed me. "What was that about?"

I wanted to ask the same thing. In fact, I had a lot of unanswered questions. Shoving past Leo, I made a dash for the front seat. I wanted to sit shotgun so I could see my mom's face when she gave me the answers I'd been seeking.

Leo groused as I jerked the passenger door open and slid into the seat beside Mom. "There's no legroom in the back!" He grabbed the door before I could pull it shut. "I'm serious, I want to sit in front."

"Get in the goddamned car." When Mom ground out the words in her don't-mess-with-me tone, Leo hopped into the back with a sulky huff.

Mom hit the accelerator, driving way too fast for the narrow cemetery lane. A couple of people had to jump out of her path. One woman shouted, flipping us the bird.

"What's the rush?" I asked. "You're going to run somebody down."

She ignored me, steering past the crowd and heading for the exit. Once we left the cemetery grounds, she relaxed, expelling a suppressed breath.

Finally—she was trapped inside the car with me, and couldn't dodge my questions. I seized the opportunity. "Did you hear what she was saying, Angelina? Did you hear her talk about dark money?"

I saw her jaw lock. After a pause, she replied: "Who?"

"Damn it, Mom, stop playing. James's girlfriend, Angelina. She said that she was in trouble. That it all had something to do with a dark money group."

Leo broke in. "Move your seat up, Kate." He shoved his knees into my back. I swear I could feel his kneecaps.

"Stop that."

"I'm getting a cramp in my leg!"

To shut him up, I pressed the button to adjust the seat. But I kept my focus on Mom. "What about the dark money?" I asked.

When she kept silent, Leo said, "I know about dark money."

I jerked around in the seat. "What?"

"I studied the *Citizens United* case. The Supreme Court opened the door when they said corporations could spend unlimited amounts of money in political races."

I rolled my eyes. He had no compelling news to share. "Everybody knows that."

Leo continued. "Then why are you asking? So now there's a ton of secret, special-interest money in politics, and no one knows where it comes from. There's like a network of dark money groups funded by billionaires. And they influence elections."

He sounded like he was parroting the BARBRI. Why my brother couldn't pass the bar exam was a mystery.

"Leo, I'm asking Mom, not you."

But he was on a roll. "So now elections are funded by a tiny part of the population, the ultrarich. The only interests they support are their own. And the unnamed dark money groups own the politicians, they tell them how to vote and what to do."

Mom acted as if she wasn't listening. Her face was unreadable behind the dark glasses she wore.

I flipped down the visor and opened the mirror to make eye contact with Leo.

"She said it had a name: Gatsby. What's a star chamber, Leo?"

My mother made an involuntary choking noise, but Leo, flattered by the attention, leaned forward.

"It was a special court, back in England, in like 1400 or something like that. They brought cases against powerful people, didn't give them any legal rights, and inflicted gruesome punishments."

I was impressed by the breadth of his knowledge. "But what's that got to do with current times?"

"Nothing. Except that the term is still around, as a symbol of disregard for basic individual rights. A star chamber is a secret meeting held by a powerful group to persecute someone."

That rang a bell. It reminded me of secret meetings I'd attended.

Mom changed lanes without looking first. A horn blared, making me jerk in my seat.

"Mom, before you crash the car and kill us, tell me something. Why do you think James's girlfriend says his death was related to dark money? And to a star chamber?"

Finally, she spoke. Her voice was terse. "How would I know? Am I a mind reader?"

She was holding out on me. I know the woman, I can always tell. "Who is Gatsby?"

Mom's face turned away to check the driver's-side mirror, so I couldn't read her expression. "Ask your brother. Apparently he's a regular encyclopedia of information."

Leo brightened. "It's probably a reference to the book by Fitzgerald, *The Great Gatsby.* Have you read it?"

"Sure, I think so. In high school."

"Gatsby was a mysterious millionaire. The book is about wealthy people living in Long Island."

I shivered, though it wasn't cold in the car. "Do people die in that book?"

"Of course they do, Kate. It's a tragedy. Are you sure you read it?"

I wasn't sure whether I'd read it, actually, but it felt like I might be living it.

"Mom, why did you run Angelina off? Are you scared of her for some reason?"

She sighed, gripping the steering wheel. "Thank God, we'll be back at the office soon. I'm getting tired of being cross-examined."

I opened my bag and pulled out my phone. "Fine. If you don't want to answer any questions, I guess I'll have to ask her."

I pulled up my contacts as Mom hit the brakes, sending

me forward so abruptly that the shoulder harness knocked the breath out of me.

Mom said, "You're bluffing. You can't possibly have her number."

"I do." I turned the screen where she could see it. "Angelina was an assault victim. One of Max's victims, pretty recently. She wouldn't cooperate with the prosecution, but I read the police reports, and I got her number from the file."

My mom snatched the phone out of my hand and tossed it into the back seat. "Leo, delete that number."

"What the fuck?" I demanded.

The car veered out of the lane as my mother took her eyes off the road to glare into the rearview mirror. "Leo, did you hear me? Delete it, now."

I quickly unbuckled my seat belt and twisted around in the seat. As I tried to grasp my brother's arm, I said, "Give me the phone, Leo."

He held it out of my reach, looking torn. "Mom? Are you serious?"

"Delete it!"

I tried to scramble over the console to get the phone back, but Leo held me off with one arm. We fought like kids. When I couldn't reach the phone, I grabbed his hair and gave it a wicked tug. He flailed at me, but I held on tight.

"Stop! Stop it, Kate, I'm serious!" he said, but he didn't release the phone. I had to crawl halfway into the back of the car before I could wrest it away from him.

I was breathing hard when I settled back in the passenger seat and checked my phone.

The number was gone.

Mom gave me the side-eye. "Buckle your seat belt. There's a police car behind us, and I don't want to be pulled over."

Fuming, I pulled the harness with a jerk. Moments of angry silence ticked by while I contemplated my mother's character flaws. No one, I thought, could live with that woman. No wonder she and Dad had split up.

And that sparked another question, one I had been waiting to pose for days. I turned to Mom with an accusing eye.

"Why did you say Dad's cause of death was 'hubris'?"

Her hands clutched the steering wheel. "I never said that."

"Liar. It's in his file."

"Stop snooping around in my office. And don't you dare call me names. If you don't straighten up right now, I will pull this car over and kick you out. You can get back on your own."

I wasn't deterred. "Victor Odom said Dad was digging into government corruption, that it involved dark money. And Victor said you knew about it."

"I don't know what you're talking about. You sound hysterical."

"Victor said you were mad at Dad for investigating, that you cussed him out. Why would Victor say that?"

Again, she heaved a dramatic sigh, shaking her head, like I was the crazy one.

I focused on my phone and did a quick Google search. When the nursing home number came up, I said, "I'll call Victor. I'll put him on speaker, so we can all hear what he has to say. Victor won't deny it. He'll confirm what I just told you."

I hit the number for Elfindale Manor. The front desk picked up and put me immediately on hold. While music played from my cell phone speaker, Mom said, "Victor won't be taking your call, Kate."

Speaking with more confidence than I actually felt, I said, "Sure he will. You'll hear for yourself. Then you'll have to open up about this."

In a tone of exaggerated patience, she said, "Victor is in a coma."

The words sent a shock through me. It took a few moments to discount her announcement. "No he's not. I just talked to him a few days ago."

Mom sounded sad when she said, "He suffered a stroke last night. I know because the staff at Elfindale contacted me. They needed to confirm that his advance directive hadn't been altered. I'm his health care proxy. I scanned a copy of his do not resuscitate order this morning."

The news shocked me into silence.

"It's tragic but not surprising," she went on. "He was extremely ill, under hospice care."

The arrangement seemed peculiar to me. "Why are you his proxy?"

"After his last divorce, he altered it, removed the ex-wife and named me. I'm the attorney for his estate."

She glanced over at my phone. The music still filtered through the speaker. "You can cut off the call, Kate. He can't talk to you."

I obeyed, pushing the icon to end the call and dropping the phone into my purse. Sinking back against the seat, I looked out the window, staring sightlessly at the other vehicles on the road.

All I could think was that people around me were dropping

like flies. Sneaking a glance at my mom's profile, her face looked like granite.

I have to get away from her.

The atmosphere in the car was so tense that it threatened to suffocate me. By the time my mother finally parked the BMW near her office, the impulse to flee was overwhelming. I jerked off the seat belt and tore out of the passenger seat. My mother called after me. "Where are you going?"

I paused, turning to face her. "Home. When you're ready to talk, to open up and tell me the truth, you can give me a call."

I strode away, swearing a private oath. I would not speak to my mother until she exhibited a genuine desire to shoot straight with me.

CHAPTER 52

I NEEDED TO talk to someone, someone I trusted. The list was short. And it did not include my mother.

I shot off a series of texts on the ride back to the city, declaring an emergency. The first message went to Steven. After I received no response from him, I hit up Millie, Rod, and Whitney.

While I sat on the New Jersey train and waited for someone to respond, my leg jiggled with barely restrained tension. The phone remained obstinately silent, so I checked it.

It was dead.

Swearing, I dug inside my bag, tearing through the contents like a maniac. Because I usually carry a charger. Almost always, in fact. But not on that day.

Across the aisle, a guy sat with his cell phone plugged in, swiping his screen with a serene expression.

I leaned over, trying to keep the panic out of my voice. "Hey, can I borrow your charger?"

He looked over, giving me a swift glance before returning his attention to the screen. "I'm using it."

"I really need it. My phone's dead, totally dead. It's important, or I wouldn't bother you." After a brief pause, I added, "An emergency, a matter of life or death."

When he didn't reply, I felt the familiar spike of temper. It sizzled down my spine. What kind of shit heel would ignore a life-or-death emergency? I rubbed the spot near my thumb and tried to chill out.

Maybe I looked truly desperate because, after a couple of minutes, the guy relented. He unplugged the charger and handed it across the aisle to me. "I need it back before we get to Penn Station."

"Absolutely. Thanks, I really appreciate this," I said.

It took a minute for the phone to restart after I plugged it in. When it lit up, I had only two responses: one from Steven, the other from Whitney.

I called Steven first. When he picked up, I jumped in without prelude. "Steven, something is messed up, very weird."

"Have you talked to Millie?" He sounded abrupt, and was breathing hard, like he was running.

"I haven't talked to anyone." I checked out the guy across the aisle. Although he didn't appear to be paying attention to me, I turned my back to him and lowered my voice. "I spent the afternoon at Max James's funeral. Steven, who is funding our group? I have to know. Is it some dark money organization?"

"I can't talk right now," he said.

"Then when? I'm seriously freaked out about this. Stuff is happening, I need to run it by you."

I heard a babble of angry voices through the phone, as if he'd wandered into a fight club. "Where are you?" I asked.

His answer was inaudible. I finally made out what he was saying. "They picked Rod up on an arrest for menacing. Second degree."

"*What?* Who did he threaten?"

An involuntary muscle twitched between my shoulder blades. This was a problem. Menacing was a serious charge, involving a threat of physical harm accompanied by a display of a firearm or dangerous weapon. It was a violation of the state penal code, not a trifling municipal ordinance.

I repeated the question. "Who did he threaten, Steven?"

There was shouting on his end of the line, and I couldn't hear the answer.

"Steven? Steven, what's going on?"

He must have moved to a quieter spot. His words were finally audible when he said, "It's a bogus charge. Larry is behind it. He called the police when Rod confronted him at work and told him to leave Millie alone. This is trumped up. It can't be anything serious."

I wasn't so sure. The charge sounded pretty serious to me. In a whisper, I said, "Did he have a gun when he talked to Larry? Did Rod threaten him with a weapon?"

Over the line, I heard Millie shriek, "Steven! Get over here!"

Steven said, "I gotta go. We'll talk tonight, after we bail Rod out. Things are going to shit. We have to figure out what we need to do."

"Right. Talk to you later. Where should we meet up?"

I held the phone to my ear, waiting for his voice, but Steven didn't respond. I checked the screen. The call had ended.

There was nothing to do but wait. But as the train carried me along, it was hard to sit still. I was edgy as fuck.

I was still debating whether I should try to call him back when my phone hummed. Whitney was calling. I hit the button, grateful to hear the sound of her voice.

"What the hell is going on?" she said.

"Oh God, I don't even know. Everything is nuts, I'm losing my mind."

"Try to calm down. Get ahold of yourself. Tell me what's happening."

I took a breath, trying to pull it together. "Okay. I just heard from Steven. He says Rod's been arrested for menacing Larry. He and Millie are trying to get him released."

"Shit, that's messed up."

"I feel like they're turning on us, Whitney. The others in the group."

"They are, and we should fight back. You sound really wound up. Is there anything else?"

I looked over my shoulder, concerned about being overheard. The charger guy was talking on his cell phone, and no one was paying attention to me. "I went to Max James's funeral today."

"What? Why did you do that?"

My thoughts were scattered. It was difficult to explain the decision in a way that made sense. "My mother was going, and it seemed like a good idea at the time. I wanted to check out Templeton because I'd read the James file. It says Templeton turned Max in to the police. Which seems preposterous."

"That's bizarre. Really suspicious." She sounded wary.

"That's what I thought. So at the cemetery, James's girlfriend was there. She grabbed me, acting paranoid, and said that someone was going to kill her. And she spouted shit about a dark money group. She even implied that my mother was involved. But Mom came up and ran her off."

"Ahhh…" Whitney's voice droned, like a long sigh.

"And you know I managed to talk to Victor Odom. Well, he stroked out last night. He's in a coma."

This time, she groaned into the phone. "Okay, kid. I need to bring you up to speed. Where are you right now?"

I looked out the window, trying to confirm my precise location. "I'm on the train, not far from Penn Station. I should be home in about thirty minutes. Do you want to come by? There's a lot of stuff I really need to talk about."

"That's the goddamn truth," Whitney said, in a tone of irony. "But Steven and I talked. We don't believe your apartment is a safe meeting place. He thinks maybe you're being watched. By our old friends in the group."

That news unnerved me. It fit the pattern of events that had occurred in the past several days. Larry had stalked Millie and targeted Rod. Maybe they were all in on the scheme. I wasn't immune. I wouldn't be insulated from harm.

While I digested the revelation, another phone call came in from Mom. I swiftly declined it.

Whitney spoke while my finger touched the screen. "We should meet at my apartment. Do you need to go home first?"

"No, that's not necessary. I'll take the subway to your place."

"You need to get here as soon as you can. I have to break some news and it's going to be hard for you to hear."

My tension spiked even higher. "Tell me now."

"Not over the phone." She paused, as if considering. I heard her sigh into the phone again. "It's about your mother."

The phone lit up as she spoke. Leo, this time. I ignored it.

"Tell me now," I pleaded.

"No, kid. Come on over. I'm hanging up, gonna call Steven to confirm the meeting place so he can be here, too. We'll see you shortly."

She hung up. I was desperate to hear her revelation regarding my mother, but it would have to wait until I reached her apartment.

I held the phone as it continued to charge. At Penn Station, I handed back the charger before I got off the train. I sped down to the lower level to catch the 1 train. It would take me to the Seventy-Ninth Street Station on the Upper West Side.

Standing on the platform, I ruminated about the conversation with Whitney, wondering what dirt she could have on Mom. Whatever it might involve, it couldn't be related to my father's death. But a tiny tendril of doubt unfurled in my head. What if Whitney knew something I couldn't bear to hear? I tried to suppress the thought. Mom was capable of some insane shit, but she wouldn't push my dad out of a window. That wasn't the revelation Whitney needed to share because it was impossible.

Wasn't it?

The 1 train rumbled up, slowing to a stop. The car was crowded. When I boarded, I made my way to a metal pole and held on to it as I mused about my mother. The train picked up speed and rushed down the track, jostling the passengers as it headed for the next stop at Forty-Second Street.

One of my fellow passengers moved to the end of the car and opened the door to the adjoining one. I watched as he exited my car. Through the open door, I spotted a familiar figure.

Larry was riding in the car next to mine.

It might have been pure coincidence. But Whitney had just told me that the group was watching me.

A wave of righteous indignation washed through me. Larry had placed Millie and Rod in peril, and now he was showing up on my commute. For reasons that I couldn't comprehend, he had launched an attack. I had a score to settle with him. I left my spot at the pole and made my way to the door between the cars.

Maybe Larry sensed my presence because he looked up before I entered and jolted out of his seat. I jerked the door open and said, "Larry! I want to talk to you."

He shoved his way to the end of the car, trying to get away from me. Moving fast, I managed to reach him before he escaped into the next car. I grabbed his shoulder and said, "What is up with you? Why have you turned on Millie and Rod? Are you stalking me now? This has to stop."

He shoved me, hard. It caught me off guard, and I stumbled backward into other bodies behind me. Someone pushed me toward a pole, and I managed to grab on to it. Otherwise, I would have landed on my butt on the floor of the subway.

When Larry pushed through the door, I followed him, making my way onto the next car just as the train slowed and squealed to a stop. As the doors opened, he pushed through the passengers and exited the car.

I almost let him go. Whitney and Steven were waiting, and we had urgent business to address. But Larry was the source of the trouble my friends and I were in. I needed to confront it head-on.

Just before the doors shut, I shouldered my way out of the

car and onto the platform. Larry was way ahead of me, so I had to run to keep him in my sights. As I tore up the steps and made my way out onto the street, I almost lost him. Because I emerged at Broadway and Forty-Second Street.

Tourist Hell. Times Square.

CHAPTER 53

AS A PERSON who lives in the city, I steer clear of Times Square. The crowds, chain restaurants, and flashy ads hold no charm for me. It's impossible to walk the sidewalks at a decent pace because people come to a standstill to look up at the sights. It's primarily a place where tourists flock together with the people who fleece them for a living.

I'd barely left the subway station before I stumbled into my first unwelcome encounter. "Hey! You wanna take a picture with a Radio City Rockette?"

The woman dressed in the skimpy sequined costume couldn't pass as a real Rockette, even to an out-of-towner. Despite the thick makeup and a huge pair of implants, she looked old enough to be a Rockette's grandma. I dodged around her.

But the brief distraction caused me to lose sight of Larry. I looked around, searching the sea of people. Just as I almost gave up, I spied a furry red Elmo character grab Larry by the hand and latch an arm around his neck.

We were inside one of New York's "designated activity zones" where costumed characters ply their trade. All around me, people dressed as Minnie Mouse, Cookie Monster, and Spider-Man solicited passersby to be photographed in exchange for tips. The Naked Cowboy stood at a distance, doing a brisk business.

A yellow Minion approached me and began to pitch a photo op. I held up a restraining hand and started running toward Larry. He was wrestling with Elmo. I was a few feet away when Larry broke away from Elmo's hold.

Elmo was a fast worker. After he lost Larry, he grabbed my hand in his fuzzy paw and tried to pull me in for the shoulder latch. "Take a picture with Elmo! You can post it on Facebook for your friends back home."

"I am home," I said. After I jabbed him in the gut with my elbow, he let go. As I darted away, he spewed a string of obscenities at me.

I followed Larry to the stoplight at Forty-Third. He was holding his phone in a heated conversation as he dashed across the street. I crossed against the light moments later, ignoring the angry horn of a yellow cab.

The tables had turned, I thought. The prey was stalking the predator. I had him on the run, pursuing him down three more blocks and pushing through slow-moving pedestrians as the garish signs flashed overhead. When I saw him sprint into Father Duffy Square, I chased him into the TKTS booth line.

The people waiting in long lines along the red steps on Forty-Seventh Street interfered with my pursuit. As I tried to maneuver past them, the theater fans moved to block me.

One angry woman grabbed my arm and said, "End of the line, bitch! We've been standing here for an hour!"

I didn't have time to explain that I wasn't in the market for discounted tickets to a Broadway show. I pushed and shoved my way through the line, keeping my eyes trained on the bald spot at the back of Larry's head.

We'd almost made it to Fiftieth Street before I caught up to him. I saw him near the subway station, bent over with his hands on his knees. He was panting with exertion as he tried to catch his breath.

I was winded, too, but hadn't lost my power of speech. I said, "What the hell, Larry? Why are you messing with us? We're all friends, right?"

Wheezing, he shook his head.

I tried again to reason with him. "Oh, come on. You've been working together with Rod and Millie for over a year. Let's iron this out."

He didn't look up. After taking a deep breath, he said in a hoarse voice, "It's out of my hands."

"Bullshit. You can call off the charge. The DA doesn't push a case like this when the complaining witness recants. Tell them it was a mistake."

He shook his head again, his chest heaving as he still struggled to catch his breath. "Sorry. There's nothing I can do."

"Are you listening to me? You can fix this."

He straightened up and walked away from me, lifting his arm to signal a cab. As a yellow cab pulled up to the curb, I let him go. I was tired of chasing Larry. Whitney was waiting for me.

CHAPTER 54

I WAS READY to get to the meeting at Whitney's apartment. I needed to talk to someone who could help me make sense of the wild turn of events.

So I headed for the subway. It had started to rain hard enough to pelt my hair and dampen my shirt. Just as I neared the Fiftieth Street station, I heard someone behind me calling my name. I figured it was a coincidence because "Kate" isn't uncommon. Still, I turned around. I was shocked to see Leo a half-block away, waving as he walked toward me.

When he reached me, his face lit up. "Kate! What a relief. Mom told me to find you."

His phone was held in a tight grip—tracking my location on Find My Friends, no doubt.

I moved away from the subway entrance so that we wouldn't block it. "What's going on? What are you doing?"

"Mom sent me. I was taking a car service to your apartment, but I got out when I saw you were in Times Square. I can't believe I found you. It's like a needle in a haystack. Guess I got lucky."

His ability to hunt me down was uncanny, but he'd picked the wrong day to do it. "Sorry, Leo, I don't have time to talk. I have to meet someone."

Without further explanation, I descended the stairs into the subway. But Leo followed, his footsteps keeping pace as he called to me.

"Kate, hold up! Mom says she's ready to talk."

Her timing was maddening. I'd been begging her to come clean about Dad, and she'd dodged me at every turn. *Now* she was dangling the conversation?

Over my shoulder, I said, "Great. If she's ready to talk, she can call me."

I swiped my MetroCard and pushed through the turnstile. There was no need to hurry to the platform because the train wasn't due for several minutes, and the station wasn't heavily populated. I'd left Times Square several blocks back, and rush hour traffic had passed.

Leo caught up to me on the platform. His face was taut with anxiety. "If you don't come with me, she'll be mad. Where are you going? Can't it wait?"

"It can't."

"Then I'll tag along, okay? And when you're done, we'll meet Mom."

"Leo!" In my frustration, I shouted his name. He turned his head away, looking hurt. With an effort, I lowered my voice. "Where I'm going, you can't follow."

Some of the people passing by turned to stare while others gave us a wide berth. I must have been putting on quite a show.

When I saw a couple shuffle away to avoid us, I said, "Let's not make a scene, okay? I have to meet with some friends. When I'm done, I'll check in with Mom. Cross my heart."

He took a reluctant step backward. With an air of resignation, he said, "Okay, then. If that's the best you can do."

Not quite everyone on the platform had edged away from us. One man stood his ground. He was a tall guy wearing a black rain parka with the hood pulled over his head. His face was obscured by a black gaiter and oversize goggles with tinted lenses.

Because I was so intent on getting rid of Leo, I didn't keep a close eye on the hooded man. Even his face covering didn't set off an alarm initially. Some people choose to wear all kinds of getups on public transportation. I've ridden the subway with Superman and Wonder Woman.

When Leo turned to walk away, the masked man stepped directly into his path. A jolt of alarm shot through me when I saw the man thrust his hand into his pocket and pull out a black rod that was about six inches long.

When the man flicked his wrist, the rod extended in length to sixteen inches. He was armed with an expandable steel baton, the kind police officers carry. Aside from the NYPD, the batons are illegal in New York. When I recognized the weapon, I shrieked out a warning to Leo, but it was too late.

As the hooded man swung the baton at my brother, Leo reflexively lifted his forearm to block the blow. He screamed as the steel rod struck his arm, and under the cry, I could swear I heard the crack of bone. Leo bent over at the waist, clutching his arm. The man struck again. The second blow was delivered to the back of his head. Leo collapsed, dropping like dead weight.

The attack had occurred in a matter of seconds, and I was on the move. I skirted Leo's huddled body and tried to land a kick to the attacker's chest, but he caught my thigh with a stinging blow—but not an incapacitating one. In an attempt to disarm him, I seized the baton with both hands, and we struggled for it. As we grappled, I tried to land kicks to his shins with my uninjured leg, but they had no deterrent effect. The guy apparently wore shin guards under his pants, as if he'd anticipated a kickboxing battle.

I was making no headway, and mounting panic was throwing me off. This was no bout of sportsmanship in the gym. The guy was considerably taller than I was, and he had a firm hold on the weapon. His eyes were protected by the tinted goggles or I would have tried to gouge them. Instead, I focused on his neck gaiter, trying to approximate the location of his Adam's apple. And then I let go of the baton, swung back, and landed a lead-hand punch to his throat.

It connected. He backed off, dropping the baton as his hand flew to his throat. The baton rolled across the pavement, out of reach. I tensed as he stepped backward. I was prepared to defend myself if he came at me, but I hoped he'd turn and run.

He ran, all right. Ran straight at me with his arms outstretched. My brain didn't comprehend his intention until it was too late to dodge. His hands slammed into my chest and sent me flying, off the platform and onto the tracks of the subway. When I landed, my head struck the steel track. I lay on the tracks, looking up. I was too stunned to move.

I heard the train before I saw it. The whistle screamed a

warning in the tunnel, followed by the beam of blinding light. My body felt the vibration as the train bore down on me. But I had the oddest thought before the engine roared in my ears and blocked everything else.

The hooded guy smelled like paint.

CHAPTER 55

"KATE. KATE, WAKE UP."

My eyes opened with an effort though the lids were heavy with sleep. I was flat on my back, laying on a hard mattress in a hospital bed.

The door creaked open and a nurse walked in, a stout middle-aged woman who smiled at me with a gratified expression. "Look who's awake! How are you feeling?"

Assessing the question, I took a moment to answer. I was immobile, but it felt like my limbs were intact. To be certain, I moved my legs, but stopped when I realized it was going to hurt. Despite my battered limbs, the worst of the pain throbbed in the back of my head.

The nurse stood at the end of the bed waiting, with a chart in hand. "How about it, Kate? On a scale of one to ten, how do you feel?"

"I feel like I've been run over by a train."

The nurse chuckled as she made a notation on the chart. I became aware that someone was holding my hand, but when I tried to look to my left, my head didn't turn. I was wearing a neck brace.

I rolled my eyes to the side. My mother sat in a hard plastic chair at my bedside, with her hand covering mine.

"Mom?" I said. Confused, I wondered what she was doing there. It took a moment for the gears in my head to start working, but when recollection struck, I gasped for breath.

"Mom, Leo. What about Leo?"

She scooted the chair closer, coming into focus. "Leo is going to be all right. He's in another room, down at the end of this floor."

"His arm?" I could picture the impact of the baton, and the memory made me wince.

"The arm was badly bruised. They were worried about his head, but the CT scan doesn't show a blood clot or fracture." Her voice wavered as she added, "Fortunately, my children inherited my thick skull."

Nodding in agreement, the nurse spoke up. "Your brother was luckier than you were. You had a concussion, a TBI—traumatic brain injury. But now that you're awake, we can keep an eye on you. The doctor thinks you're going to be just fine."

The nurse patted my foot before moving to the side of the bed to take my vitals. In a hushed voice, she said, "The *Post* said you're the third straphanger to get shoved onto the tracks this month. Do you recall anything about it?"

When she raised the question, a jumble of impressions seized my brain: the impact on the tracks, the sound of the oncoming train, the flash of light followed by darkness. Did I recall being carried out of the subway, strapped to a hard plastic stretcher?

In my mind's eye, I saw the faces of first responders from the fire department and NYPD, and a young EMT bending over me who looked like he was scared to death.

My mother's voice was icy. "No unnecessary questions, please. I don't want anyone upsetting my daughter."

The nurse shrugged, unoffended. "It's pretty upsetting to everyone. The *Post* says the subway attacks are the 'new normal.' Personally, I'd like to give up on the subway, but how am I going to get to work? So I've started carrying one of those self-defense kitty cat key chains. And I won't hesitate to use it."

The nurse checked an IV bag attached by a long tube to a catheter in my arm. "How's the pain, Kate? The doctor gave you a PCA. Are you familiar with it? It's patient-controlled analgesia so you can give yourself a dose of pain medication when you need it." She picked up the handheld button and displayed it to me. "Do you need a dose?"

I needed something. Maybe the painkiller would serve. When I gave a stiff nod, the nurse pushed the button and left me alone with Mom.

After the nurse exited, my mother stood beside my bedside. Keeping my hand in a tight hold, she said, "This is my worst nightmare. Both of my kids in the hospital after being attacked. It's what I've been trying to avoid for the past three years."

I blinked as I tried to read her meaning. The pain medication hadn't had time to take effect, but maybe my head was still fuzzy from the TBI because I didn't understand what she was saying.

She dropped her voice. "You've been asking about your father, about the circumstances of his death. I know you suspect it was foul play. I should have been up front with you. I think you're right, Kate." She drew a shuddering breath before she spoke the next words. "I believe he was murdered."

Though I had long suspected it, it was a shock to hear my mother speak the words. I swallowed, unable to frame a response, but she didn't seem to require one.

"I tried to convince Morris to drop it, to leave it alone. I told him he was courting danger. Not just for himself, for all of us."

I was growing more confused. Mom had finally opened up, after I had begged for the information. But her statements didn't provide any clarity.

"Mom, are you talking about the manslaughter trial? Did you tell him not to testify? Because you know there was no way he could just drop that."

She gave me an impatient shake of the head. "It wasn't the NYPD case I was concerned with. He could survive that. It was the corruption investigation. He'd stumbled onto a witness who opened up about the dark money funding judges and politicians. After Morris cracked open a window into the people who pull those strings, he refused to back off or look away. It was bound to end badly. I told him so, over and over, when he confided in me."

I tried to absorb her revelations, but they made little sense in my fuzzy head. "Why didn't he tell me? I was in the DA's office, I could've helped him. But he never mentioned the corruption, just the trial. He was worried about the testimony, he told me that."

She scoffed. "He was protecting you from the truth. Your father never sweated testifying under oath. That wasn't his crisis. He had information on judges and public officials who were on the payroll of people with so much wealth and power that they can't even be identified. Morris wanted to shine a light on that. But it can't be done."

The opioids were starting to take effect. The stark disclosure my mother made bounced off me. I began to feel chatty and upbeat. "So he wanted to bring down a criminal enterprise? That's totally in character. What a great guy he was." I smiled at her, wanting to continue the conversation.

She gave me a wary look. "You're getting high. I can tell."

It occurred to me that she might be correct. As an experiment, I stretched my legs. The movement didn't hurt as much as it had when I first awoke.

I found my handheld remote and used it to elevate the head of the bed. A happy idea struck me. "When Leo and I get out of here, we should all go somewhere. Maybe Florida? We could rent a condo in Fort Lauderdale, just hang out on the beach and soak up the sun. What do you think, Mom?"

She sighed, shaking her head. "I tried to protect you. I tried for years to get you to work for me, so I could insulate you. Your father said that he was determined to find out who the players were, whose hands were dirty. He intended to tell you when the time was right, but he never got the chance. Do you understand?"

I did not understand. Dad encouraged me to become an assistant DA. He cheered me on. If I was working with bad guys, he would have told me so. I thought so anyway.

But I didn't want to talk about corruption. I wanted to talk about the beach. Back when Leo and I were in undergrad, my mom had taken us to Florida on spring break. At the time, we were horribly embarrassed to be seen on the beach with our mother while the other spring breakers were enjoying a bacchanalian revel. In my hospital bed, it made me laugh out loud to remember it. The sound of my laughter bounced against the walls of the tiny hospital room.

The nurse stuck her head through the door. I was happy to see her again. She seemed like a really fun person. I waved at her, even though the movement of my arm caused the catheter to twist in my vein, pulling the plastic tube. But I didn't mind it, not at all.

The nurse spoke to my mom. "Ms. Stone, do you mind stepping out? Dr. Salinas is here to see your daughter."

I beamed. "Dr. Salinas? That's great."

My mother's face looked troubled, but she let go of my hand. "Okay, I guess I can leave her for a bit. I'll go check on Leo. Kate, we'll talk later, when you feel up to it."

"I feel great. Tell Leo I said hi."

She gave me a final glance. Before she left, I noticed that her mouth was pinched into a glum expression. I closed my eyes to block out the unhappy sight.

CHAPTER 56

AFTER MOM LEFT the room, I thought I had only blinked my eyelids, but I must have dozed off again. Because when I came to, I saw a figure in a white lab coat toying with my PCA. From the side, the doctor kinda resembled Whitney.

When she turned to face me, I squeezed my eyes shut and opened them again, to be certain it wasn't a vision conjured up by the drug I had been given. Because the doctor *was* Whitney, in a crisp white jacket, with a stethoscope hanging around her neck.

"Is this a new look?" I meant to sound sardonic, but my voice was raspy and weak.

"You're awake!" She reached for my forearm and patted it, right under the tape that held my IV catheter in place. "I heard all about your travail. Poor girl! Did you know there's a video of it on the Internet?"

My forehead wrinkled. It seemed like I had heard about being featured on video before. Was a fistfight involved? At the courts building? Had the nurse told me? I couldn't recall.

343

Whitney propped a hip onto the side of the narrow bed. We were a little close for comfort, to be honest, but I was in no position to scoot. She said, "The video showed you getting slammed off the platform. You literally disappeared from view. And then, a moment later, the subway came down the tracks. How did you survive it, my precious girl?"

My voice rasped again. "I fell between the row bed and the rails."

"And the cars passed right over you. Wow. Incredible."

She rose from the bed, walked to the door, and peeked out. There was activity in the hallway. I could hear it: voices raised, feet running down the tiled hall in soft-soled shoes. She pushed the door shut, muffling the noise.

Returning to my bedside, she reached for the IV bag, appearing to study it.

"Whitney, you're not supposed to mess with that. It's got my pain medication."

"Right. Gotcha." She picked up the handheld dosage control for the PCA. "Are you feeling okay?"

"Yeah. Well, considering."

She shook her head with a rueful expression. Reaching out, she brushed my hair off my forehead and spoke in a voice that was almost tender. "I hate to see you like this. It wasn't my idea, I promise. I never wanted you to suffer."

As she leaned over me, I could see the photo ID that was clipped onto the pocket of her lab coat. The plastic card contained a stern headshot of Whitney, but in bold letters was the name: Salinas, S, MD.

My voice sounded silly, even to my own ears, as I said, "You are not Dr. Salinas."

When she laughed, it came out like a sigh. "There was an old TV ad—maybe you've heard of it? 'I'm not a doctor, but I play one on TV.' So I'm playing the part today."

She slipped her hand into mine. Her fingers were cold. "How about another drop of painkiller, honey?"

I shifted on the bed, still achy. "I can't have it yet. You have to wait between doses. That's how that thing works. So that a person can't overdose."

Whitney sat at my bedside, appearing to be lost in thought. Her facial expression flickered, as if she was conducting an internal debate. At length, she said, "I'm glad I'm handling things now, so it will be smooth. Painless. I argued against the prior plan, but Gatsby overruled me. Gatsby likes things to look arbitrary or accidental. A hit-and-run, a suicide. A subway shove."

"Gatsby?" My fuzzy head scrambled to put two and two together. "Whitney, we got hooked in with some scary people, you need to be careful. Do you think the leader put Edgar up to this? It had to be him. I smelled the paint on him when he pushed me."

"Honey, don't be too hard on Edgar. He was just following orders."

"He tried to kill me. I told the police to go look for an artist named Edgar. Bring him in for questioning, find out why he'd do something like this." When I gave my brief statement, the police had asked me for his last name. But I couldn't provide one. I'd never heard Edgar's full name in all of the weeks of our association. I told them about Larry, too, because I suspected that our chase through Times Square was part of the scheme. He and Edgar must have been working in concert.

Talking about Edgar's murderous attempt made my head hurt. I was becoming agitated. I struggled to sit upright, but Whitney pushed me back onto the pillow.

Her voice was calm and reasonable. "Sweetheart, the police are looking for a crazy man, not an artist. They have the subway video of a man who looks like a vagrant, someone who lives on the streets."

Laying back on the hard bed, I could envision Edgar's appearance on the subway platform with the hooded jacket and the dark gaiter. Would the police really confuse him with a homeless person? What about the baton he carried?

She huffed a regretful breath. "Gotta be honest—I'm going to miss you. But this is the better way. You'll go to sleep. They'll find you and think it was medical error. Hell, the hospital may even try to cover it up to avoid a lawsuit. No one will attribute anything to our group, so we'll be in the clear. And you won't spend months or years looking over your shoulder like your dad did."

Even in my drugged head, it registered that her friendly delivery didn't disguise a threatening speech. I grabbed the remote that sat on the mattress and pushed the nurse call button.

She continued, sounding wistful. "You were a talented girl. Gatsby thought they could use you. But you make problems, Kate. Digging up old bones, insisting on unearthing shit that needs to be left alone. Remember when I told you about my doll, with the rotten breath? It was supposed to convey a message. I was trying to drop a hint."

While she talked, I had repeatedly pressed the call button but gotten no response. I picked it up and held it to my mouth.

"I need help! Call 911. This is an emergency!"

The device was silent. I tried to raise my voice, but it sounded weak and tremulous. "This is Kate Stone. There's a fire in my room! Fire!"

Whitney tsked. "I disconnected the call button, honey. It's not plugged in."

I struggled to sit up, but when I tried to slide my legs to the floor, they wouldn't cooperate. She had strapped my lower body to the bed.

I tried to shout, though the volume I produced was a pale imitation of my normal voice. "Help! Fire! Fire!"

Whitney said, "Kate, no one is coming. A guy down the hall just flatlined. From an air embolism."

My throat threatened to close, but I croaked out, "Leo?"

"No, not your brother. It's another guy, some old dude. I did that for you as a farewell gift. You always had a soft spot for your brother."

My chest sagged with relief to hear that Leo had been spared. I should have given thought to the plight of the anonymous victim down the hall, but there was no time. Whitney's hand was hitting the button of my patient-controlled analgesia. "I'm giving you more of this opioid to chill you out. I reset the machine, so you can have a little party in your head on the way out." She gave me a rueful smile.

I shouted again: "Nurse! Security!" But my voice had lost its power. My hands clutched the buckle at my hips, struggling to unfasten the nylon strap securing me to the bed.

She grabbed one of my hands. "None of that, Kate. You need to lie down. It works best that way. I'll shoot a nice round bubble of air into your vein, and it will all be over."

I screamed, making a hoarse wail, but no one came to my rescue: no voices in the hallway, no footfalls approaching my door.

Whitney released my hand to pull a syringe from her breast pocket. I watched, frozen with horror, as she pulled the plunger down.

In a gentle voice, she whispered, "Are you feeling that happy juice yet?"

I was starting to feel it. On top of the dose the nurse had administered, the painkiller packed a punch. It was sending me into a spin like I was trapped on a bizarre carnival ride.

Whitney bent over my arm, trying to insert the tip of the syringe into the catheter. I bent my elbow, blocking her effort. She turned to face me, wearing a stern expression.

That's when the rescue arrived. It was a spark of anger, sizzling in my brain. *How can you do this to me? You said we were like family!*

Struggling to hold my arm steady, she said, "Kate. Stop that."

The spark of anger crackled and spread, and I clung to the feeling. I had one shot, one brief chance before the drugs or the syringe laid me out. I focused on her face. Nose? Cheekbone? Eye socket? Jaw?

Stay away from the teeth, a voice whispered. It sounded like my dad.

As if she had heard the voice, too, Whitney bared her teeth, looming over me with an angry glare.

You can't overthink this, or you'll blow it, the voice warned.

I grabbed her ears, pulling her head back. Because of the double dose, my sprained wrist didn't hurt at all. Without hesitating or giving her a second to recover, I pulled her head forward with all the force I could muster. And I smashed her nose against my cranium, right at the point where my forehead and hairline meet.

Blood shot out of her nose as she dropped to the tile floor. I started to lose focus and was in danger of blacking out. But a jolt of fear replaced the anger, enabling me to set to work on the straps securing my lower body. I managed to get them unfastened, though it felt like I was moving in slow motion.

When I lunged out of the bed, I almost slipped on the syringe, which lay on the floor by Whitney's inert body.

On shaky legs, I knee-walked to the door and pulled it open before I collapsed, spilling out into the hall.

I heard the tapping of soft-soled shoes running down the hall. When a young man dressed in scrubs reached me, I grabbed his ankle and held on tight. "Call the police," I said.

He knelt down, tugging at my hands. I tightened my grip. "911," I said. It sounded garbled, even to my ears.

When I heard the sound of my mother, I thought it might be a hallucination. But she looked real when she shoved the orderly away and shouted for help. When she lifted my head and demanded to know what I was doing on my back, that felt real, too. I babbled a slurred account of Whitney's attempt to send a bubble up my arm as the hospital personnel gathered around, talking in excited voices.

The last clear thought that spun through my head was that I wished I could thank my dad for teaching me how to give a Glasgow kiss.

CHAPTER 57

THE BURNING SUN was blocked by a green umbrella, the soles of my feet were coated with golden sand. Lazily, I stretched before sitting up in my beach chair.

I was totally relaxed, almost drowsy. When I looked out from the shade of the umbrella, I saw two red-haired children run into the surf, followed by a tow-headed boy. The blond kid reminded me of Leo at that age.

My mother's voice interrupted my reverie. "Leo. Leo! Your back is burning!"

Leo was stretched out on a beach towel in full sun, outside the protection of an umbrella. His head was pillowed in his arms until Mom called his name.

He lifted his head. "I'm fine, Mom."

With a dogged expression, she grabbed a bottle of sunscreen. As she scrambled out of the beach chair next to mine, she said, "If you don't get under your umbrella, I need to rub this on your back."

He looked so horrified that I had to intervene. "Mom, for God's sake. He's an adult."

She wheeled around. "You children don't understand this Florida sun. It's not like summer in New York. You could end up in the hospital with sun poisoning."

She squirted a jet of white lotion onto her hand while Leo jumped up and scrambled back to the protection of his own umbrella. Her efforts frustrated, she settled back onto the chair next to mine, swiping the sunscreen onto my leg.

Frowning, I wiped it away with a beach towel. "Mom, we're not infants. You have to quit babying us."

She sighed. A beer can jutted out of the sand directly beside her chair. She picked it up and took a healthy swallow. "Your father always accused me of being overprotective. Maybe he was right. But as it turns out, I had plenty of cause to be that way."

Turning to me, she pulled her sunglasses down the bridge of her nose and pinned me with a piercing stare. "Am I right?"

I couldn't win that argument, so I broke eye contact, bending over the beach bag to hunt for my phone. When I unearthed it, I checked my messages.

Mom pushed the sunglasses onto the crown of her head. Her face relaxed as she stared out at the surf. "This getaway was a good idea, Kate. Glad you came?"

"Yes, Mom." I was glad, and it had been a good idea, despite the fact that I had proposed it in a drug-induced state of delirium.

She glanced over at me before returning her focus to the water. The waves pounded on the shore, and the sound was calming. A sense of ease washed over me.

In a tentative tone, she said, "So is there anything else

you want to ask me? Any unresolved baggage, something we haven't yet covered?"

"No, don't think so." I was only half listening because I was busy reading a text from Millie. She and Rod were hiding out in Missouri, spending time with her family. I snickered at her description of their interactions with the small-town locals.

"We'll never know who forced your father through that window. Can you make peace with that?"

That question caused my thumbs to freeze on the screen of the cell phone. *Could I?*

I still wanted to know. Specifically, I wanted to identify them so I could exact revenge on the people who'd dropped my father on his head on the sidewalk in New York. But it seemed highly unlikely that I would ever discover the identity of the perpetrators.

If Whitney knew, she wasn't telling. After she was taken into custody at the hospital, she sang like a bird, at first. She owned up to the attack on me and the other patient on my floor. But she told the investigators she had acted alone, denying any knowledge of the subway assault or the band of vigilantes.

I told the investigators she was holding out. That there was more, involving dark money and a power circle behind her activities. They claimed they had asked her about it. Maybe they did. Shortly after that, she was charged for the crimes at the hospital. The DA filed one count of murder, another of attempted murder. Her attorney entered an insanity plea: lack of criminal responsibility by reason of mental disease or defect. The case won't come to trial for a long time. Most days, I try not to worry about it.

Mom's voice broke into my reverie. "I mean, I have my theory. But there's no point in obsessing over it."

Finally. Was she going to share the theory? I shot her an expectant look. "Well? Enlighten me."

"I always suspected Victor."

The accusation sent a jolt through me. I pushed back. "Victor was Dad's best friend. His partner, for over two decades. He was loyal to Dad."

"You were too young to see him for what he was. Your father could never see it, either. While we were married, Victor hit on me every time Morris's back was turned. Victor was only loyal to Victor. If someone offered the right inducement, Victor could be bought. Or if he thought Morris's investigation was some kind of threat to him personally, he'd stab him in the back. Or push him through a window."

"But how could you be his lawyer if you suspected that?"

"You know that old saying. Keep your friends close and your enemies closer. That makes a lot of sense to me."

I looked away, trying to absorb the information. Mom gave me a quiet moment before she went on. "I would have liked to hear Victor admit it, but there's no chance of that now. He's comatose. They've put him in hospice care."

She heaved a deep sigh. "Maybe it's enough that we're still here. Still together, unscathed." Mom paused before adding, "Well, mostly unscathed."

She was right, wasn't she? We were lucky. Leo and I had survived the attacks and recovered from them. If we were distinctly edgier, somewhat more paranoid than we had been prior to the subway station incident, well, it could have been much worse.

My phone pinged. It was from Steven, checking in. He was still in the city, laying low. He said he missed me and asked how long we were staying in Fort Lauderdale. We texted back and forth. He said some sweet things. In response, I suggested some activities we might try when I returned.

Mom nudged me. When I looked up, she was giving me a serious eye. "Do you think that vengeance group has disbanded? I haven't heard anything concrete from the investigator. But I know that the NYPD hasn't apprehended the artist yet, or any of those other reprobates you described. Are you worried about that?"

"No. I'm not worried." It was a half-truth at best. I spent hours stewing over the whereabouts of my former cohorts. But I wasn't worried at that particular moment because my eyes were on the cell phone. Steven had sent another text. He enthusiastically welcomed my proposition, and added to it. The message gave me a flush that wasn't caused by the Florida sun. I was so enthralled with the description that I ignored an incoming phone call.

Mom flashed an impatient glance my way. "Who's calling? People are so inconsiderate. Don't they know we are on vacation?"

I checked the number. It was familiar. My voice held a note of trepidation. "It's the Manhattan DA's office."

The phone pinged to let me know that someone had left a message.

I played the audio recording. Bill Parker's voice came through the speaker, sounding exuberant. "Kate! Just wanted to share. It happened, finally. I'm being promoted. They're giving me the spot in white collar that I've been hoping for."

As the message went on, his voice dropped, as if he didn't want to be overheard. "The position is conditional, though. Rubenstein has heard about my struggle with anxiety. The word got around in the office, I guess. So he says I can only work in the new job if I join a support group to get help for my anxiety problem."

As I listened, a funny reaction buzzed in my head.

Bill's voice was eager as he wrapped up the message. "So I was wondering whether you could recommend any support groups because I know you've been there, right? Anyway, let me know if you have any leads. Have fun in Florida!"

I hit the arrow button again and listened to Bill's voice mail a second time.

White collar

Support group

Rubenstein

"Oh my God."

Mom looked over at me and lifted her sunglasses. "What now?"

Holding the phone in a death grip, I locked eyes with her. "It's Rubenstein."

I scrambled out of the beach chair so suddenly it tipped over into the sand. But I didn't stop to right it. I needed to get to the hotel room to start packing.

As I ran across the beach, kicking up sand, my mother's voice followed me, shrill and loud. "Where are you going? Kate? We have dinner reservations!"

I wouldn't make it to dinner, not that night.

I had to get back to New York.

ACKNOWLEDGMENTS

Bringing *Renegade* to the page was great fun, and some people provided excellent assistance along the way. Many thanks to the team at Assemble Media, including Jack Heller, Brendan Deneen, and Caitlin de Lisser-Ellen. I'm grateful to my agent, Jill Marr of the Sandra Dijkstra Literary Agency, for her friendship and support. And I owe a huge debt of thanks (and undying loyalty) to Alex Logan, my editor at Grand Central Publishing, for the inspiration, motivation, and guidance she provided through each draft of the manuscript.

ABOUT THE AUTHOR

Bestselling author Nancy Allen practiced law for fifteen years as Assistant Missouri Attorney General and Assistant Prosecutor in her native Ozarks, trying over thirty jury cases. She served on the faculty of Missouri State University for fifteen years, teaching law classes. She is the author of the Ozarks Mystery series. With James Patterson, Nancy is coauthor of *New York Times* bestsellers *Juror #3* (2018) and *Jailhouse Lawyer* (2021). *Renegade* is the first book in her Anonymous Justice series.